Hope you enjoy my

Deborah Langley

Stardom

by

Deborah Caren Langley

Stardom

This edition published by Inscape Solutions Limited

A catalogue record for this work is available from The British Library

ISBN:	Softcover	978-0-9935930-4-8
	eBook	978-0-9935930-5-5

My name is Deborah Caren Langley and I grew up in Blackpool, England. When I was at school I was always involved in school activities like choir, dance classes, even after-school events like weekends away camping, canoeing or hiking. As a child I enjoyed school, I had lots of friends and my parents always encouraged me in every way and in everything I did. I had a great childhood.

When I left school I worked in a sweet factory as a machinist wrapping lollipops and hated every minute of it. I decided to go to college, where I studied Childcare, and subsequently worked with children for many years. Even so, my real passion was creative writing and I really wished to be a writer. So one night I sat down and started writing a book (and then I put it away for many years). Never in my wildest dreams did I think that it would be published but it was! You could say my dream came true.

Apart from my family, nothing has given me so much joy so I've kept going. This is my second book – I hope you enjoy reading it as much as I did writing it.

Acknowledgements

I would like to give a huge thanks to my publisher, Nigel Wilkins, because I wouldn't know what I would do without him. So thank you Nigel.

I also would like to thank my very good friend from America, Trisha Achenbach. She has supported me 100% – as has my good friend from Australia, Carolyn Findley, again 100% support.

I must thank all my family and friends for their support.

Last but not least, always my mum and dad, Love you both, miss you everyday. XXX

Thank you all from the bottom of my heart.

Prologue

Everyone dreams of being famous but for Desiree Beaumont this became a reality, she took the world by storm. From a pretty little girl, Desiree became a beautiful woman and then one of the world's biggest sex symbols.

With demons to fight, this woman goes through hell but can she bounce back? Will she ever be really happy?

For all romantics, everywhere.

Chapter 1

Blackpool, England 1965

Frantically packing a bag in the dead of night, desperately trying not to wake her drunken husband, Carol Louis left her home – leaving her 5 year old daughter sleeping in her bed. Before walking out of the door she kissed her daughter tenderly, streams of salty tears rolled down her face as she whispered "I will come back for you baby girl, I promise…"

Desiree was such a pretty little girl with the biggest brown eyes you had ever seen. She had waist-length chestnut blonde hair and the cutest smile. Everyone commented on what a beautiful little girl she was, how she would break so many hearts.

She was such an easy child. She had a love for old movies and particularly liked all the glamorous ladies, the Hollywood stars, like Maryann Morton, Lena Thomson and Ramona Hammond. She would happily sit and watch them in their beautiful dresses, with their stunning make-up and hair; she wanted to be just like them. She was always such a happy little girl, always smiling. But her life wasn't what it seemed.

Once, Carol and Desiree had been shopping when a grey-haired lady stopped them. Desiree was such a chatty little girl, she began to tell the lady how she wanted to be on telly when she grew up.

"Would you, sweetheart?" The lady asked, smiling down at her.

"Do you think I will be allowed?"

The lady nodded. "What a beautiful little girl! What's your name?"

"Desiree Louis" she said proudly.

The lady smiled at Carol and told her she had a delightful child.

"Thank you" she replied proudly.

They said goodbye and carried on down the aisle. As they walked along, Carol took hold of Desiree's hand. Desiree turned and waved to the lady. Carol looked down at her, she could see she was deep in thought.

"Desiree?"

"Yes Mummy?"

"You look miles away there, Sweetie"

"I was thinking about when I go on the television"

"Oh?"

"Do you think I can? Like that lady said?"

"Oh Darling, I think you can do anything you want when you grow up."

Desiree looked up at Carol and smiled at her.

"Do you think I will be as beautiful as you?"

"Oh Sweetie, that's a lovely thing to say, you will be very beautiful…"

Carol had met David in 1958 at the Blackpool Mecca on a rock 'n' roll night, David had spotted Carol from across the dance floor. Her big brown eyes with her thick black eyeliner shone as she stared back at him. She thought he was so handsome with his Rockabilly look, 6ft tall with sandy blond hair and slate grey eyes staring at her. Her long black hair framed her face. She was so beautiful he had to go over to her. He asked her to dance and from that night their romance blossomed, it had been the best two shillings he had ever spent.

He was one of the gentlest men she had ever met. They soon fell in love and got married and Desiree was born June 10th 1960. David was a doting dad. He had a beautiful wife, a beautiful daughter and everything was wonderful, *he had it all.*

When Desiree turned two, David had started going out with his workmates, once, twice a week at first. Carol didn't mind until slowly it became three, even four nights out. She found out he had started gambling and drinking with his friends. Things became hard with money, debt collectors started to appear at the door. He started to change. He began to drink more, and became very abusive, hitting Carol more and more frequently.

Carol was desperate to keep the wolves at bay and had two jobs on the go to bring money into the house. Things were hard. She would go to work with bruises on her face, trying to hide them with make-up but everyone knew what was happening although Carol would defend him. He constantly accused her of seeing other men and when she became pregnant with their second child he was convinced the baby wasn't his.

Carol was into her seventh month of pregnancy when David had come home very drunk. He took one look at Carol, shaking her head and rolling her eyes and flew into a rage. He grabbed at her but she pulled away, hitting her stomach on the side of the table. The shock caused her to go into labour early. Sadly the baby was stillborn. Carol was so devastated at losing her second little girl she couldn't take anymore, she just had to leave.

She frantically packed a bag and, trying desperately not to wake him, Carol left her husband, her home and her 5 year old daughter still asleep in her bed.

David had always adored Desiree and had never raised his hand to her.

Now, as she grew up without her mother she had to learn how to fend for herself. She had to, David was always drunk, and if he wasn't then he was sleeping it off. When he had his friends round, Desiree was in the way so he would make her go into her bedroom. She would keep coming out which annoyed David so he started locking her in her bedroom. She would crawl under the blankets and cry herself to sleep, usually hungry.

She was often in dirty clothes and wasn't clean, she began to smell. She would wet herself she was so scared when David shouted. As time went on he started using his hand, then it was his belt. She would be covered in bruises and was admitted to hospital on many occasions. Eventually the social services got involved and took her away from her father making her a ward of court, placing her in the children's home. She was such a frightened little girl, she would sit on the bed with her knees up, her arms rapped around them, rocking back and forth, tears rolling down her face.

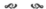

She was pleased that she had been taken away from David but she didn't like the Children's Home. The bigger girls bullied her although that was the least of her worries. She hated her father and she hated her mother for leaving her. If there was ever a child raging with pent up aggression it was Desiree.

As she entered her teens she started to mix with the wrong crowds, smoking, drinking and stealing. She became rude and hard to handle. She was expelled from school for slapping a teacher across the face. The teacher had called her to the front of the class and shouted at her, ridiculing her in front of everyone. Her father had shouted at her just the same, usually followed by his hand and that was enough. She ran away regularly, she was such a long way from being the little girl who wanted to be on television.

Social services placed her into foster homes but she would still run away. One time she had been stealing food out of the kitchen and storing it up until the night she climbed out of the window and took off, hitching lifts from strangers to get away. She got as far as Lancaster were she found an old barn that had fallen into disrepair and was abandoned. As she opened the creaking door cobwebs covered her face. It was raining heavily, the barn was damp and cold, it had an awful fusty smell to it but it was better to be in there than outside.

As she stepped further inside, she saw some old bales of hay and she could hear the birds cooing in their nests. As she settled down in the hay to try and keep warm the barn door opened slightly. Desiree covered herself up with the hay to hide. Peering through the hay she saw a beautiful brown and white border collie standing there. It was so timid it took her all her time to coax her over. She gave her some of her food and eventually she sat with her. They kept each other warm that night. The next morning as the sun shone through the timber Desiree woke and found that the dog had gone. It wasn't long after that the police found her and took her back to Blackpool, back to her foster home.

Soon she was in one foster home after another and it came to the point where nobody wanted to take her. She ended up being placed back in the children's home. The girls no longer bullied her because she would fight back viciously. She was getting herself in to all sorts of trouble, she was starting to spiral out of control.

Not long after, Desiree and a group of her friends stole a car and went cruising round in it. They had been in the car smoking dope and eventually got caught driving recklessly. They were all taken to the police station and charged with theft. One of the boys had been charged with possession of cannabis.

Nobody really knew what to do with Desiree. She would go in to town with her friends instead of school, messing around and making a nuisance of themselves.

"Hello, Desiree"

Des was stood on a statue waving her arms about acting stupid.

She looked down, "Do I know you?"

"We have met"

"Don't think so, lady"

"Oh we have, remember you wanted to be on television"

Desiree suddenly realised who this old lady was. A few years had passed so she was a lot older and so frail she walked with a walking stick. Desiree got down from the statue and told her that dream was dead, she'd had it well and truly knocked out of her.

One of the lads that Des was with shouted to her and she shouted back.

"Yeah… yeah… I'm fuckin' coming…"

The lady cringed at her language. She was so disappointed she put her head down and walked away wondering what had gone so wrong. She turned in time to see Des throwing milkshake at a shop window, laughing and running off as the shopkeeper came out. Later that night Desiree got arrested for being drunk and disorderly and damaging shop property. She appeared in court and was sentenced to do community service for sixteen weeks, cleaning up in the park. It gave her plenty of time to really think about what the lady had said to her in the shopping centre: where was that girl who had longed to be on television with the beautiful dresses? Why was that dream dead? – why couldn't she be on television?

1976

As Desiree turned sixteen, her life was about to change forever. She left the children's home and she decided to leave Blackpool to put her past behind her. She got herself a cheap day ticket costing about three pounds, heading for London. She didn't have much money and she didn't have an easy time of it. The first few weeks she slept on the streets. No one would give her a job and she didn't have anywhere to live. Then, finally, a lady gave her break. She gave her a job cleaning her house and let her stay in her spare bedroom.

Grace was a widower and she had seen Desiree curled up in a corner, sort of wedged up the ally between two houses. She saw she was cold, hungry and her clothes were dirty. She felt so sorry for Desiree that she took a leap of faith and took her home. Desiree was so grateful she was determined to sort her life out and make something of herself. Thanks to Grace she did just that, she eventually got herself a little bedsit. It wasn't much but she made it her own. She managed to get herself a job in a shop stacking shelves in the afternoons so she could still clean Grace's house in the morning.

After her shift in the shop one day, she walked up the high street and noticed an advertisement in the window of a big posh restaurant, 'Waitress wanted– Apply within'. She straightened her hair, brushed herself down and went in. She asked one of the waitresses about the job and then Bob Archer, the owner, walked in and looked her up and down.

"I've come about the advertisement in the window" she said nervously

"Have you got any experience?"

"No sir, but I learn quick"

"Hmmm, OK darlin', I'll give you a chance"

"Oh… Thank you, sir"

"Tomorrow at six, don't be late"

"Thank you again"

She worked in the restaurant in the evening. She was now working three jobs, as many hours as she could, so she could save enough money to get her photographs done to build a portfolio. She worked hard for her money. Grace pointed out that she wouldn't be able to keep this up she was working morning afternoon and night Desiree told Grace she would be alright. She'd always dreamed of being a movie star.

"You are going to make yourself ill my dear"

"I'll be fine"

Grace told her she was going to let her go. Desiree looked her in the eyes.

"I can manage, Grace, really – I don't want to let you down"

"Des I didn't really need a cleaner… I just wanted to give you a helping hand, my dear."

Desiree was so grateful, she gently kissed her on the cheek and told her she would always find time to pop round and visit her.

Desiree felt she owed Grace a lot, she was the only person to give her fighting chance. By this time Desiree was eighteen years old and stunning in every way. Beautiful looks, gorgeous figure and very shapely legs – she made heads turn as she walked down the street.

One fateful night Jake Summers came into the restaurant with a party of guests. Jake made his name by taking photos of celebrities and making girls' dreams come true by turning them in to famous models. He thought Desiree was absolutely stunning. He could not believe his eyes when he saw her, he thought she had such potential. He asked Desiree if she had ever done any modelling

"No, never," she answered looking at him warily.

"Would you be interested in doing some?"

"I don't know you..."

Desiree thought he was just another fella trying to spin her a line… she was used to that. She wasn't having any of it and dismissed him. Jake continued to watch her for some time. He noticed how the men reacted around her, how they would break their necks looking at her. Jake was persistent… This girl was beautiful and he wanted to get her on his books… She could make him a lot of money.

"What's your name, Darling?"

"I don't mean to be rude, but I don't even know you so why would I tell you my name?"

"I know you don't know me, but you are going to, please, tell me your name"

"My name is Desiree Louis… Happy now?"

"Yes, thank you! Umm, Desiree Louis…. That is a beautiful name for a beautiful girl!"

Desiree laughed and thought 'no chance – you don't impress me mate'. He smiled at her and told her who he was and that she could be famous. She'd never heard of Jake Summers and was very suspicious.

He gave her his card and told her to come along to see him the next day. She took the card from him and put it in her pocket. But was he who he said he was? She wasn't so sure. Jake hoped she would turn up… He thought she had it all.

Des did some checking. She asked her boss if he knew Jake Summer.

"Do I know Jake? Hell yeah… Everyone knows who Jake Summer is… "Why?"

"He's given me his card"

"Don't ya know who he is?"

"No… Who is he?"

"He's an agent for famous models, Des"

"Yes he told me that but I thought he was just coming on to me" She couldn't believe she'd nearly blown it. 'Thank heavens he was persistent,' she thought.

Next day Desiree skipped work at the shop and went to the studio and asked the girl on the desk if she could see Jake Summers.

"Have you got an appointment?" The girl said, looking Desiree up and down.

"Hmm… No"

"Well, No – you can't see him then.."

"But he…"

"He is a very busy man" she snapped.

Desiree felt so disappointed. She turned round and was just about to walk out of the door when Jake came through to the reception.

"Miss Louis"

Des turned back around.

"Mr Summers"

"Where are you going?"

"Hmmm"

Jake turned to the girl and asked her why she hadn't told him that Miss Louis had arrived. The girl lowered her head and told him she was sorry. Jake asked Des to follow him through. She smiled and started to follow him. As she passed the girl she smirked at her.

Jake introduced her to Marcus Wade. Marcus was a photographer and he was gobsmacked when he saw Desiree. He couldn't wait to take some photos of her. She jumped at the chance. He took some head shots of her first then asked if she'd consider doing her photographs in swimwear, including some bikinis. She said she would and went to get changed.

Marcus told Jake that she was so stunning.

"She's very photogenic – just look at these," flicking through the photos he had just taken.

"When I saw her, man… I couldn't believe my eyes well… my jaw dropped and hit the ground – the men around her, they couldn't take their eyes off her. I bet their profits went up when she started working at Archers!"

"She has got everything Jake!"

"Yeah she has… She is going to be so big… The world isn't going to know what's hit it!"

"Yeah, I think you could be right!"

Desiree came out of the dressing room with a towel round her covering up a light green lattice detailed swimsuit. She was a bit nervous.

"Right baby girl, get rid of the towel and let's get some pictures" Marcus said excited.

Desiree took the towel away slowly revealing her beautiful figure and Marcus and Jake's jaw dropped.

"You are perfect!" Marcus gasped. "Pose for me baby!"

"How do you want me to stand?" She asked nervously.

"Anyway you want… Just pose for me babe!"

Desiree soon got the hang of it and did some great poses: head tilts, pouts, throwing her head back with such style. Marcus was so excited about this girl. She was amazing… Where had she been hiding?

"More Babe…. That's fantastic"

She smiled a full beautiful smile and gave a mysterious but knowing look.

"Oh yeah baby that's it… keep it going… Oh yeah, beautiful"

"How would you feel about changing the colour of your hair?" Jake asked as Marcus handed her a red, very skimpy bikini. There wasn't much to it.

"What colour are you thinking of Mr Summers?"

"Black…"

"Yes, I like the sound of that"

Jake smiled at Marcus and nodded. Des went to get changed.

At this point his other new client came in. She was the new up and coming singer Lori Miller. She was about to take the music world by storm and she was having photographs done for the cover of her first album.

Desiree came out with her bikini on. Marcus looked at her apologetically.

"Shit! I've overbooked myself!"

"That's OK… I don't mind waiting," Desiree smiled as she wrapped the towel back around herself.

"Thank you, Desiree"

"Thanks… That's very nice of you," Lori said smiling at her.

Desiree and Lori were the same age and both were new in the industry. Lori had longish blonde hair that flowed round the top of her shoulder. She had a different look to most of the singers already out there and she wore a tight black bodices and leather jeans. She had the biggest blue eyes, a nice shapely figure, she was going all the way to the top. She was going to be a big star in the future. Marcus took lots of photos of Lori. She was a natural and did some great poses and gave Desiree some ideas.

"Yeah baby… that's fantastic!" Marcus enthused.

Jake looked around him and couldn't believe his luck.

"Lori babe, move your hand to your head and push your hair up!" Marcus ordered.

Lori moved her hands to her head pushing her fingers through her hair, as Marcus had said and letting it fall, licking her lips at the same time.

"Oh Yeah Baby… beautiful… keep it going"

Lori Miller had always wanted to be a pop singer. She would stand at the mirror for hours and pretend to be a famous singer though her parents wanted her to get a good education and become a doctor or something, but her dream came true. She auditioned for a TV talent show called *Youngstars* but never got on screen – she got signed straight away by a recording company called Coliptoss. She had a long way to go but she was finally on her way!

Desiree sat and watched until Marcus had finished taking Lori's pictures and they had a break. Desiree and Lori got talking until Marcus stopped them…

"OK Desiree, back to work"

Desiree posed for lots of pictures that day. Marcus just wanted to take more and more photographs, Lori stayed around and watched as she and Desiree had arranged to go for a burger after the photo shoot.

"You are incredibly beautiful, Desiree" Marcus said.

"Thank you!"

Jake had discovered Desiree Louis and wanted to make her in to a worldwide sex symbol.

He had no idea just how big Desiree was going to be when he signed her up for a 2 year contract. After the photo shoot Desiree and Lori headed round the corner for the burger bar.

"What are you having, Des?"

"Hmm... I'll have a cheese burger and fries with a milkshake, I think"

"Yeah... sounds good"

They sat and talked and Lori asked why Desiree wanted to be a film star.

"I don't know I just do...I can't explain... It's just something in here..." she said putting her hands to her chest. "Why did you want to be a singer?"

"I want to be famous and rich with lots and lots of money... not there yet!"

Chapter 2

Copenhagen, Denmark 1978

Staffan Ottesen , Edvin Lykke and Delmar Schmidt were all born and lived their lives in Christianshavn, a district of Copenhagen in Denmark. They were friends at school and grew up doing everything together. They all liked rock music, especially 60s Rock, and went to all the concerts they could – *Zillion, Sharp Edge, Fallen Magic* and *Black Thorn*. They all even got girlfriends pretty much at the same time.

After leaving school they all went to the local college, then on to Frederiksberg University. Staffan was a bright young man studying Science. At a local food and drink festival, they met up with Lucas, from Frederiksberg, and Barny who came from the village of Sovang. Barny was also studying at the university and they had been talking about their favourite bands. Staffan fancied himself a bit of a rock star and he wanted to form his own band. The discussion had made him think about this more.

Eventually, he put an advertisement up in the music room at the University. He had already asked Edvin and Delmar as he knew that they both could play a wicked guitar. Now they needed a drummer and a keyboard player.

Several people turned up to audition as the drummer but Staffan wanted a real heavy beat, a rock band beat. Barny turned up.

"What about me?"

Delmar asked if he could even play the drums. Barny took the drum sticks off Edvin and spun them round his fingers. 'Can I play the drums?' he mumbled to himself.

He sat down and blasted out the beat of a song from *Sharp Edge*. Staffan's jaw dropped and he told the guys they had just found their drummer – now all they needed was a keyboard player. The guys went out that weekend to see a band playing at the local pub and, lo and behold, there was Lucas on keyboards. They had found their keyboard player, even if he didn't know it yet.

And so their rock band was formed. They called themselves *Dragon Skull* and Staffan's girlfriend, Farina, offered to manage them. She took lots of pictures and plastered them all over the campus. Staffan's powerful voice brought a big audience in and eventually they developed a fan base.

Staffan was now nineteen years old and stood six feet tall. He had long blonde hair with beautiful, piercing blue eyes. It was like looking into the ocean looking into his eyes. He had always wanted to be a rock star, just like his childhood rock idol, Paul Best from *Sharp Edge*. He could play a mean guitar and also wrote his own songs, along with his friend Edvin. Staffan's mother and father had always encouraged him musically as they could see he had a real gift.

Staffan, Edvin and Barny were waiting for Delmar and Lucas to finish their classes. While they waited. Barny was flicking through a magazine. Suddenly his mouth opened and his eyes widened. Edvin nudged Staffan and they asked him what he was looking at. He turned the magazine round to face them.

"Wow!" Staffan grabbed the mag from him and told them that he would meet this girl one day.

They asked him how he planned to do that and he said he didn't know but he would meet Desiree Louis one day, she had to be the most beautiful girl he had ever seen. Farina coughed Edvin and Barny suggested that he rephrased his last statement. Staffan put his arm round Farina and kissed her.

Farina got them a gig at a sports hall in Valby. It only took them eight minutes to get there and they arrived early so they had time to set up their equipment. At that time, they only had two small amps and their guitars drums and keyboard were all second hand they did the job – that's all that mattered.

They didn't pack the crowds in liked they hoped but they earned about 50 krona so they were happy with that. Farina managed to get them a few more gigs in the city centre, Vesterbro and East Amager. The more gigs they did they more of a crowd they got. Girls went crazy over them. Farina didn't like that the way they would get hold of Staffan, kissing and pulling him. He didn't mind, he felt he could get used to it. It soon came between them and Farina called it a day on their relationship and they went their separate ways.

Alberto, who was Barny's friend, recorded them one night while they played and sent tapes into a few record companies, who didn't even bother to play them. They'd not heard anything back from any of them and Delmar was getting very frustrated. Staffan told him they couldn't just give up, that they were all disappointed but they had to keep trying. Nobody had said this was going to be easy.

Then they entered a band competition at the university. They came second but what they didn't know was that one of the producers from a record company was there and he liked what he saw. With a different name, some new equipment and some help he could have a winner. He approached them and asked if they had any demos. Staffan quickly said yes. He'd been working on a new song and they just needed to put some music to it. Fredrick Svenningsen gave them his number and told them to call when they had got it all together.

Staffan and the guys went back to their dorm and got to work on the song. They worked all through the night, they were probably in for some complaints from the rest of the dorm but they really didn't care. Fredrick liked it instantly and made sure it was recorded. The song went straight in the charts and quickly hit number one. Everyone wanted this record. It also kept *Connection*, another new band trying hard to break through, off the top slot.

Vancouver, Canada 1978

Johnny, Hadley, Callan, Lance and Paul were playing in a Canadian band from Vancouver called *Connections*. Johnny was also a very good looking young man who could play guitar and write songs, along with his friend Hadley. Johnny and Hadley had met at work, both working at the same hardware store, and had formed a duet. They played the bars and clubs at the weekend.

They met Callan in the local food store where he was on the checkout getting shouted out by his boss about his attendance and time keeping.

"Shove your fucking job up your fuckin' ass – you'll be fucking sorry when I become a famous guitarist! " He stormed out and headed to the burger bar over the road.

Johnny and Hadley overheard what Callan had said and they made their way over to join him. They were intrigued about his guitar playing.

"Hey buddy, we heard you say you could play guitar," Hadley said, nudging his arm.

"Yeah that's right, what the fuck about it?"

"Well we are interested to hear about it" Johnny said.

Callan quickly changed his cocky attitude.

"Yeah…right on man, take a fuckin' seat and I'll tell you about it"

Callan was a little rough round the edges and said things how it was. They sat talking for hours until the girl in the burger bar told them if they weren't eating they would have to go.

"Keep your fuckin' panties on, sweet cheeks"

"Don't call me sweet cheeks, shit face!"

"Wow baby, that cuts deep"

"If you're not eating you gotta go"

Johnny said "I'll order something… OK, happy now Darlin?"

"OK" She smiled at him.

"Hey, why the fuck were you nice to him, but not to me?"

"Cause you don't look like him, now do ya, sweet cheeks?"

She swiftly walked away with her nose up in the air.

"Fuckin' bitch"

She quickly turned around, stuck her middle finger up at him and mouthed *'Fuck You'*.

"Now back to business" Johnny said, asking Callan if knew anyone who could play drums and keyboard.

"Hell yeah, I know this guy Lance – he plays a mean fuckin' drum beat"

"Keyboards…?" Hadley enquired.

"Yeah Lance knows Paul – he works in a radio station."

"That's what I'm fuckin' talking about… Can we meet them?"

Callan told them he would arrange it but Lance was already in a band.

Hadley shook his head.

"How the fuck is that gonna work?"

Johnny said, "Let's just meet them first."

A few days passed before Callan could arrange for Johnny and Hadley to meet Lance and Paul. They all met up and Johnny and Hadley heard Lance and Paul play. Lance told Johnny that his band was going nowhere, they had been a total disaster at their last gig and he would love to join their band. Paul played keyboards really well – what he could do with those keys was out of this world and as a bonus, he had all the contacts. *Connection* was born.

Desiree got together a great portfolio and Jake started showing her photos about. Soon there was a lot of interest in her and she started to get some part-time work modelling clothes and swimwear. Soon he managed to get her on the cat walk at *Fashion Flair* fashion week. There were going to be some big names there so it would be a golden opportunity for Desiree. Jake had been told that his long-time friend Matt Adams would be there with his latest lady, Terry Maddox. Adams was in England for a film festival where he was up for Best Director. Des had never heard of him, she was more worried about how nervous she was when she got on that cat walk. She was convinced she was going to trip or fall off.

Clyde, the Fashion Flair director, was well known for being hard on his models and told Desiree to get out there and do her stuff. She confessed to being really nervous.

"If you don't get your act together you're done, end of the road, lady"

Des didn't like his tone, it reminded her of her father.

"I want to see sexy, smouldering and moody. Rada show her how it's done, she clearly isn't a professional"

Rada smiled at Desiree, "Don't take it to heart, he's always like that"

"He's very rude"

Rada Bazanov was a pro at this. She knew all there was to know about being on the cat walk. She told Desiree how to get rid of the cat walk nerves.

"Just think to yourself that you are at home practicing in front of the mirror block everything else out"

Matt Adams had not been paying much attention to the show, he was only there for Terry as she had wanted to go to the fashion show. He just happened to look up over his glasses when he saw Desiree. He sat with his mouth open. Terry nudged him, she had picked several dresses she liked, particularly one of the ones Desiree had been modelling, hoping that it would look as good on her as it did Des. Matt was moaning that he'd had enough and wanted to go. On his way out he looked at Desiree and winked at her.

Meanwhile, there were drinks and canapés after the fashion show. Gavin Clements was there from the rock band *Zillion* who had been around from the early seventies. Des was stood on her own feeling very out of place and uncomfortable when she heard a voice in her ear.

"Can I get you drink?"

She looked up at Gavin, "Hmm, yes please"

He took her over to the bar – well if that's what you could call it. It was just a table with drinks on it really with a young man serving them

"So you are Desiree?"

"Hmm, yes… and you are Gavin Clements"

"Yes I am… Jake told me all about his new model"

"I don't know about model – I'm a lot smaller than the other models"

"What you lack in height you make up for with everything else" he smiled at her. She smiled back.

Jake made his way over with Collin Tyler

"Sorry Des," he said, apologetically.

"That's OK, Gavin has been keeping me company"

"Hey Gavin"

Gavin smiled and gave Jake the thumbs up.

"Gavin, you know Collin don't you?

Gavin said he did and shook his hand. Jake then introduced Collin to Des. Collin's eyes lit up and told Jake he could see what he meant. Collin Tyler was very interested in her. Jake wasn't really sure about Collin having Desiree on his books. He had a bad reputation with models.

"Leave well alone Collin!" Jake warned.

Collin looked at Jake and winked "Bring her to the studio tomorrow, Jake"

"OK – but like I said"

"Oh Jake, come on"

Next day, Jake dropped Des off at the photo shoot with Collin and true to form he promised her the world for a price… She had to sleep with him.

In spite of her past, the one thing she had managed to keep hold of was her virginity. He was simply there to exploit her. Collin bedded every new girl on his books. She had come this far, she wanted to be famous so she did what she thought she had to do to get on. Her very first time wasn't to be what she had planned at all. After a session, Collin asked Desiree to stay late… She knew what it was for. He was all over her and when he found out she was still a virgin, he wanted her more.

"Hey Babe… I'll make your first time special!" He promised.

But it wasn't… She hated it… His hands were all over her and she cringed when he touched her. After she left him she scrubbed herself violently. She hated him touching her but she so wanted to be famous and she had come so far… She wasn't letting it go now. She was very naive in the sex department, Collin was in his late thirties and he knew exactly what he was doing. When Jake found out what Collin had done he told him to back off Desiree.

"You are a dirty bastard I told you to leave well alone!"

"Hey… These silly bitches want to be famous – I might as well have a bit of fun out of it!" He gloated.

"Yeah they do… It's their dream and you promise them you will get them there and then exploit them! I don't want you near Des… She's not coming to you again!"

"So why is she any different?"

"She is and I'm warning you… You keep your fucking distance!"

Collin immediately took Desiree off his books and she was just so relieved.

"Why didn't you tell me Des?" Jake asked her quietly.

"I thought I would lose all this!"

"Fuck me Des, you're beautiful… You didn't need to do that… Never feel that you ever have to do that again!"

"OK" Des replied solemnly.

"Anyone ever tells you that's what you have to do, you tell me…OK?"

For the first time ever she trusted someone…. Jake…. Jake had grown very fond of Desiree and he wanted to protect her.

He arranged for Marcus to come back to take some more pictures and he was more than happy to be Desiree's photographer. With his help she started getting on the covers of more magazines. People had started to notice Desiree Louis… but she still had a long way to go before she was a big star.

Early 1979 she had changed her appearance. She had got rid of the chestnut blonde hair and dyed it jet black. She still kept it waist length, she had her hair line changed and her eyebrows reshaped and she'd even had her teeth whitened. She had also changed her surname from Louis to Beaumont… She was finally getting her life where she wanted it and she was happy.

Gavin Clements had been in touch with Jake over Desiree to ask if he could have her in Zillions' latest video.

"Video, wow"

"Yeah she's perfect"

Jake told Gavin he would talk to Des about it when he saw her. Jake did ask her about the video she smiled and she would love to do it, but she didn't know what she was doing. Jake told her not to worry about that so she finally agreed. Gavin was over the moon when he heard she would do it.

Jake took her to the set where they were shooting the video and Gavin explained what they were after. All she had to do was dance with him and sit at a table holding his hands. The song was called *'Leaving me alone'*. She was so excited she couldn't wait to start.

Before shooting the video with Zillion, Desiree had gone round to see Grace. When she got there, all her family were there. Grace had been admitted to hospital two weeks earlier as she found out when she rang the doorbell and her son came to the door.

"Oh Hello… is Grace here?"

"She's in hospital"

"Oh I'm sorry to hear that. Is she alright?

"Hmm… Can I ask who you are?

"Sorry yes, I'm Desiree"

"Miss Louis… I'm Grace's son, Malcolm"

Malcolm explained that Grace had had a very bad fall and would not be coming back to live here; the house was going up for sale. Des was so upset, she hadn't seen her for a while and felt so guilty. Malcolm asked her to step in for a minute as he had something to give her and disappeared.

Desiree looked confused as to why Grace's son would have something for her. When he returned, she discovered Grace had bought her a beautiful necklace in the shape of a star and on the back it read, *'Desiree, My Superstar – Love Grace'*. She'd bought it when Desiree had done her first photo shoot. Malcolm handed her the box and as she opened it her eyes widened. When she read the back, her eyes began to fill up and astray tear ran from the corner of her eye. Malcolm asked if she was alright.

"This is so beautiful. Your mother was so kind to me, I'll treasure it" She removed it from the box and put it on.

Malcolm smiled then suddenly Grace's other son Patrick and daughter Stella appeared. Malcolm introduced them to Desiree. She told them she was pleased to meet them and told them she'd love to thank Grace for the lovely gift if they wouldn't mind.

The next day Desiree went to the hospital to visit Grace. She had bought the biggest bouquet of roses she could find. Grace looked so frail, but as she looked up at Des, a smile swept across her face and she held out her arms. Des gently kissed her on her cheek. Grace was full of bruises where she had fallen.

"Can't leave you alone for a minute!"

Grace mentioned the necklace to her so Desiree held it away from her neck for her to see.

"Thank you so much, Grace – I'll never part with it"

She told her what had been happening, how she had given up her jobs in the shop and the restaurant. Now she was going to appear in a video and for the first time she had money to spend and people wanted to know her. It was all going to take some getting used to. She was getting invited to parties and all sorts of functions. They talked for hours. Grace was so pleased for her. Sadly that was to be the last time Des saw Grace.

Milton Keynes, 1979

Lori started touring, kicking off in Milton Keynes with a big line-up of famous singers and big girl groups like *Sugar Pop* and *Miss Naughty* – there were lots of bands and singers. Lori was having the time of her life and couldn't wait to see Des to tell her all her news – she had started seeing the pop singer Scott Daniels. Girls went crazy over him he was so handsome, he had short spiky dark hair and slate grey eyes, Lori had managed to hook him and was keeping him.

She also managed to get herself on the front page of the newspaper while on tour. She and Scott had been caught half naked in the lift of the hotel they were staying at. Scott was on his knees and Lori's panties were around her ankles Needless to say they made headline news. The cameraman got a great shot of Lori's expression – pure lust to say the least. It was all over the front page. Desiree was really shocked when Marcus had read it out to her.

"She is going to get some teasing over this Marcus"

"I thought she might somehow"

"She'll never live this down," Des said laughing.

Desiree met up with Lori after she had come back from touring. They had a ladies night out and Des asked Lori about Scott and wanted to know all the juicy details! Lori told Desiree that she couldn't believe it when the lift doors opened and there they all were with their cameras bulbs flashing from every angle, she could barely see. They were half naked and Scott was on his knees and they couldn't get the lift door to close fast enough.

"He's so hot. It just happened"

"Hmm yeah…. In the lift! Couldn't you wait?"

"No! He just pounced on me and one thing led to another!" Lori laughed again and shrugged her shoulders. "What can I say? What about you?"

"What about me?"

"What about men…what about sex…? Don't you miss it?"

"Hmm no…" Des answered, shaking her head. "My first experience… It's put me off forever. He made my skin crawl" she said, referring to Collin

"You were a virgin?"

"Yes… I hated it….

"He was just a slime ball and the next time will be different!"

Desiree wasn't convinced and wasn't in a hurry to do it again!

Chapter 3

Australia, 1978

Riley's mom had remarried, giving him a stepdad, Terrance Pollard. Riley's real dad had died when he was a baby and he had been given his mom's maiden name as was usual at the time. He didn't really remember his real dad – all he did know was that he didn't like his new one. Terrance would put him down at every opportunity, telling him he was a delinquent and would never amount to anything. Instead of encouraging Riley, Terrance would refer to him as a waste of space because he was in the school band. Riley liked rock music and wore his hair long. He would play his records loud and played guitar along with the music and sang to his life-size poster of Desiree Louis. This was a girl he really wanted to meet – she was his number one pin up.

When he left school his first job was at the crematorium, keeping the gardens straight and the graves tidy. He quite liked the job. It didn't pay much but he had a place to practice his singing and guitar in the old hut at the back of the cemetery. Terrance would kick him out of the house when he practised because he couldn't stand the noise. Riley formed his first band with his friend Rob and they played bars and clubs but soon flopped and the band broke up.

He was not going to give up though, he always knew he would make it. First, he met Warren through work, then a friend of his, Julian, who could play the drums. Together, they held auditions for another guitarist. Tim turned up and played a *Sharp Edge* song like real pro – they made their mind up that Tim was in. They were just packing up when a scruffy looking guy, long hair ripped jeans and T-shirt, came in. How he had heard about the audition they didn't know.

"Came for the audition"

"They're all done mate"

"Crikey… your fuckin' pullin' my chain!"

"Nah"

Ricky put his case on the table and pulled out a trumpet and blasted out a Zillion song. Riley's eyes widened.

"Fuck me, mate… you can play that bastard"

Ricky smiled a crooked smile. "Sure can."

"You're in, bud"

They all wrote down some names and threw them into a bucket and agreed that the first name to come out of the bucket would be the band name. They asked Riley's boss to pick and out came 'Lightning'. *Lightning* it was… they started working the clubs and bars. Terrance just laughed. He thought Riley and his band were a joke – how wrong could he be.

At the beginning of 1980

Dominance had finally hit the big time and took the British and American charts by storm. *Connection* also hit the charts and when the bands met up they became good friends. They were both having such a fantastic time. Girls would flock around them… What could be better than loads of screaming young girls grabbing pulling at their clothes wanting to sleep with them? Some girls would give them blowjobs just to be at the after gig parties. By this time, Staffan had changed his name from Ottesen to Templeton.

Riley's band *Lightning* had just entered the charts. Staffan and Riley didn't get on. The rest of the band got on with him, Johnny and his band also got on with him but, for some reason, Staffan and Riley took an instant dislike to each other and would snarl at each other at every opportunity, publicly insulting each other on several occasions.

Desiree started getting more offers from other rock groups like *Snakeskin, Devil Red* and *Iron Vengeance*, all wanting her to appear in their videos. She loved every minute. Jake was inundated with requests for Des to be in videos. The rock stars loved Desiree, she was just perfect for what they wanted with her rock chick look. The rock videos really got Desiree noticed and she became a pin up for a lot of young lads (and older ones) with her sexy poses and her beautiful looks. She was on posters, bill boards, magazines… you name it, she was on it!

Lori had grown her hair longer and permed it. She dyed it outrageously pink and purple. She had become such a big attraction, she had become a pin up girl herself. Guys went crazy over her long legs and sexy outfits – she was way ahead of the times. She was also back on tour, this time in Europe, so Des had some time to herself. With no photoshoots and no rock videos to do, she told Lori she would fly over to see her in concert. Lori was so excited.

"You could come on and sing with me, Des… we could do a duet!"

"No…" Des laughed, "I'm coming to watch you!"

"Yeah come on… It will be fun!"

"But I can't sing"

"You can"

"Well… I can… a bit!"

"Right that's sorted then"

"Yeah, OK, it'll be fun!"

Lori introduced her friend on stage and they did a duet together. Des had a fantastic time and the publicity didn't do either of them any harm. When Lori got back from her European tour she went round to Scott's to break up with him. She'd read in the paper that he'd cheated on her with a fan. The press had got hold of the story from the fan herself and Scott was expecting her. He knew he was in deep shit and tried to make out the fan had made it up!

"No Scott… Bullshit!"

"Lori, you know what it's like babe!"

"Bullshit… She was interviewed!"

Scott got hold of her and pulled her close and pressed himself against her. He kissed her moving down her neck starting to open the buttons on her top.

"Get your fucking hands off me!" She shouted.

"Come on babe… It didn't mean anything!"

There it was he had admitted it, Lori saw red and hit him over and over again. Scott took hold of her hands trying to stop her. She was quite strong and it took him a while to grab her hands.

"Fucking hell… Calm down you silly cow, it was only a shag!"

"Fuck you! You fucking prick!" She screamed storming out slamming the door behind her.

She crabbed a taxi and went straight to Desiree's hotel up to her room. She broke down in to tears as soon as Des opened the door.

"I hate him, he's such a bastard."

Des took hold of Lori to console her. Des told her he would come back grovelling, trying to make it up to her and she would forgive him. Scott had really hurt Lori but she wasn't going to let him know it. She had fallen head over heels in love with him and couldn't believe he'd done this to her.

"Would you forgive him?" Lori asked.

Des smiled at her and shook her head. "But *you* love him"

Yes I do love him… he has hurt me, so fuck him – Tonight we are going to party and I'll show him"

Des looked at her. "What?" She asked.

"Clubbing my friend… and we are going to party hard!"

They went out nightclubbing and partied till the early hours. They really partied hard that night, drinking and dancing with some more than willing young men. They give the press something to think about too, when they filled condoms up and lobbed them over the roof top. Next day, the press printed that they were out of control They suffered the next morning though as they were very hungover. Lori had stayed over at Des's hotel suite.

"Morning Des" she said holding her head.

"Don't shout, please," Des pleaded.

"Des… I whispered" she said in a croaky voice.

"No you didn't! And I blame you for this!"

Lori laughed, "Ahhhhhh!!! Ohhhhh!!! my friggin head!"

Des ordered some coffee from room service they both sat there holding their heads and wishing they hadn't bothered!

"Shit what did we do last night?" Des asked softly.

"I don't fuckin' know – it's all over the front pages, though"

"Ohhhhh… shit!!! Who ordered the papers?"

Lori handed the paper over to Des.

"I don't know, me I think. Des looked at the paper, "Oh shit, do you want to know what we did?"

Lori shook her head nervously, "No… no, don't tell me"

"Apparently, we were throwing johnnies filled with water off the fuckin' roof top and shouting obscenities at the press…"

They both sank into a heap on the floor. They knew that the press would be waiting for them and they were right. Jake and Will were not impressed with either of them. Jake wanted to know what Des was playing at and Will told them they were not giving the right impression to their fans. While they both sunk into their chairs trying to bury their heads, Lori realised she didn't really want to be a 'clean cut singer', she wanted to be a bit of a rebel.

Lori still hadn't forgiven Scott and was about to meet Riley She'd gone to meet her agent, William Radford. After her meeting she went to a club and bumped into Judy Blake, an actress who had just made her film debut. Lori was sat having a drink with her when Riley came in. He spotted Lori and went over and introduced himself. Judy left Lori talking to Riley and headed back over to the group of people she was with. Lori and Riley got talking when Riley had mentioned he was a big fan of Desiree's. Lori asked him if he'd ever met her.

"No… I would love to meet Desiree Beaumont!"

"Would you?"

"Yeah… most men would!"

"I see… is that why you have come over here, to get me to introduce you to Des?"

"No…not at all"

Lori wasn't quite so sure about Riley.

"Why don't we go grab something to eat and see whose bed we wake up in?" Riley said confidently.

"What?… well, you're sure of yourself"

"Yeah… defo! Don't want to waste time, do we?"

"Well you don't…obviously!" She said as she smiled at him, shocked at his directness.

Lori liked Riley and said that she would love to go get something to eat with him. She enjoyed his company but he didn't beat around the bush, he said what he meant and she like that about him. He asked if he could see her again and she said "yeah why not?"

They started seeing a lot of each other. Scott was so jealous he couldn't stand it. He kept calling Lori telling he wanted her back. He told her she'd taught him a lesson, now it was time to forgive him. She was driving him mad. She told Scott it was all finished between them. She was seeing Riley and she liked him. Des was concerned that Lori was seeing Riley on the rebound.

"What's he like?" She asked

"He's funny… He makes me laugh"

"Well that good"

"The sex is good, actually very good – he certainly knows what he's doing!"

"You're sleeping with him really…?"

"Oh my God Des, don't be such a prude – Yeah I'm sleeping with him and he is *fantastic* in bed!"

Des laughed…as Lori eyes had glazed over.

"Scott keeps ringing me… I don't know what he's playing at"

"You're with Riley and he doesn't like it?"

"Tough. He should have thought of that when he screwed that girl!"

Des had to leave Lori as she had a photoshoot. She was sat in her dressing room putting her make up on ready for Marcus when Jake came in.

"Des there's a woman out here claiming to be your mother!"

Des turned round quickly. "What?"

"She wants to see you!"

"Not interested Julian! Tell her to go away!"

"Just see her – even if it's to tell her to fuck off!"

"Why?"

"I don't know… Are you not intrigued a little?"

"No!" She said sharply.

"No… Really Des, I think you are…"

Desiree looked at Jake. She wasn't really sure but then she agreed and Jake went to get the woman and brought her to Des's dressing room.

"Desiree… Oh my God, you are so beautiful!"

"Am I Carol…?"

She recognised her straight away. She knew she was her mum. She was older, time had taken its toll on her; her beautiful black hair was starting to go grey and was like straw. She looked as if she'd had a hard life. Her clothes were old and faded, the heels on her shoes were worn down and looked as if they would to fall off if she took another step.

"Yes you are very beautiful … I'm your mum, not Carol"

Desiree gave her a steely glare. "I have no mum!"

"I understand why you feel the way you do!"

Des stood up and turned to her.

"You left me with a man that beat me so much he put me in hospital several times, I ended up in homes but that's OK it taught me a valuable lesson… not to trust anyone"

"Desiree…"

"You think you can turn up now and be my mother? I don't fucking think so!" as she stopped Carol in her tracks.

"I was always coming back for you!"

"When?… Now I'm famous you mean?"

"I'm your mum!"

"I have no mum and I have no dad!"

Desiree went over to her purse and took the money she had in it and threw it at Carol. "Now fuck off!"

"Des… Please!"

"No…. Do I have to get security to throw you out?"

"No… I'm sorry I will never bother you again!"

"Good…Now get out!"

Carol put her head down and walked over to the door she turned back to Des.

"Remember when you asked me if you could be on television and I told you, you could be whatever you wanted to be"

"No" She said abruptly, remembering everything about her mum.

"Well Baby, you did it and I'm so proud of you… I'm so sorry for leaving"

Des stormed back over to Carol and shouted in her face, "But you didn't come back for me, did you? You left me with that monster!"

"I'm sorry," Tears started falling down her cheeks.

"Get out!"

Carol opened the door just and was just about to walk out when Des shouted.

"You forgot your money…"

"I didn't come here for money" Then she left.

Desiree looked at herself in the mirror. Tears were forming in the corners of her eyes. Her mother showing up like that had brought a lot of bad memories flooding back, memories she didn't want.

Desiree had massive issues with trust and once she thought she couldn't trust you, nobody could change her mind. Des could never forgive her mother.

Chapter 4

Lori and Riley's relationship drew to a close. They'd had a great few months together, it was very short lived and they parted friends. Lori was still in love with Scott and Riley wanted to meet Des. They had very different agendas, they had fun together and they'd enjoyed each other but they were never going to get married and live happily ever after. They were the hottest couple in town for a while, though Scott wouldn't leave her alone until he got her back. He told her that he would never cheat on her again. She told him he shouldn't promise things he couldn't guarantee. He swore he meant it.

Lori had been asked to sing the theme song to '*Friday Night*', a new film that was in the making. She jumped at the chance as the film was set to be a blockbuster. When the single came out it went straight to number one, keeping *Dominance*'s and Connection's songs from getting to the top slot. She was asked to attend the film premiere which Desiree was also attending.

When Des walked in to the crowd in a royal blue, figure-hugging dress with plunging backline and sparkling gems encrusted all over it, heads turned. Matt Adams had seen her from the other side of the crowd, he would have liked to have met her. Unfortunately, he was way too far away to speak to her, nobody could get near her.

Flashbulbs were popping everywhere, questions were flying at her from every angle – every newspaper; magazine and reporter wanted a piece of Desiree.

Staffan Templeton had seen Desiree on the cover of a magazine. He thought she was the most beautiful woman he'd ever seen and he wanted to meet her. He had told the Edvin and the guys that he wanted to meet her years before and now he told them he was going to marry her one day.

"In your dreams, Staffan" Edvin sniggered.

"I am, I'm telling you… I will marry Desiree Beaumont!"

"You'll be lucky just to meet her let alone have any sort of relationship with her… Well it's not happening!" Delmar said, laughing.

"Oh guys… faith… I'm going to meet her and I'm going to marry her! You wait and see…"

The guys found Staffan really funny. Meeting Desiree Beaumont was a dream for most men and here was Staffan telling them he was going to marry her. As for Staffan, he was determined he was going to meet her. He was not, however, the only one who wanted to meet Desiree Beaumont. Riley Watson was also very interested in her and wanted to meet her.

When Staffan found out she was staying at the same hotel as his band while they were on tour he got very excited… He couldn't wait.

"Hey guys…! Guess who is going to be in Vegas at the same time as us?"

"Who…?" asked Barny.

"Desiree Beaumont, no less!"

Delmar and Edvin said in unison, "Fucking hell – you're joking!"

"No I'm fucking not. And guess who will be meeting her?"

"No fucking way Staffan… You won't get fucking near her!" Lucas said.

"Yeah I fucking will. She will be in the same VIP bar as us and she's mine! We are famous so why won't I get near her?"

Desiree was in Vegas for photo shoot and Staffan was determined that he was going to meet her.

After their concert the band went into a private bar just for VIPs and there she was! Wearing a low halter neck, black mini dress, with beautiful shapely legs, her hair up and showing off her beautiful tanned back she sat, slowly getting drunk. Men were all around her. Staffan scanned her body from her head to toe. He just had to take a chance and go over.

He pushed in front of all the other men.

"Hi" he smoothed confidently.

Desiree stopped talking to all the men that were crowded round and looked at Staffan.

"Hi there" she said smiling at him.

She had seen him on the TV and in magazines and she thought he was gorgeous.

He just stood looking at her with his mouth open. Looking into her big brown eyes outlined with black eyeliner, her long eye lashes fluttered as she licked her full red glossy lips. He took a deep breath....

"I'm Staffan Templeton"

"Yes... I know who you are!"

She said as she sat confidently playing with a strand of hair that was dangling at the side of her face, continuing to smile at him.

"Do you?" He said nervously.

"Yes of course... You are the singer from the band *Dominance*!"

"Yeah... Yes I am. You are very beautiful!"

"Thank you" she smiled at the same time thinking what a sexy accent he had.

"I believe you have been in some rock videos, but not one of ours?"

"Yeah...I have been in a few... Would you like me to be in one of yours?"

"Oh God yeah... even more so, if you have to touch me!"

"Really.? You'd like me to touch you?" She said laughing.

"Oh fucking hell, yes...Oh I mean..."

Des laughed again. "I know what you mean!"

She found him funny and she found him really attractive too.

"Are you laughing at me?" He asked smiling at her.

"Yes"

"And why is that may I ask?"

"You are funny"

Edvin, Delmar, Lucas and Barny watched eagerly. They wanted to see if Staffan could actually pull this off. They couldn't believe that she was talking to him and she seemed to like him. They talked and talked.

He couldn't believe that he'd finally got to meet her. He was hooked. He turned his head to the guys and grinned like a cat that had got the cream.

"Fuck me he's actually done it!" Edvin muttered.

"Yeah, he's a lucky bastard!" Delmar smiled.

She leaned into him.

She whispered "I'm going to the pool are you coming?"

"OK…Yeah… But why are we going to the pool?"

"We are going swimming… You can swim can't you?" She asked, licking her lips seductively.

"Yep…" He gulped deeply.

"Come on then!"

They headed for the pool and, when no one was watching, Desiree slipped her dress off and jumped in. All Staffan could do was look at her longingly.

"Come on!" She shouted, taking her thong off and putting it poolside.

She excited him… He thought she was crazy and out of control.

"Get in there with no clothes on?" He asked incredulously.

"Yeah… Come on… Take your clothes off!"

"OK then!" He shrugged.

Desiree didn't have to tell him twice! Staffan took his clothes off and jumped in with her. They messed around in the pool, naked their bodies touching every now and then. Staffan wanted more… much more. He eventually plucked up the courage to get hold of her and pull her closer to him. He moved his hands round her body and leaned in to kiss her. She kissed him back, their naked bodies becoming more intimate, pressing against each other.

"Oh shit," he sighed, "I want you here and now, Desiree!"

She had really turned him on. He kissed her more passionately… more intensely… He pushed her towards the side of pool and pressed up against her. She wrapped her legs around him and moved her finger gently down his back, pulling him closer to her, sighing as he made love to her right there in the pool. She couldn't believe she was doing this.

"Oh yeah babe, that feels so good," he whispered as they moved in rhythm together.

The sex was hot and passionate. She had never felt like this before.

Grabbing some towels that were lying around, they bundled up their clothes and sneaked back in to Staffan's room where they continued what they'd started. They couldn't keep their hands off each other as they fell on the bed. He pulled her to him firmly, running his hands over her body, taking her breath away. His fingers excited her. His mouth tantalized her.

"Oh yes... Oh..." she sighed with every movement.

When she touched him she sent him crazy. He moved his mouth slowly up her body, easing himself between her thighs and made love to her. He didn't stop, forcing her to climax over and over and eventually they fell asleep in the ruffled sheets.

The paparazzi missed this one but they had got them in the pool together naked and of course it made the headlines.

HOT NEWS

DESIREE BEAUMONT AND ROCK SINGER STAFFAN TEMPLETON IN VEGAS PLAZA POOL NAKED TOGETHER

The next morning Staffan woke first and watched Desiree sleeping, trailing his fingers across her skin. He had this feeling that he'd never had before. This girl had stolen his heart and she wasn't getting away. He had fallen in love, he knew he had. 'Could I fall in love that fast?' He thought to himself? *Yes I can,* he thought looking at her.

Desiree opened her sleepy eyes.

"Hi" She said, smiling at him.

"Hi, yourself," he said, smiling back at her.

She moved her fingers over his chest as he kissed her forehead.

"Say something in Danish to me"

"Hmm.... *Jeg tror jeg er forelsket I dig*"

She smiled. "And what does that mean?" She asked.

"I think I am in love with you!" He looked at her and smiled. "I'll order some breakfast!" He said, jumping out bed.

She smiled back at him. "Can I use your toothbrush?"

"Yeah... use whatever you want!"

"Really? I'll keep that in mind."

"You're not going to disappear on me are you?" He asked.

"Disappear?" She asked inquisitively.

"Yeah… This wasn't just a one night stand was it?"

Desiree shook her head. "No"

"Good I'm glad… I want more of you!"

Room service came and they had their breakfast. Des jumped into the shower and Staffan followed her. Steam filled the room as the water cascaded down their bodies. Their eyes met and he pulled her to him, kissing her softly. The water covered their naked bodies. The kiss deepened and they made love again, very hot and passionate.

Desiree got dressed quickly as she had to get to her photoshoot. Staffan had sound checks before his next gig but he asked her if he would see her later.

"Yeah, definitely"

They met up after they had finished. Staffan had hired a motorbike.

"Where are we going?"

Staffan smiled at her. "We are going for a ride."

He took her hand, led her to the motor bike and got on, holding his hand out to her. She threw her leg over the bike revealing her beautiful shapely legs. She wrapped her arms tightly around his waist as he rode off, screeching the tyres behind them as they headed towards the Grand Canyon. He rode to the Watch Tower. The view was overwhelming. They looked out over the rock layers, all the vibrant colours and the Colorado River flowing through the centre. It was so beautiful, Staffan wrapped his arms around Des's waist and kissed her cheek whilst they admired the view.

"Why don't you come to watch the gig tonight? That's if you want to!"

"Yeah… that would be fantastic!"

"Great I'll tell security that you're my guest… Not that they would refuse you anyway looking like you do"

Des turned to him smiled and kissed him tenderly.

"We better head back"

The headed back to the Plaza. Delmar Edvin and the guys were in the bar. Staffan took Desiree to meet them. They all stood gaping at her with their mouths open, not knowing what to say – she was just so stunning. She found their reaction quite funny and smirked.

Saying bye to them, she pulled Staffan to her kissing him seductively biting his lip at the same time. He automatically went to grab her but she smiled again winking at him and told him she'd see him later. Staffan sighed and smiled.

"Oh you will… man, you're one sexy girl"

Edvin smiled… "Well?"

"Well what?"

"Come on, Staffan"

"I'm in love and she's coming to the gig tonight!"

"Fuck me… You did it… You said you would"

"I told you I'm marrying her!"

The guys were totally dumbfounded – they couldn't believe he'd got her. He said he would… and he did.

Chapter 5

Desiree and Staffan became a hot item, hitting the headlines week after week. They were most definitely the hottest couple around. They became very close, Desiree's Danish rock star did not disappoint! The sex was electric. Des had fallen for Staffan in a big way, she had never been in love before. Collin had left her cold, he repulsed her; he had taken away the one thing she wanted to be special.

She had this romantic notion about what her first time would be like. Staffan ticked all the boxes with all his long shaggy, permed blonde hair and big piercing blue eyes, his beautiful tanned masculine body. He wore an earring and a chain round his neck; she just thought he was so hot. Des couldn't get enough of him and vice versa.

It was pretty clear that the couple had fallen in love and there could be talk of a wedding.

Des was scheduled to appear on the Desmond Cowley talk show, she and Staffan had been in the news quite a lot with rumours about their romance and Desmond wanted to know all about it. Laurence Warren and Steven Russell were also appearing on the show.

The Desmond Cowly Show

Desmond had talked about the film the new film starring Laurence Warren and Steven Russell, it was set to be a blockbuster. Vivian Towers also had a role in the film alongside Millicent Lee and Jenny Blake. Desiree was so excited about meeting Laurence Warren and Steven Russell, she stood quietly at the side of the stage and watched. Then, when Desmond said her name, she suddenly got nervous. She'd never been on television before, this was her first ever interview.

"Now we have a real treat for our male guests tonight... Desiree Beaumont, Ladies and Gentlemen"

The audience clapped as she sauntered on looking every bit the sex symbol wearing leather jeans and leather waist coat, her hair flowing down her back swishing round her waist, smoky grey eye makeup that made her big brown eyes stand out. She was simply stunning.

"Hi, Desiree"

"Hi"

"Welcome to the show...Now you have taken the world by storm with your beautiful looks, beautiful figure – you're also very much in demand for rock videos."

Des smiled. "Yeah... It's happened so fast"

"Now what made you want to be a model?"

"I didn't... I wanted to be a film star... This just happened. I have been so lucky, I can't thank Jake Summers enough for making all this possible."

"Do you like doing the rock videos?"

"Oh yeah... It's great... Lots of good looking men!" She giggled.

"Now what we really want to know about is the man in your life!"

Desiree laughed "Hmm" and continued to smile coyly.

"There are rumours that you've been seeing Danish rock singer Staffan Templeton from *Dominance*"

"Hmm yeah... We've been seeing a lot of each other, that's right"

"We want to know if it's serious"

"Ha-ha... Well we like each other and that's all I'm saying..."

"You're not giving anything away here!"

Desiree smiled and shook her head.

"We will just have to see…"

"Well good luck with the rock videos. It's been lovely having you on the show Thank you for joining us, Desiree…. The beautiful Desiree Beaumont Everyone…."

Dominance were touring Brazil and the guys watched Desiree's interview before they went on stage. Edvin told Staffan that this was what he was going to be asked about on his interview next week.

"Yeah I know…"

"Well they are gonna want to know all about you and Des"

"Yeah…and I'll tell 'em"

"Des is hot news… They can't get enough of her. You and Des together now that's really hot news….

"Yeah… I know it'll be fun!"

The following week it was Staffan's turn to be grilled about his relationship with Desiree. Everyone wanted to know all about them and how serious they were.

The George Vernon Show

When Staffan had his interview with talk show host George Vernon that was exactly George wanted… The low down on him and Des.

"Well girls, tonight we have the sexy singer from *Dominance*, Staffan Templeton with us … we also have actor Darrel Rawlins and the lovely Fiona Howard….

The studio filled with screams from the crowds of girls in the audience as soon as George mentioned Staffan's name.

"Staffan Templeton everyone"

"Staffan… Hello"

"Hi George"

"Well *Dominance* is storming up the charts with *'Rock with me'*"

"Yeah its doing really well… We are really pleased"

"I believe you're doing a European tour soon?"

"Yeah we're looking forward to it"

"And you and the guys have a world tour on the cards as well?"

"Yeah… That's right no rest for the wicked" He threw out a throaty laugh

"I need to ask you about your love life Staffan – all the ladies want to know if… Are you still free or not?"

Staffan tilted his head to the side and smiled.

"It's been said that you and Desiree Beaumont are quite an item… Is it true?"

Staffan smiled again and said, "Yeah it's true… So no, I'm not free"

"What's it like seeing such a sexy lady?"

"Well what can I say…? She is so freakin sexy!"

"Many men would love to be in your shoes"

"Yeah, she's a beautiful girl"

"Is it serious?"

"Hmm" He smiled.

"I hope so… I think so… Yeah…" he said trying not to give too much away.

"Do we hear wedding bells?"

"Um, we will have to see, early days yet!" He smiled again.

"Well thank you Staffan for coming on the show…good luck with the tour it's been a pleasure. Staffan Templeton everyone… next we have the very talented actor Darrel Rawlins and the lovely Fiona Howard.

Chapter 6

Staffan wanted to live with Desiree so he decided to ask her to move in with him. He said they could buy an apartment together in New York.

She looked at him in total amazement.

"Is it too soon, don't you want to, Des?" He asked, concerned.

"Yes, of course I do… but are you sure?"

"I told you, I love you…I want to spend my life with you"

"You really love me, Staffan?"

"Yeah… I do"

"Nobody has ever loved me," she whispered.

Staffan looked at her confused. Then Des sat and told him all about her childhood. After Carol had left… how David started taking it out on her and all about when she was twelve how he beat her black and blue, and was admitted to hospital on regular occasions with severe beatings. The most awful thing of all, how he said the most terrible things to her. How he would tell her she was ugly and that she would never find anyone to love her. How Social Services had to make her a ward of court, how she ended up in home after home.

Staffan couldn't believe what he was hearing. He was horrified.

"How could anyone not love you, Des?"

Des shook her head. Sadness taken over by the hate she felt for them both.

"Well they didn't!" She cried bitterly.

"Do you remember your mother?"

"Yes she was so beautiful, I think he beat her."

"So why leave you with him?"

"I don't know, but she did."

"Well, I love you, Des"

Des smiled flung her arms round his neck and kissed him and told she didn't want or need to talk about this anymore

"Now, about this apartment…"

She told him she would get onto the apartment hunting straight away. She suggested that they put Jake on it. Jake asked his real estate friend, Mark, to find them an apartment. Mark found them an apartment block overlooking gardens and he offered to be their trustee to set up a private sale. It had a beautiful fountain with a lovers sculpture in the middle of it.

Des loved it. It was just perfect, lots of security (you even had to have a pass to get through the gates into the grounds). The apartment itself had two big bedrooms with en-suites, an open plan fireplace in the lounge with original brick and beams, leading to a beautiful fitted kitchen. It didn't take long for Des and Staffan to move to New York and in to their apartment. When Staffan was away, she took some time to learn some Danish dishes so she could impress him. He was impressed, as much with the fact that she had taken time out of her busy schedule to learn Danish cooking.

Staffan and the guys had been in the studio all day. It had been uneventful but Staffan had come home very frustrated. However, when he arrived home to the aroma of Chicken Amangur with Copenhagen Potatoes and all the trimmings. She'd even baked coffee cream puff muffins and dill bread. Staffan was really impressed.

"Wow babe, something smells good"

"Do ya like?" She smiled.

"I love it…" He said, taking hold of her round the waist with one hand and playing with her hair with the other, kissing her. "You…You amaze me!"

Des smiled and kissed him back she giggled.

"How was your day?"

"Shit! We couldn't get *Seconds Away* done, it just wasn't flowing."

"Is that going to be the new single?"

"Yep, but the music, the beat isn't fuckin' coming so we recorded *Dirty Diary"*

"Wow that sounds good. The other one will come, baby –I know it"

Staffan and the guys asked Des to be in their new video for *Nights Alon*e and *Dirty Diary*. Staffan didn't want anyone else and Barny, Edvin, Delmar and Lucas thought it was a great idea. Staffan wouldn't be natural with anyone else so Des was the obvious choice. She said 'yes' straight away – she was looking forward to it.

"*Nights alone* is a love rock ballad," Staffan said, smiling at her.

"Sign me up!" She smiled.

"I get to touch you!" He said, rubbing his hands together and grinning like a Cheshire cat.

"I think I can handle it," she said, tilting her head to the side, fluttering her eyelashes and licking her lips seductively.

Staffan laughed. "You're going to drive me crazy, you know that don't you!"

"You bet Baby!" She said playfully.

After the first few days of filming, Desiree had really teased Staffan. He was going home extremely horny. As they packed up to leave, Staffan grabbed her and kissed her longingly.

You teased me more than you needed to" he murmured huskily.

Des laughed "How much can you take baby"

"I'm going to take you home and ravish you now!"

"No! You are going to feed me before you do anything to me!

"Oh I see… You can tease me all day, but you want me to feed you before I can ravish you?" He smiled.

"That's right, Buddy Boy!"

"I think you have a nerve"

"Yeah… but just think… If you feed me, I'll ravish *you*!"

"Right... come on out the door. You will eat fast won't you?" He said chasing her out laughing.

As she'd promised she took him home and ravished him. She pushed him down on the bed using her teeth to unzip his jeans slowly. Looking down at her he stretched his hands out to get hold of her, moving her body out of his reach to tease him more, she moved her fingers into his jeans pulling his manhood out. Slowly she whispered her tongue over the tip of it making him groan. His whole body stiffened up, she was driving him to insanity. His mouth was dry, his hands were clammy and his breathing was heavy. He quickly reversed the position. He moved down her body, pulling her panties off and pressing his swollen dick against her, pushing her thighs open with his knees, his passion was intense. Her lips parted as he kissed her throat, 'uh-uh-uh' she groaned. Staffan grabbing her buttocks made her even more responsive, moving back and forth in a steady rhythm. His passion spilled from his body to hers. Eventually they crashed down, limp and breathless in each other's arms.

They had been living together for a few months and Staffan had fallen head over heels in love with Desiree. He decided he was going to ask her to marry him as soon as they had time enough on their own for him to ask her properly. Although they were still very young, he just wanted to be with her.

They had both been very busy. Staffan had been touring with his band all over Europe. Desiree had been doing photoshoots or the rock videos in Europe but they never seemed to be in the same place at the same time. Staffan had planned how he was going to propose and all he needed was to have Des in the same place as him. Finally, their work schedules came together and they managed to be in Paris at the same time. This was it. Staffan was going to ask Desiree to marry him. He arranged a romantic dinner and he was planning to ask her on one knee, to be really romantic. Des had really missed Staffan and suggested that they order room service and spend the night in bed..

"No, we can't do that"

"Yeah? Oh yes we can!"

"Des, I've got a surprise and we have to go for dinner!"

"What have you planned?" She said eagerly.

"I can't tell you that, otherwise it wouldn't be a surprise"

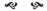

"Oh Yeah!" She said, crinkling her nose up giggling.

They sat down to eat when the waiter came over with a bottle of champagne. Staffan kept grinning at her.

"Why do you keep grinning at me Staffan?" She asked.

"No reason," he answered but continuing to grin.

"Staffan, if you don't tell me I'm going to wind you up!"

"What… *sexually* wind me up?"

"Yep…!"

Staffan winked at her and smiled. Des looked at him quizzically. 'You've asked for it,' she thought as she flicked her shoe off and stretched her leg out. She placed her foot on his groin and started rubbing her foot rhythmically up and down. She could feel his manhood growing beneath her toes…Staffan looked at her and smiled.

"Des, you are making me go stiff!"

"I warned you," she said, doing it all the more.

"OK… Do you want to know what I'm up to?"

"Yeah… Yeah…Come on… Give!" She smiled.

Staffan got the waiter's attention. He appeared at their table and placed a plate with a silver cover in front of Des. She looked at it and at first thought it was her dessert. At this point, Staffan got down on one knee next to her. Desiree's eyes widened with excitement and she began to bite her bottom lip. He took the silver cover off the plate and there was a beautiful diamond ring, bigger than she had ever seen. All the staff in the restaurant gathered around to watch, intrigued to find out what her answer was going to be.

"Will you marry me, Des?" Staffan asked

Des suddenly got very excited and started to grin.

"You want to marry me Staffan?"

"Yes. You are the most beautiful woman in the world I'm head over heels in love with you…"

"Oh Staffan… Yes, I will marry you!" She said with tears in her eyes.

Staffan placed the ring on her finger and smiled at her. "I love you"

Des smiled shyly, looking down at her diamond ring. Leaning over to him she kissed him gently. "I love you, too…" she murmured.

All the waitresses sighed with happiness. Everyone in the restaurant went over and congratulated them. Finally, they all stood and drank a toast to the young couple, remarking how much in love they looked.

Staffan confessed that she had made him the happiest man in the world, but there was a little matter that was standing to attention under the table.

"How do I do we get out of the here? You have created a monster in my pants that I've now got to hide. You made me very horny rubbing me up!"

Desiree burst in to a surge of unstoppable giggles and took hold of his hand.

"Come on… I'll hide you"

"You'll hide me?" A smirk grew over his face.

"Yes"

They managed to get to the elevator without anyone noticing. He made her stand in front of him so she could feel his hard budge in his trousers. He pressed himself against her suggestively. As they approached their room Staffan couldn't keep his hands off her any longer. He grabbed her, picking her up. He smiled longingly at her as he threw gently her on the bed. She flicked her shoes off. His eyes admired the view, he was in such a hurry to get her naked. He ripped the buttons off his shirt so he could get it off quicker…

"Do you want all this?" She asked, running her fingers down his body

"It's mine already"

Des giggled as she traced her finger over his lips. Staffan grabbed her finger gently with his teeth, sucking it suggestively. Staring at him, smiling like sin, she rolled on top – pulling his hands above his head. Slowly but gently she made her way down his body with butterfly kisses. She stopped at his navel, looking up at him with her lustful brown eyes, then continued to move her mouth lower down his body. He started to breathe faster, biting his lip.

"Hmm… oh yeah… huh…"

He groaned with pleasure as she sat on him and rode him like a cowgirl.

"Oh Fuckin' Hell, Des… Ohm… Oh Yeah… Yeah…"

He reversed the position. and she responded with a wild excitement running through her body. His tongue circled her nipples as he thrust back and forth, her hips following his rhythm until she arched her back in climax. Staffan's eyes rolled to the back of his head as he came hard.

"Oh Man!" He said, trying to catch his breath.

Chapter 7

August 1981

A few weeks after Staffan had proposed, he and Desiree decided to sneak off and get married. They'd only told Lori and Scott what they were planning. It all happened so fast. They flew to Vegas and got married in the White Chapel. They had asked Lori and Scott to be their witnesses and met them there. It was so hush hush. For their reception they all went out for dinner and no-one was any the wiser. They spent the week in their hotel suite; they just wanted to spend the whole time together before letting the world know..

"I just want to stay here with you forever" Des said snuggling up to him.

Staffan kissed her softly. "Do you know how much I love you, Desiree?"

Des smiled with contentment

They spent the week in their room, not going down to dinner or going anywhere – they just ordered room service. Somehow the press had managed to find out where they were. They knew the floor they were on but not which room, until Staffan opened the door to let a waiter in. One reporter spotted him, Staffan had never seen anyone run so fast. All of a sudden flash bulbs were flashing like crazy. It took Staffan all his time to close the door.

There were reporters running from everywhere.

"Well, they know where we are now!"

"Yeah, but they don't know we got married"

"I think they might…"

"Not for sure though"

Staffan laughed and sat on the bed, gently kissed her and told her she was the only women he would ever love.

"I don't think they are going to give up now until they get the story"

"Well, they will have to wait – we're on our honeymoon"

The press finally did get a photo of Des standing at the window. They just couldn't wait to get the big story on the couple. What a scoop this would be! There were already so many rumours circulating about the couple being married and they wanted it confirming. They followed them to the airport. When they flew back to New York, the American press was all over them at the other end… photos for this paper and that paper… it was great publicity.

"Staffan, are you and Des married?"

"Yes… we were married last week"

"Come on Des, show us your ring!"

And of course Desiree obliged. She stuck her hand out, her fingers twinkling as she show off her wedding ring, white gold set with diamonds to match her engagement ring. Staffan just had a plain white gold band.

"What's it like to be married to one of the most beautiful women in the world Staffan?" One reporter asked.

"You mean *the* most beautiful woman in the world… and it's fantastic!"

Questions were flying from all directions… They wanted to know everything.

"It was very hush, hush" she giggled.

Even when Desiree and Staffan jumped into their car and drove away the press was still all over them, running after the car to get more photos. When they got home they flopped on the couch…They'd had such a tiring day and they were exhausted. Suddenly the phone rang it was Jake.

"Did you forget to tell me something?" He asked, annoyed.

"Oh Jake… I'm sorry…. It was a spur of the moment!"

"You know this is not going to go down well with the fans… yours or Staffan's! Men dream of you, being with you…. girl's dream of being with him…. This could damage both your careers – you should have kept this a secret" he scolded.

"Jake … it was kept quiet … We are in love!"

"Are you happy Des?" Jake asked.

"Yes…."

"Good… Then I'm happy for you…oh and Marcus has told me to tell you no babies! He doesn't want you ruining that beautiful body!"

"No worries there… Not yet!" She laughed.

"Right… See you tomorrow, babe"

Staffan and Des went to bed. They both had really heavy workloads as from the next day. As he cuddled in to her he told her that as soon as her saw her on the front of that magazine he knew he was going to marry her. Des smiled. She had never felt like this about anyone before. Staffan was her first love. She had got to where she wanted to be. She was famous, she had the love of her life – she still wanted to be a film star but that could all wait. She'd had such an unhappy childhood but now she was happy and wanted to be a good wife.

Desiree headed into the studio the next day for a photoshoot and Staffan headed off to meet Delmar and the guys. They were setting off on a tour visiting states like Pennsylvania, Tennessee and Florida.

"Hi babe, let's get them clothes off" Marcus said smiling at her.

Desiree went and got changed into some very sexy underwear.

"Des, how would you feel about no bra?" Marcus dropped in casually.

"You want me to show my boobs?" She asked aghast.

"No… I want you to cover them up with your hands … but be seductive… lick your lips, you know Babe!"

"OK … fine…"

"Yeah" he said excited. He didn't think it would be that easy.

Des came from the dressing room with a robe on. Marcus had dug out a big fur rug and he wanted Des to lay on it posing with just her thong on, with her hands covering her breasts. They were the sexiest photos she'd ever done and she looked fabulous. It had been a long shoot and she had done shots with and without the bra.

Des liked this line of underwear. She liked the tie knickers and the front fastening bra. She had already put in an order for this line for herself except she wanted her thongs to clip at the sides instead of tie.

"Oh babe, you are amazing!"

"Marcus, you see hundreds of girls!" She smiled.

"Oh baby, not like you… The camera loves you… You are just breathtaking"

"Can we take a break, Marcus?" She asked.

"Yeah… sure…"

Des was taking her break with a glass of water, relaxing, when Marcus shouted out that she had a call. It was Lori. She'd rung to tell her that she and Staffan had hit the front page on every newspaper around the world.

"Oh my… Really?"

"Listen Des I'll read it out to you…"

Dominance was well into of their tour. They had been on the road for about eight weeks when they called into a diner for something to eat and drink. In the booth next to them was a very loud and boisterous group of guys. They were especially loud when they opened the mag that Desiree was in.

"Hey, look at this!" One of the lads shouted as he held up a big centre page poster of Desiree with her new sexy look.

"Fuck me….! She's some piece of ass," said another.

"She is so fuckin' hot!"

"Yeah… what I'd like to do with her… Fuck me, man!"

Another lad wanted to see the picture and grabbed it.

"Desiree Beaumont… she is so fucking hot… look at them legs and her body… fuck!"

"Staffan Templeton is one lucky bastard… he gets to lay her every fucking night!"

"You'd fucking bottle it if you had the chance to be with her… you wouldn't know what to do!" His mate laughed.

"Fuck you…I know exactly what I'd do!" Delmar turned round and said, "Guys come on… that's Staffan Templeton's wife you're talking about."

"Yeah we know and she's so fuckin' fit…bet you wouldn't say No!"

One guy said, "That's … Delmar Schmidt…" then Staffan turned round and the guys realised that they were talking to the band.

"What photos are you looking at guys?" Staffan asked.

"Desiree's new ones… they have only been released today…. She is so hot… you are one lucky bastard!"

"Yeah… don't I know it!" He answered smugly.

Staffan looked at the photos. Desiree's gorgeous face looked back at him seductively, in just her thong on a fur rug, her hands barely covering her breasts. He was not happy.

When they got back, Staffan told Desiree he didn't want her doing any more pictures like that.

"Staffan…"

"I don't want men…"

"*Staffan…*" she said, interrupting him.

"I had to sit and listen to a group of young horny guys saying what they wanted to do to my wife," he explained.

"Staffan… what did you see when you saw me on that mag all that time ago?" She asked.

"No, Des" he said, shaking his finger at her.

"No…. what did you want to do to me?"

"It's not the same…" he spluttered.

"No?"

"No…. I knew I was going to marry you!"

"Not in the pool you didn't"

"Oh Yeah I did."

He walked over to her, put his arms round her and kissed her.

"You're mine for ever… never forget that!"

He lifted her up in his arms, kissing her. He walked into the bedroom and threw her on the bed looking down at her. His eyes scanned her body as he removed her shirt.

"You're so fuckin' hot, Baby"

He ran his hand down her body. She arched her back as he touched her, moving his hand across her breasts, down the shallow curve of her stomach, his mouth kissing her thighs. Her body shook as he ran his tongue over her legs. She had tingles running up her spine. He looked up at her and smiled, his eyes on fire with passion as he took his jeans off. She reached for him.

"Oh baby, Yeah" he whispered as he eased between her thighs and began to make love to her.

As they moved rhythmically together Staffan gave moans of pleasure.

"Ohm… yeah baby… yeah" Des moaned as they climaxed together.

He rolled over on to his side and looked at her, both still breathless.

"I was so fucking jealous when I heard them guys…"

"Nothing to be jealous about Babe… nothing at all…"

And in no time at all they had fallen asleep in the ruffled sheets, their bodies wrapped round each other.

.Before they knew it, Staffan was going on tour again. He missed Des when was away, especially when he knew he was away for months this time. The guys had some really heavy sets to do. Delmar would get lost in the riff of the music and the beat of the drums, his eyes shut and swaying from side to side, it was like he was on another planet. Night after night they would go on stage to fans chanting their names, girls screaming, pulling at their clothes – endlessly signing autographs, records, posters and T-shirts for their fans. They loved every minute of it but it was tiring.

After the tour had finished they flew back to New York. They had earned some time off and all Staffan wanted to do was spend it with Des. He got in the limo and sank into the back seat, so tired that he shut his eyes and sighed heavily. As his limo approached his apartment block there were crowds of girls waiting. When they saw the limo, they started screaming.

"STAFFAN…. STAFFAN …. I LOVE YOU …"

They were waving photos of him, pushing their faces up against the limousine tainted windows, even pushing their breasts against the windows. Staffan smiled, shaking his head. The gates opened and the limo drove though with Security struggling to hold the hundreds of screaming girls back.

Des was at the Global Magazine Awards with Jake. Staffan had forgotten that she wouldn't there. He had ordered a big bouquet of red roses for his return and planned to grab a bottle of champagne and put it on ice next to the bed.

He laid the roses carefully on the floor, making an arrow pointing toward the bedroom, and waited for Des. Unfortunately, he pretty soon fell asleep.

When Des finally did get home, she saw the roses and followed them. She was so happy to see him. She slipped out of dress and slid in to bed next to him, gently kissing his head. He opened his sleepy eyes.

"Hmm" he murmured.

"Hey baby,"she whispered softly.

"You're so late"

"I know.... I missed you"

"I had champagne on ice, but it's all melted"

"Oh baby I'm so sorry"

"Hmm come here"

He turned over onto his side and put his fingers through her hair, gently brushing her cheek. He was so jet lagged that his eyes shut and he fell back to sleep Des simply kissed him and snuggled into him like spoons. Next morning she was up making Staffan his favourite Danish pancakes with cherries for breakfast. She woke him by kissing him gently.

"Hey." He smiled softly.

"Breakfast is served"

Staffan sat up for Des to place the tray on his knees she climbed back into bed next to him pinching his cherries.

"I've missed you so much, Des"

She kissed him on the cheek and told him she'd missed him too. He told her that breakfast could wait and raised his eyebrows at her. She smiled at him as he moved the tray out of the way and moved closer to her, pulling her down into the bed. His hands moved over her curves, as he kissed her. She responded eagerly. His mouth moved down her body, making her arch her back as he ran his tongue down her legs to her toes and made his way back up flicking his tongue over her skin.

She looked at him from beneath her long eyelashes, her heart racing. She beckoned him with her finger and he slowly made his way up her body. She pulled him to her, kissing him passionately and slowly reversed their positions. She made her way down his body, hovering over his manhood. His eyes burned with wild anticipation. His breathing was ragged. She excited him so much he just wanted to take her but she made him wait.

She teased him even more, moving on top and easing herself down. She moved slowly on him, making love to him. He wanted to come but she wouldn't let him. He grasped her hips, pushing her further down on him.

"Oh Baby I'm gonna come"

"No, not yet," she whispered.

"Fuckin' Hell Des, what are you trying to do to me?" as he tried to hold out.

"Drive you insane baby with desire" she laughs.

"Oh 'um, baby you're doing that"

He couldn't take it anymore, he had to come.

"Arrrrr oh Baby Yes… Yes … Yes!"

Her legs stiffened as she came at the same time. She collapsed on top of him as he lay puffing and panting, trying to get his breath and kissing her gently, stoking the curves of her body. As they lay caressing each other, Staffan mentioned that he had some time off and suggested they should go away – no press, no managers, just the two of them. She had nothing on for a few weeks and thought it was great idea, so that's what they did.

They took time out in the Seychelles, on Mahe Island. They managed to get a small but beautiful beach house with a winding path to the beach. The blue ocean lapped gently on the sand stretching towards the horizon, the beach cradled a warm, shallow bay with the back drop of the beautiful mountains. It was heaven. They made the most of their time together.

Running round play fighting, Des jumped on his back whispering how much she loved him and nibbling his ears gently. As he ran in the warm refreshing sea with Des on his back he suddenly let go of her. She slid down his back and he turned to her, pulling her close.

" I love you, Des – I want us to have children and grow old together"

"Yes, that's what I want too"

Over the weeks, they'd stroll hand in hand along the beach in the moonlight, take moonlit swims and then lay on the hammock, gazing into each others' eyes, just cuddling one another. Des cooked all Staffan's favourite meals. It was just nice to be alone together, no flash bulbs, no microphones stuck in their faces and no questions being fired at them. All too soon, however, it was over and they had to go back.

That they'd managed to keep the press off their trail could have been because Johnny was about to marry his girlfriend, Amy. That was big news. They were having a lavish white wedding. Staffan and Des were on the guest list along with other big names. The wedding was being held at the Empress hotel in New York. Anyone who was anyone would be there.

Chapter 8

At a music awards evening, Staffan and the guys had been nominated for biggest selling single. As ever, Desiree looked stunning in her white, floor length, backless dress that was covered in pearly diamantes around the bust area which shimmered as she walked. Men were simply captivated by her but it was Staffan who had her on his arm.

Johnny and his band were there. Both bands had been nominated for awards. Johnny Barren had also just got married himself but he soon noticed Desiree, He thought she was really beautiful. Riley and the guys were also there. He spotted Lori and Des talking to Denzel Middleton, a fashion designer, and decided he'd interrupt them. He sauntered over, very sure of himself.

"Hi Lori" he said smoothly.

"Hey Riley" she responded, leaving Des talking with Denzel.

"How are things? I hear you and Scott are back together"

"Yeah… we got back together"

Denzel had gone off to mingle and Des turned to Lori, smiling at Riley. Lori introduced Riley.

"Riley, this is Desiree"

"Yes I know…." He turned to face Des. "You are my pinup girl – I've wanted to meet you for so long," he smiled, looking straight into her eyes.

"Oh, really… I'm very flattered?"

As she smiled back she realised just how good looking he was, she could understand what Lori had seen in him. Staffan had spotted Riley with Des and Lori and casually walked over. He didn't want Riley anywhere near Des. He stood behind Des, wrapping his arms around her waist and kissing the back of her neck, all the while staring straight at Riley to make sure Riley was clear on who belonged to who.

"Staffan…!" Riley smirked.

"Riley" he answered, giving him the coldest look he could.

"You have a beautiful wife. You need to keep a tight hold or someone might steal her away…"

Des smiled at Riley.

"I don't fucking think so" Staffan said and gave him another frosty look. He didn't like the way Des had smiled at Riley.

Staffan took hold of Des's hand

"Come on girls, let's go back to the table"

"Bye, Riley" Des said and she smiled at him again.

Riley smiled straight back at Des and told her he would see her around.

"Don't think so…. bye, Riley" Staffan said sarcastically.

Scott had also seen Riley with them and went over and told him to stay away from Lori.

"Hey man, we had our time, that's over… I have a new interest now"

"If you're talking about Des I'd seriously think again, Staffan would kill you!"

"Well, she might find me more satisfying. Lori did!" He said, grinning broadly.

Scott looked at him and shook his head. He felt like punching him but chose to ignore him instead. Riley smiled and shrugged his shoulders.

"She'll be mine one day… I'll make sure of it" and he strutted off back to his table.

Andy Marsh was also there with his band, *Eclipse*. They had made it big the year before *Dominance, Connections* and *Lightning* and he had even been voted sexiest man the year before.

He wanted to talk to Desiree so went over and asked her about being in their new video. Des said she would love to do the video and would be in touch with him about the details in the week. She would sort it out with Jake who would set it up with their agent. Andy was delighted and looked forward to working with her.

That night both *Dominance* and *Connections* won awards. They had a great night and *Lightning* also picked up the award for Best New Rock Band. The rest of the evening they partied at the after awards celebrations. Staffan took Des to the crowded dance floor holding her close. He noticed Riley looking over at them. He did not want Des getting to know Riley and he really didn't want her appearing in his videos. He knew Riley was interested in her, he had been watching her all night… he couldn't take his eyes off her.

Staffan pulled Des tighter.

"I hate it when I can't touch you…it drives me crazy… You make me so horny. Just looking at you makes me horny"

"Good, I hope to always have this effect on you"

"Oh Baby – I don't think there's any doubt about that!"

Staffan told Des he was going to the bar but actually went over to Riley and warned him to stay away from Des.

"Or what, Staffan? Whatcha gonna do? – She can talk to who she likes… She'd look really good in one of our vids… I might ask her"

"Just stay away from my fuckin' wife" He growled at him.

Riley laughed, "Why, do you think I'm a threat?"

"Fuck you, Riley… just stay well clear of her"

Staffan and Des danced and drank and only had eyes for each other. They were seen as the perfect couple, very much in love. Staffan had told the press that he had met his soul mate. She was his best friend and she always would be. Des was quoted as saying he was the sexiest man she had ever met and she'd never loved anyone as much.

A freelance writer from 'See Ya' magazine spotted Des and went over. He wanted to do a feature on Des and Staffan at home together, pictures and story. Des was happy to do it but she needed to discuss it with Staffan first. Staffan agreed to do it. Michael Crossly wanted to set this up soon before the band went on tour. Within a week Michael had set everything up he and his photographer went round to Des and Staffan's apartment.

He asked them all the usual questions about how they had met, how they managed to fit everything into their busy schedules, did Des cook when she was at home. He got a full story and lots of photos of them together, lots of photos of them kissing and folding their arms round each other. They were a very loving couple and were just so natural together, giving each other little loving touches. He got a tour round their apartment and took plenty of photos of it, it was very much a home.

The Cara Jakes Show

The guys were scheduled to start another tour Staffan and Delmar was appearing on the Cara Jakes show. The audience were mainly women and they went wild when Staffan and Delmar went on. Lori Miller and Vivian Towers were also on the show.

Cara had already interviewed the ladies so now it was Staffan and Delmar's turn. The ladies in the audience went crazy, screaming madly as soon as they walked on.

"Staffan Templeton and Delmar Schmidt everyone..."

"It's great to have you on the show"

"Great to be here"

"You guys have another big tour on the cards, won best selling single and you Staffan, you recently got married."

"Hmm... yeah to all of those"

"Tell us what it is like being married to the very sexy Desiree Beaumont"

"Hmm... it's great!" He grinned

"Yeah she is a very sexy lady, how do you cope with all those men drooling over her? Do you get jealous?"

"Yeah, but it's me she comes home to..."

"You're not the only rock star that got married recently are you?"

"No... Barny out of the band has just got married and our good friend Johnny Barren from *Connections* has just got married as well.

"Delmar what about you? No lady in your life?"

"No, not at the moment – but I'm open to offers," he laughed.

"There you go ladies"

A girl in the audience shouted 'I LOVE YOU DELMAR...'

Delmar smiled, " Thank you darlin"

"You guys have got a new single coming out and there's a video. Is Desiree appearing in it?"

"Hmm, yeah she is"

"Yeah, she's great to work with. We all love Des, she's so easy to work with," Delmar interrupted.

"It must be fun"

"Yeah it is and Staffan gets to spend more time with his wife"

"Well it's been great having you on the show and good luck with the tour and congratulations on your marriage to Desiree. Staffan Templeton... Delmar Schmidt... Lori Miller, and also the wonderful Vivian Towers everyone.

Chapter 9

Des had been working long hours and needed some time off so she asked Jake to rearrange her work diary to give her some time with Staffan. She suggested to Staffan that she went on tour with him. He was delighted, the more time he could spend with Des the better.

When he was on stage she would stand at the side and watch him. She would sing and dance to the songs herself. When he came off he would go straight to Des, he was so pleased she wanted to be there.

“What do you think, Babe?” He asked one night.

“Fantastic!” She enthused as she took a full grip of his ass.

“Des, are you after my body?” He asked sexily.

“Yep… it’s those sexy moves you do,” she whispered into his ear.

“Hey… they were all for you!”

“Yeah…yeah … I’ve seen you do them before!” She giggled.

“Always for you, Babe”

“Guys… Get a room!” Edvin said.

“Got one and that’s where we’re heading!” Staffan said, taking hold of Des’s hand.

"See ya guys... got a hot date with my wife!"

"Hey Staffan...!" Edvin shouted.

"Yeah...?" he said turning back.

"We had an idea... Why don't we put Des on as a special guest to sing with us? Actually Delmar suggested it..."

"Would you want to, Des?" He asked looking at her.

"It could be fun. Why not? Wouldn't hurt would it?"

"She can sing... I've heard her with Lori when she went on a gig with her"

"OK, Yeah" Staffan said enthusiastically.

"Fans will love it, especially the men!"

Staffan curled his nose up at that. Des looked at him and laughed.

"What?"

"You...!"

"So, I'm jealous... you're mine, all mine!"

"She needs a sexy dress to show off that sexy body," Barny said.

Staffan looked at him. "Sexy dress?"

"Yeah, if you want her to rub against you, she needs to dress sexy"

"Yeah, now you're talking!" Staffan said, rubbing his hands together and grinning at her.

"Hmm guys, I *am* here. I'm not some sex object!"

Staffan took hold of her and kissed her. He turned his head to the guys

"Yeah, Guys!" turning back to Des, "...only *my* sex object"

Des laughed and playfully slapped his shoulder.

"And talking of which Desiree, let's go!" Staffan said rubbing hands and giving her that sexy look.

Des grabbed him round the waist and kissed him. They both shouted 'See ya guys' and left. When they got back to the hotel and ordered hot dogs with fries,key lime pie and a bottle of bubbly from room service. They lay on the bed in just their underwear. After they finished eating Staffan stared at her.

"What ya doin'?"

"Admiring the view" His eyes scanned her body.

"You want me, don't you?" She said laughing.

"Yep"

Des laughed as she kissed him sexily, gripping his lip with her teeth.

"How much do you want me?"

"This much…"

He grabbed her, his fingers making their way down her body from her neck, down between her breasts right down to her navel. He unclipped her bra and flung it away. He gripped her panties with his teeth and slowly pulled at them. Finally they were skin to skin. He looked up at her with desire in his eyes. She sighed as he moved his tongue up the inside of her thigh. She felt giddy with excitement.

He pleasured her with his tongue until she moaned with delight. She couldn't wait any longer, she wanted him to make love to her. He manoeuvred himself between her thighs and pressed himself into her. Their lips locked as they moved in frenzy together, their sweat mixing together as he thrust himself against her making her groan even more. He eased back slowly only to thrust again, harder. Her mouth opened and her legs stiffened as she began to orgasm but he wouldn't let her as he wanted her to come at the same time as him. They were both breathing heavily as he thrust in to her again and again. Finally, they climaxed together. Sweaty and out of breath they lay back looking at each other panting, getting their breath back.

On the last set of every gig, Staffan would introduce Desiree on stage. Fredrick thought it was a brilliant idea and the men loved seeing Des up there. They got some really good reviews and Staffan got to sing with his wife. He did his sexy moves up against her and she did some sexy moves of her own. It drove Staffan crazy. He didn't know how he managed to keep his hands off her. She knew the songs and it was fun…. they had a great time together.

After the tour they went away for a few days on their own although the press was never far away. They really loved Desiree. Every opportunity they would try and get photos of her. Staffan would get frustrated with it at times, when they got time to themselves, which didn't happen too often, he just wanted to be left alone. They were very much in love and they were always kissing, cuddling and touching each other. They were very happy.

Not long after, they were scheduled to have an interview together on the Cara Jakes Show.

"We have Staffan Templeton and Desiree Beaumont on the show tonight folks… Staffan and Desiree everyone…."

"Hi Des, Staffan..."

They both said hello and smiled.

"You both look great. Marriage must agree with you, so tell us what it's like being Mr and Mrs Templeton"

"It's great," Staffan said smiling.

"What do you love the most about Desiree, Staffan?"

Staffan laughed coyly and said, "Everything..."

He took hold of Desiree's hand and squeezed it affectionately.

"Desiree, what do love the most about Staffan?"

"Oh let me see..." she smiled. " Just about everything I think!"

"You're both very busy people. What effect do you think that will have on your marriage?"

"Hmm... we will deal with whatever comes up..."

"I've got ask about children, is there any sign of little feet coming into your life soon?"

"Hmm... No not yet. We have talked about it but we both have really hectic lives at the moment. Maybe in a couple of years." Des said, smiling, and Staffan nodded in agreement.

"So Desiree are you doing any more rock videos?"

"Oh yes, definitely"

"Staffan, things are really great for your band – you seem to be picking up those awards. You're also touring England soon, is that right?"

"Yeah, we're touring England for 30 weeks with *Connection,* so we are looking forward to seeing Johnny and the guys. Also, *Eclipse* are joining us for 15 weeks of the tour so we're looking forward to seeing them as well"

"Well thank you both for coming on the show and good luck to both of you ... *Mr and Mrs Templeton, folks....*"

Chapter 10

The few days they'd had together were soon over and they went back to their busy schedules. Des met up with Lori who had some big news of her own. She was getting married to Scott!

"Oh Lori, I'm so pleased for you"

"I can't believe it… He just asked me," Lori said excitedly.

"Oh, I know you are really hooked on him!" Des smiled.

"I heard you were on the stage with Staffan and the guys, singing!"

"Yeah it was fantastic… Staffan is one very sexy mover… he did some very suggestive moves up against me on that stage," Des giggled.

Lori smiled. "And did that by any chance turn you on, Des?" She teased.

"Oh, did it ever!" Des laughed. "I had to do some back… he wasn't getting away with that!"

Lori laughed "You love him so much don't you?"

"He's the best thing that ever happened to me. I'll never loved anyone like I love him"

They ordered lunch they both ordered chilli philly steak bake with a glass of white wine, while they waited talked about Lori's wedding plans.

She said she wanted to have a marriage like Desiree's because she'd never seen anyone look as happy and that was down to Staffan. She wanted to feel like that with Scott.

Lori announced to the press that she was getting married to singer Scott Daniels. They made front page headlines and they were photographed looking very much in love. They had been dating for some time and had planned a big beach wedding. Anyone who was anyone was going to be at that wedding, they were so excited. They were flying their parents over. Everything was going to plan, everything was perfect.

A few weeks later Des got a call from Andy Marsh, the English rock star from the band *Eclipse*. They had already spoken about doing the rock video at the awards and Des had loved the idea. She'd agreed to do the video with Andy and the guys and they were all very excited about it.

A week later they got started. It was terrific and Des and the guys had a great time. Des was so much fun to be around.

Staffan went to the studio where they were filming. He was a bit jealous of Andy, especially after seeing them doing some of the video. Andy had to move his hands up her legs and kiss her. It looked a little too real for Staffan's liking. After all, Andy was a good looking man with long, blonde permed hair… just Des's type and she seemed to get on with him a little too well.

She reassured Staffan that he was the only one for her. He knew he was being stupid. Surely, Andy wouldn't do that – he had his own lady.

"Good… keep it that way" he muttered as he kissed her hard.

"You're the only sexy blonde for me." She smiled, "Now take me home and I'll prove it to you!" She giggled.

"Come on then, let's go!" He laughed, rushing her out of the door.

When they arrived home Des pulled him into the bedroom and pushed him up against the wall. She kissed him teasingly, gripping his lips with her teeth as he took her in his arms. He lifted her leg up as she ripped his shirt open, digging her nails gently into his chest.

"Aagh," he moaned as she started kissing him, moving her mouth down his body, opening his jeans.

"Ohhhh Baby, Yeah!" He cried, licking his lips.

"Oh fucking hell…. Let me…" He swallowed hard, trying to get his words out.

"No…you just stay there," she said sexily looking up at him.

"Des, you're driving me crazy…" as he gave out long drawn out groan.

"Good… stay there!" She ordered.

He placed his hands behind him, resting on the wall "Ahhhhhh, fuckin' hell, hmmm…"

He couldn't take any more he grabbed her and reversed the position, slamming her up against the wall, lifting up her skirt. Moving his mouth down her body she responded eagerly. He made his way back up her body, bending her over. She braced herself with her hands on the wall as he pressing himself between her thigh. She pulled his hand over her breasts while the other gripped her hip, she felt a burning sensation in the pit of her stomach like a *Lightning* bolt shooting through her body. In a frenzy they moved against each other until neither of them could take anymore and they climaxed together. His head pressed against hers as they collapsed in a hot, sweaty heap on the floor, panting like two animals trying to catch their breath.

"Oh Man, that was fantastic!"

Des smiled, "Oh Baby you never disappoint."

"I'm glad to hear that"

He took her hand to help her and as she got up he grabbed her and kissed her passionately.

"I love you Des"

Chapter 11

1982

Staffan and the guys were on tour. They'd been gone a few weeks and Des was at a photo shoot for her calendar. She was taking a break and just happened to pick the newspaper up. She didn't normally read the paper but there it was front page…

The paparazzi had been hanging round the hotel trying to get sneaky shots of *Dominance*. Finally, they had got the shot they had been waiting for. A beautiful blonde in a mini-dress looked suspiciously like she was leaving Staffan's hotel room in the early hours of the morning. The picture appeared to show the leggy blond in the doorway kissing him passionately.

When Des saw the picture she went berserk. She knew girls went crazy for Staffan but this photo was a different thing. This girl was touching him and they appeared to be looking lustfully into each other's eyes. She couldn't control her anger and jealousy and trashed the dressing room. Jake ran into the room taking in the scene. He tried to calm her down and told her to go home and think logically but Desiree could not get her head round this. Out came the demons, the trust issues.

Seeing this girl all over Staffan. She felt this was different. Thoughts of her father telling her no- one would ever love her came flooding back and she really believed Staffan had cheated on her. When he got back she was waiting, ready for him….

"Des, Babe, where are you?"

She ran out of the kitchen like a raging bull. She hurled a plate at him, hitting his head. Staffan reeled with the pain and shock, blood dripping down his face.

"Fucking hell, Des… What's wrong?"

"You cheating bastard!" She hissed through clenched teeth

"What the Fuck?" He asked holding his head.

"I saw you, you bastard, with that girl!"

"No….no…. You have got this wrong!" He said, putting his hands up in front of him.

"Fuck you!"

"Des… I didn't…"

She started throwing more stuff at him but this time he ducked. He tried to grab her but she just kept hitting him.

"Des… Stop… baby stop! You're acting like crazy bitch… Fucking hell!"

He eventually grabbed her and pulled her down to the floor and sat on top of her. He took hold of her hands and held them down

"Stop, Des"

"Fuck you!"

She managed to get her hands free and slapped him across the face.

"I hate you!" She swore.

"Des… I didn't, I swear"

"We're finished" she said matter of factly.

"No Des, please listen!"

"I want a divorce!"

"Des… That girl…" He stopped in mid-sentence *"Divorce?"*

"GET OUT!" She screamed

Staffan got to his feet.

"Divorce…? No…. I haven't done what you think. You need to listen to me before you make the biggest mistake of our lives"

"GET OUT… I don't want you anywhere near me… You Bastard"

Staffan left and booked himself into a hotel for the night.

He thought if he left her alone she might calm down. Hopefully they could talk next day and then he could explain. Next day, however, she still wouldn't listen. There was simply no talking to her. Staffan couldn't get her to change her mind. They had only been married just under twelve months and he didn't want a divorce so he tried talking to Jake.

"What were you doing with that girl?" Jake asked

"She was just a fan. Fuck knows how she found out my room number – I know how it looks but…"

"Did you sleep with her?"

"No… no… she wasn't even in my room …"

"Des went berserk… She trashed her dressing room"

"Yeah, she trashed the apartment and she cut my fucking head open. Look at the fuckin' cut on my head. She doesn't normally read the papers… Why did she have to see that one?"

"She just picked it up, and there you were!"

"Fuck me… I just don't fucking believe this."

"Will you talk to her for me?"

"I'll try"

Jake tried to talk to her but she wouldn't listen. Staffan had hurt her so there was no going back. She filed for divorce and had the papers delivered to Staffan straight away, she didn't waste any time.

When Staffan received the divorce papers he couldn't believe it. He rang her to try to talk to her again but she wouldn't talk to him.

"Des, please listen…"

"No… Just sign the divorce papers"

"Des, I love you so much. Please don't do this"

"Sign them!" She repeated harshly.

"I love you Des. You are making the biggest mistake of our lives. We had plans, we wanted children, and we were supposed to grow old together…. Des, *please*"

"Just sign the bloody papers" she cried.

She slammed the phone down on him and sat down, a river of tears rolling down her face as she cried and cried, her eyes red and puffy. They felt so heavy, the sadness in her eyes shining through. Then the defence mechanism kicked in again, hard, no-one would ever make her feel like that again.

Staffan had no choice but to sign the divorce papers. She wouldn't give an inch and they were divorced quite quickly.

Edvin and Delmar really worried about Staffan. He was struggling with the break up from Desiree and wasn't the same man. He was so sad, he simply wasn't himself. When the band went back on tour he just went through the motions, putting on an act for the fans. He saw other girls but he wasn't really interested, he just wanted Des. He could've had any girl he wanted but Desiree Beaumont was the only one.

They were in rehearsals and Fredrick came in with the newspapers. Staffan had gone to get some drinks and when he reappeared, the guys were studying the papers. Edvin opened the centre pages and there was Desiree.

"Wow guys… Turn to the centre pages!"

Barny, Delmar and Lucas looked wide-eyed at the centre page.

"Fucking hell… She looks good!"

"I wonder if Staffan has seen these"

"Seen what?" as he walked over to them.

"Des's new pictures"

"No…"

"She looks sensational!"

"Let's look then…"

"Are you sure you want to?"

Staffan nodded his head and took the paper from Edvin. Des was on a motor bike, totally naked. You could only see her from the side and she wasn't actually showing anything but the pictures were sensational. *She* was sensational.

Staffan's jaw dropped and his eyes widened, "WOW… Fuck me!"

"She looks fantastic doesn't she?" Edvin remarked.

"She's a work of art… She always has been"

Seeing Des in the paper had set Staffan's heart racing but feeling heavy at the same time. He couldn't believe that he had been so happy, had had his perfect girl and in one second it was all gone all because of a stupid picture.

Desiree was just as sad without Staffan and she missed him but couldn't think about her feelings. She'd buried them, they were gone – well, that's what she kept telling herself. She put all her pent-up frustration into her work. She had to be at her best all of the time. The public had to see her perfect, not even a hair out of place. There was a great deal of interest in Desiree's life. In spite of her confident persona in the public eye, behind closed doors she was insecure....

Lori caught up with Des. She'd been on tour for months so she hadn't seen her. She still couldn't believe that Des and Staffan had broken up, they always seem so solid. She didn't believe for one minute that Staffan had cheated on Des. There must be a simple explanation for what the papers had printed. She'd seen the picture; it did look incriminating but cheating on her? No!

"Des did he really cheat?"

"I saw him Lori, that girl was... I don't want to talk about this"

Lori saw the old Des creeping back, hard and suspicious of everything, keeping everyone at a distance, not letting anyone in. Lori wondered how Staffan was taking all of this, she knew there was no one else for Staffan but Des.

Lori's wedding was coming up and she wanted to know if she should invite Staffan to the wedding.

"Lori, it's your wedding, you should invite who you want"

"I don't want to make you feel uncomfortable... or him for that matter..."

"I'm sure we can behave like adults"

"I think he and the guys are on tour anyway"

Des really hoped that Staffan was on tour, she knew she couldn't face him. She knew that Lori and Staffan were friends, she didn't want to make things awkward, so if he was to be there she would just have to be a big girl and deal with it.

Chapter 12

Thing were about to get worse for Des. She was in the studio with Marcus when Jake rushed in.

"Des, you need to see this babe…" he said as he handed her the newspaper.

"Jake I don't read the papers, you know that…"

"Well your gonna want to read this, babe."

Des picked up the paper. Her father had seen her in a feature and he'd gone to the press to let them know he was her father. She scanned the pages with horrified eyes.

"No… No… No!" She threw the paper to floor and clenched her fingers into a fist.

"Des,… darlin?"

"No… I hate that fucking man…. He made my childhood a living hell

"You need to do a press conference"

She wasn't listening to Jake, she was just thinking about the man who had hurt her so much as a child.

"He is nothing to me… NOTHING!"

"Des, you need to talk to the press."

Des gave a press conference and told them that man would never be in her life. She hated him.

"Des, why do you hate your father so much?"

"He was not a father. Fathers don't hurt their child like he did"

"Des, will you see him again?"

"NO…"

"He wants to see you,"

"He can rot in hell for all I care"

She got up and walked away. She didn't want to talk about him any more.

It was all over the paper the next day. Within the next few days her father flew over. He'd received some money from telling his story and he wanted to see her, he *demanded* to see her. Jake took him into her dressing room.

"Hello, Des"

Des turned round, "GET OUT"

"Oh baby girl, is that a way to greet your old dad?"

"JAKE… GET HIM OUT!"

"I want to talk to my daughter alone"

"NO JAKE!" Desiree shouted shaking her head with sheer fear on her face.

Jake said he would wait outside the door. Des shook her head disbelievingly, she was shaking. She was scared of this man, really scared. He walked towards her and she trembled with fear.

"Stay where you are. Don't come near me"

Waving his hands he coldly said "Well Desiree. Did you get all this on your back?"

"GET OUT…" she screamed.

"You're a whore just like your mother…"

"What do ya want?"

"Money…!!! Daughter of mine… money"

"You got money from the newspaper when you sold your story, and don't call me your daughter"

"I need more and I reckon you owe me"

"I owe you shit"

"I told you, you wouldn't get anyone to love you. Even your rock star husband ended up in bed with some other bird."

Biting her lip nervously, trying to stop it from quivering her voice was shaky.

"Why are you doing this?"

"You look like her, your whore of a mother"

"No wonder she left you. You drunken bastard, look at you. You're disgusting"

He lunged at her grabbing her by the throat and slammed her against the wall, winding her when her back slammed against the wall. He squeezed his fingers round her neck. She was choking and started to feel faint. She managed to let out a weak scream.

"She left you, you little bitch"

"AHH" she was gasping for breath, her heart was beating so fast she thought he was going to strangle her.

Jake heard Des scream and rushed in. He grabbed David and told him to go or he would have him arrested and if he ever came near Desiree again he would get a restraining order slapped on him.

"Has he been in your knickers, Des?"

"GET OUT" she screamed shaking as she tried to get her breath back.

Jake called security and had David removed from the building. Des was shaking like a leaf and tears rolled down her face. Jake took hold of her and hugged her, telling her he was sorry.

"He will never come back…He will never bother you again, Des"

"I hate him… I HATE HIM"

David had pressed so hard on her neck that he'd raised bruises her. His finger marks looked like she had a necklace of love bites.

"Oh fuckin' hell, Des…" Jake said looking at her neck.

"I told you Jake, he's a bastard. He would have strangled me"

"Oh babe, I'd no idea how bad it really was"

Jake suddenly understood why Des had trust issues. Why she was so hard and put up barriers, keeping people at a distance.

"This is nothing Jake, I've had black eyes broken ribs, broken arms. In and out of hospital"

Jake took hold of Des and hugged her again.

"Never again, Des"

He wanted to have her checked over by the doctor but she told him she was fine and there was no need.

Des had been invited to a Lightning concert and their manager, Cooper Bancroft, had asked Desiree if she would like to be in the stars' pit. Des told him she would love to.

When Riley heard she was coming he got really nervous – normally he was very confident with the opposite sex but this was Desiree Beaumont, his all-time pin up girl. When Cooper came backstage on the night of the gig, Riley was pacing up and down, mumbling to himself.

"What's with him? He's not normally nervous"

"He's knows Des Beaumont is in the stars' pit.

Riley suddenly rushed over, "Tell me she's out there"

"Wow, man!"

"She's out there right?"

"Yep, she's in the pit"

Riley leapt up in the air throwing a fist pump.

"Oh man, Yes… Yes …"

He peered through the stage curtains from the edge and there she was, looking every bit a rock chick – leather jeans and leather waist coat. Riley looked back at the guys.

"Oh man, I could end up with a stiff dick just looking at her "

"Woah…woah…woah… Fuckin' hell, Riley"

"I'm gonna ask her out on a date"

"You reckon"

"Yeah man she'll come, in more ways the one if you get me"

"Keep fuckin' dreamin" as they ribbed him

Cooper laughed "Ready to rock guys"

The music started to blast out, the drums pounding out with a hard rock beat. The crowd went wild roaring and chanting ' *Lightning… Lightning… Lightning…*'.

Riley ran on stage and shouted, 'ARE YOU READY TO ROCK' and the crowds just went wilder still.

"Well, let's fuckin' rock then"

After their first song he announced that Des Beaumont was in the building. The guys in the audience cheered and Des gave them all a wave. Riley sang a song just for Des, as he sang he pointed at her she smiled at him and blew him a kiss and he pretended to catch it.

After the concert, Riley rushed to freshen himself up, spraying deodorant and splashing on aftershave, putting a fresh T-shirt on as fast as he could so he could get to the VIP lounge. He knew Des was in there but what he hadn't realised with all his rushing he had put his T-shirt on the wrong way round. Tim tried to tell him but Riley had just ignored him he had spotted Des and swallowed hard.

"Hi there"

"Hello… I was just asking Cooper if you were still here"

Cooper pointed subtly to his T-shirt but Riley couldn't make out what he was trying to tell him, so he shook his head and turned back to face Des who was talking to him.

"It was good seeing you again, Riley"

"You're not going?"

"Sorry I can't stay long … I'm flying out to the UK tomorrow"

"Oh I see"

Cooper pointed at his T-shirt once again Riley looked down at his T-shirt.

"Oh, Fuck me!"

Des looked at him speechless and then giggled.

"Oh shit, I didn't mean… Oh shit, my T-shirt is on the wrong way round"

He kept spluttering, totally tongue tied. Meanwhile, Des was laughing uncontrollably. Riley winced with embarrassment.

"I must look a total prick"

In-between giggles she smiled,"What does it matter?" then she moved in closer to him and whispered, "I put my knickers on the wrong way round yesterday"

"No you didn't – you're just saying that to make me feel better!" He pulled his T-shirt over his head.

Des couldn't help but giggle at him but she soon stopped when she saw his body. She gasped in amazement.

"I'm real glad I've made you laugh," he said, smirking at her.

"Oh Riley, I'm so sorry"

"I like it when you laugh, it's so sexy"

"Oh it's a shame I have to go – but I do have to go"

"Yeah I know… maybe we'll see each other again soon?

"Yeah …that would be nice… nice body by the way" she mentioned winking at him telling him she would see him soon. "Bye for now"

As she walked away she turned and smiled at him. Riley watched her as she went thinking this woman could bring a grown man to his knees.

She had made his night telling him he had a nice body. He was going to make sure she was going to enjoy it.

Chapter 13

Lori and Scott's wedding.

Lori's wedding took place on a secluded part of the beach in San Marie with their reception held at the adjoining hotel, the only one for miles around. They had booked the big dining hall, filled with round tables decorated with pink and white flowers on each table, subtle lighting around the room leading out to the beach through glass sliding doors which were left open. In between a row of roman columns decorated with silk sashes, a scattering of white and pink rose petals led up the aisle to a beautiful pink and white arched altar on the beach.

Lori's dress was a long, white, halter neck affair which flowed elegantly over her curves. Her hair was twisted and pinned in to a side pony tail resting on her shoulders with flowers cascading down through it. She looked absolutely stunning. The sun was beating down, glimmering over the ocean as it crashed against the rocks in the distance, seagulls flying overhead in the clear blue sky.

She held her bouquet as her father took her by the hand. A tear of joy escaped from the corner of her eye. Her dad looked at her and smiled.

"I'm so proud of you, Lori"

She smiled back at her dad as they started to slowly walked down the aisle. Passing her mum and Des, she gave Des a cheeky little grin. Des was so happy for Lori, a little pearl-shaped tear ran down the side of her face.

As Lori reached Scott she thought how handsome he looked in his white shirt and white trousers. Love for Lori shone in his eyes. He took her hand and smiled lovingly at her. As they exchanged vows, Des couldn't help thinking of Staffan. He had hurt her so deeply, all the while she thought nothing could ever have come between them.

Soon, everybody made their way into the dining hall for the reception. The room buzzed with excitement and the press was invited to take some pictures of the wedding and then some more of cutting the beautiful pink and white six-tier cake. They took lots of photos, they even got some of Des, looking stunning as always. It wasn't hard for Desiree to look beautiful it was just so natural. She was in a beautiful purple dress, the straps crisscrossed at the back leading all the way to her waist. She had swept her hair to the side where it cascaded in curls. She had gone to the wedding with Jake, his wife Sandra, Marcus and his partner Larry. She didn't want a date… She wasn't looking for romance… even though it was about to find her when she arrived back home.

When she got back to New York, Riley Watson bumped into her while she was having lunch with her friend Ellen Warren. He spotted her as he came into the restaurant and went straight over to her.

"Miss Beaumont"

Des looked up and there was Riley standing in front of her. His long straight dark hair nearly touched his waist. His tanned and beautifully toned body looked extremely good in a black T-shirt and leather jeans. His big brown eyes searched her face for recognition.

"Hello," She said, smiling at him.

"You do remember me, don't you?"

"Of course I do …"

He smiled at her, so pleased she'd remembered him.

"It's so nice to see you again" She said, continuing to smile at him.

"Well you could see more of me if you wanted to," he said with a cheeky grin. "I spotted you when I came in"

Desiree laughed. She thought he was funny and she'd always liked men who could make her laugh.

"I would like to talk to you about being in our latest video"

"Yeah, OK, that would be good. I'll give you my number. Ring me and we'll fix something up"

"Ripper… I'll do that," he grinned at her, then took her hand and kissed it whilst looking straight into her eyes.

"I'll be in touch" he said with his beautiful Australian accent.

Ellen looked at Desiree and smiled. "WOW, has he got the hots for you, or what, babe?"

"He is very good looking" Desiree giggled.

"Oh my God, isn't he? Isn't he the one Lori was dating?"

"Yeah…" Des replied laughing. "I've been told he's very good in the sack!"

"Is he really? Is it time for Des to start dating again?" Ellen giggled.

"No… No… I'm not ready for all that again."

Des and Ellen finished their lunch then they headed for the shops for some retail therapy and talked about Lori's wedding.

The following week Riley rang Des about appearing in the video and finally, Des said she would do it. He was really pleased and they set a date some weeks later for filming.

In the video, he got to get up close to her, kiss her and touch her. They filmed the sequence on a bed and he had to wrap his arms round her. He got to move his hands up her legs and kiss her quite passionately with Riley loving every minute. Des enjoyed doing the video, too, she thought Riley and the guys were lovely and great to work with. They had lots of fun filming and none of the guys could get enough of Desiree. They released with the single, as soon as it had been edited

Staffan saw the video on the music show *KarocK* and he was livid. He grabbed the nearest glass and threw it across the dressing room just missing Barny's head.

"Fuck me, Staffan"

"Sorry Barny"

"What the fuck's wrong?"

"Fucking Riley… He's got Des in his vid," he said, clenching his fists.

"Staffan that's what she does and she does it so well, I might add. Staffan my friend, you and Des are divorced. Why don't you have some fun… see girls… lots of girls?"

"That's the thing Barny. I didn't want to be divorced. I didn't want girls"

"Oh my friend I'm sorry. I really am… but I don't know what you can do"

"I'll get her back"

Not if Riley had anything to do with it, he really had the hots for Des. He wanted her… and the bonus was it would upset Staffan no end. As the weeks went on Riley started sending Des flowers, chocolates and champagne. He rang her several times to ask her out to dinner but she kept refusing. Jake mentioned that he was very keen. Des just smiled and shook her head.

"No…no…not happening"

Then out of the blue Riley turned up at the studio where Des was doing a photo shoot. He'd decided that if she wasn't going to go dinner with him then he would do lunch and took a picnic basket with him.

"Hi Riley"

"Jake"

"What you doing here?"

"Desiree has refused dinner several times so I've come with lunch!"

Jake smiled, "Des… Ha. You do know that she and Staffan have only just recently got divorced."

"Yep"

"Have you not thought that she's just not interested?"

"Nope" Riley grinned.

Des made her way over.

"Riley," she smiled. "What are you doing here?"

"Well you have refused dinner several times so…. I thought lunch?"

"Oh," she giggled. "Is that lunch in the basket?"

"Yeah… lead me to your dressing room and I'll set it up!"

"OK Riley… you've worn me down… lunch it is. Give me an hour"

Des went back to her shoot and Jake took Riley to her dressing room.

"You are one persistent bastard!"

"Yep"

"Staffan ain't gonna like it," Jake said shaking his head.

"I wasn't asking his permission. Staffan and I might not get on but we do have one thing in common."

"Desiree," said Jake, rolling his eyes.

"I liked Desiree at the same time as Staffan but he happened to meet her first and now he's blown it. I won't – She's not going to be able to resist me, Jake!"

Jake wasn't so sure about that, he knew Desiree.

Riley set up lunch then went to watch Des on the monitor. He couldn't believe his eyes. She just had a silk sheet over her covering her vital bits. The way she moved her hands up her body, her legs. As she stretched her leg up in the air she sent a shiver up Riley's spine. His eyes widened, fixed on her, his jaw dropped. He didn't think anyone could get their legs up that high. She was more beautiful than before somehow and the sexy poses she was doing just made him want her more. He could understand why Staffan was so crazy about her.

When Des finished her photo shoot Riley took her hand and led her to her dressing room.

"Wow, Riley"

"Desiree Beaumont, we have chicken, cheese, ham, salad, French bread, potato chips, fruit. Oh, and a bottle of chilled wine"

"Oh wow, this is lovely Riley" She was very impressed.

They sat and ate the gorgeous lunch Riley had prepared and talked. He was funny and charming. Des liked him. Des liked him very much….

"See what you are missing? We could have so much fun."

"Oh Riley, you are so sweet"

"So…,what about dinner?"

"OK Riley, dinner," she said defeated

"Tomorrow at 8… I'll pick you up" He smiled at her, staring into her eyes.

"Riley…Riley?"

"Yeah… I was just thinking. I hope you can do CPR because you take my breath away."

"Oh Riley, that's really cheesy"

"Yeah I know," he grinned.

They both started laughing. He was going to have her he was going to win her over, she was going to be his.

Chapter 14

Riley picked Des up and took her out for a romantic evening. He was absolutely smitten with her. She looked so sexy in the white minidress she wore. He couldn't believe his eyes when he saw her. She smelt so good… the smell of ylang-ylang… so sensual. He took her to Orchard Bloom, a lovely little restaurant in Rhode Island. He had asked for a table in the corner surrounded by candle light so they could have some privacy. He didn't want people coming up and asking for autographs from either of them, he wanted Desiree to himself. They made small talk at first about tours and photo shoots.

Then Des said, "You must have thousands of girls after you"

"I suppose there are a few."

"Why have you not got a girlfriend, you are very good looking"

Careful with his words he said, "I've not got the girl I want yet"

Des smiled at him as he poured her another glass of wine He was such good company, he was so nice, funny and charming. She was glad he had talked into going out with him now. As they finished eating, he leant over and told her he so wanted to see her again. She said she'd love to, on condition that she cooked dinner. He agreed and the next evening he arrived promptly with a beautiful bouquet flowers and a bottle of wine.

She had been cooking most of the day and he entered to the smell of Italian chicken. She'd made with side salad accompanied with garlic bread and for desert she had prepared a vanilla cheesecake.

"Hope you like chicken"

"Yes it all smells fantastic"

Over the next few weeks they had a lot of dates. Riley took her to see the Brisbane Cats, his favourite football team, who were playing the New York Raiders. She'd never been to a ball game before. They went go-karting and Des had the time of her life, they had so much fun racing round that track. They were also spotted together in Gold Dreams night club on the dance floor hand in hand, looking in to each other's eyes swaying from side to side. They didn't seem to notice anyone around them, they were transfixed on each other.

It wasn't always easy seeing each other. They had to fit in round their busy schedules. He wanted to see her as much as he could and he kept the girl fans at arm's length, not always easy given his job as the sexy rock star, but he was determined not to make the same mistake as Staffan.

The paparazzi were lying in wait for them every time they went out. It was all over the papers. It was big news and they became quite an item. They had been in the restaurant having dinner and again the papers had got some great pictures of them.

When they got back to Des's apartment she offered Riley a drink. His mind was on more than a drink… he wanted more, but he was trying hard not to blow it. He sat slowly drinking the glass of wine she had given him, thinking how sexy she looked. He thought he'd better go, but as Des walked him to the door he pulled her close and kissed her hungrily. He wanted her so much.

"Hmm Des… I better go… I don't want to… but…"

"Well don't then," she whispered huskily.

He rested his forehead on hers. Des smiled at him and closed the gap between them. He kissed her and moved her back, shutting the door behind him with his foot. Still kissing, Des pulled him back towards the bedroom. Riley began to kiss her more deeply as he undressed her, one bit of clothing at a time. He looked at her with a big grin sweeping across his face… pleased with himself. He caressed her body making her arch her back. Her whole body surged.

"Mmmmm" she moaned.

She removed his shirt, running her hands down his chest towards the top of his jeans and opened his button. Pulling down his zip, he eased out of them and laid her on the bed.

"You're every man's fantasy... I want you so much..."

"Make love to me, Riley"

That was exactly what he wanted to hear. She had really turned him on. He bent his head to hers and kissed her. Their bodies hot and sweaty, he kissed the small of her neck. Goose bumps ran up her spine as he moved his mouth further down, running his tongue over the arches of her body. He was driving her crazy.

"Oh God, Riley... ahhh"

"Oh Yeah – you don't know how long I've wanted this, baby."

He moved his hips between her thighs and began to move slowly, rhythmically, making love to her. His fingers interlaced with hers as he pushed himself deeper into her. Her head swam with dizziness, he was everything she imagined he would be.

Riley woke Des early the next morning by moving his finger up and down her back. He couldn't sleep, he was so happy to wake up by her side he couldn't believe he had finally got to be with her.

"Good morning, Beautiful"

"Morning"

She slid out of bed and slipped on her robe when Riley grabbed her hand.

"Where you going?"

"Making some coffee... I need coffee in the morning. Stay there!"

Riley smugly lay back in bed, placing his arms round the back of his head smiling to himself. This was exactly where he wanted to be.

The paparazzi had been outside Des's all night waiting to get the shot that would rock the world.

When Staffan read the newspaper he was seething and in his temper he thumped the mirror, slashing his hand wide open on the broken shards. He already hated Riley but this had just made it twice as bad. It was about to get even worse.

Des was on a video location with the rock group *Black Rose.* Riley had gone to a music awards night where he spotted Staffan and went over. Staffan, Delmar and Barny were sat with Johnny's wife Amy and the guys.

"Hi guys," Riley said – taking in Staffan's hand all bandaged up.

Riley had gone over for one reason only, to wind Staffan up, rub his nose in it about him and Des.

"Hi Riley," Johnny replied.

"Hey… Staffan how ya doin'? What have you done to your hand?"

"Something got in my way…" Staffan growled

"Have you heard the news about me and Des? We're quite an item now"

Staffan looked at Riley and nodded, "Yeah, I heard you're dating my wife."

"Ex-wife I think that is…yeah, ex-wife… Man she's hot… she's real hot!"

Staffan's face went blood red with anger. Riley had touched a nerve alright. Staffan was about to get up when Amy grabbed his arm.

"Don't bite," she whispered.

Johnny interrupted, "Why don't you fuck off, Riley"

He moved Riley away, seeing how angry Staffan was getting.

"Hey Johnny, I just came over to say Hi mate…"

"No you fucking didn't… Why wind him up?"

"Because I can…" he sniggered.

Staffan didn't bite so Riley disappeared, disappointed.

"He's a fucking dick and I'll show him… He's gonna regret rubbing my nose in it about him and Des…"

Johnny and Amy looked at him. "How?" They asked in unison.

"I'll get Des back. He wants to fuck with me"

"But Des is going to be hurt in all of this," Amy said.

Amy, I love Des and I want her back. But him… fuck him!"

"You and Des are divorced. You couldn't get her to talk to you. How is this even going to happen?" Amy asked.

"I want Des and it *will* happen. He won't fuck with me again"

Two weeks later Des was due to appear on the RM awards show for rock groups and she had been asked to present awards to *Eclipse*, and *Connections*. What she didn't know was that she was going to be getting an award herself.

She had been voted *Rock Video Goddess of the Year.* This was a new category and Des was the first ever winner. Andy Marsh had been asked to present it to her. Lori had also been asked on to present an award to *Dominance* and *Lightning.*

Des was looking forward to it. She wore white leather jeans so tight they looked as if they had been sprayed. She paired them with a very revealing glittery top, not leaving much to the imagination. Lori was wearing tight denim jeans and strappy bodice. They both looked stunning. They posed for sexy shots together on the red carpet. The press loved them… Flash bulbs were going off from all sides. They both left the press wanting more.

Staffan noticed Des as soon as he walked in.

This would be the first time that Staffan and Des had been in the same room together since they'd got divorced. Des was still hurting over Staffan supposedly cheating on her and she didn't forgive easily. The press were watching for something… anything… between them.

After all the bands had received their awards, Andy announced the new award for Rock Goddess:

"And the award goes to Desiree Beaumont" Andy shouted.

Des looked stunned, putting her hand to her face, 'Oh My God'. She was so flattered that she had won, she'd never won anything in her life. Riley kissed her and told she was the best there was. She gently brushed his face with her fingers "Thank you darlin"

There were lots of congratulations going round, lots of loud music, drinking and eating. Riley and Des were sat together at a table looking very loved up. The cameras were on them. Anything they could get on Desiree, they were getting it. Riley only had eyes for Des.

"You look fantastic…" He whispered in her ear sending a shiver down her spine.

"So do you," she said as she started playing with his hair. Riley moved closer and kissed her longingly. Lori looked at them smiling, sitting down.

"Hi guys!"

"Hi" they said in unison.

"Des, can I talk to you a sec?" Lori said prodding her.

"Yeah, sure"

Riley grabbed her hand.

"Don't leave me," he said blowing kisses at her.

Des smiled and kissed him. "You're mad"

"Yeah, about you"

Des went to talk to Lori.

"What's up?"

"I think Scott is cheating again"

"No Lori, he wouldn't"

"Oh Des… we both know he would…"

Des put her arms round her friend. She told her she hoped he wasn't, she knew how that felt and how much it hurt when you love someone that much does that to you. Scott appeared and put his arm around Lori's waist.

"Hi Des…"

"Hi Scott"

"Hey Babe, where've you been?"

"With Des… Where've you been?"

"Over there looking for you. Come on Baby, let's dance"

Des looked at Lori and smiled. Lori smiled back and headed to the dance floor with Scott. Staffan had seen Lori leave Des and thought this was his chance. As Des headed back to Riley, Staffan grabbed her and pulled her into a quiet corner.

"Des…"

"Leave me alone, Staffan"

"No, I want you to talk to me"

"Nothing to say"

"Oh Baby, there is…"

"No there isn't – now let me go."

She pulled away from him but Staffan grabbed her again and pulled her back.

"Des, please…"

"Let go!" She said through clenched teeth.

Johnny was walking past, saw them together and shook his head. Riley was looking for Des. He'd seen Lori but there was no sign of Des.

"Hey Johnny, have you seen Des?"

"Heading to the ladies, Buddy..."

Johnny thought it was easier to lie. He was friends with both Staffan and Riley.

Riley put his thumb up, "Thanks". He went back to the table and sat talking to Tim and Julian from the band.

"Talk to me Des," Staffan continued.

"No..."

"Fucking Hell, Des..."

Des narrowed her eyes. "Let go..."

Staffan finally released his grip and she pulled away and walked back to Riley.

Staffan put his head down and went back to his table. It was only two tables away from Des and he couldn't help keep looking over. Riley sensed he was watching them and deliberately took hold of Des, looking over her shoulder straight at Staffan. He was goading him, hoping he would react. Steam was coming out of Staffan ears but he kept his cool, thinking to himself 'You'll get yours!' Amy went up and sat next to him and asked him if he was OK.

"No... He is heading for a fuckin' slap."

"Staffan, just don't bite."

"If she would just listen to me..."

"Maybe she's still hurting herself?"

"Why is she with him? She's going to listen to me, Amy ...I'm going to make her!"

Johnny asked him if he had spoken to Des. Staffan shook his head.

"I've not given up yet, she'll have to talk to me at some point"

Johnny smiled at Staffan and patted him on the back. Amy looked Staffan up and down. She felt so sad for him. She could see how much he loved Des and how much this was hurting him. Seeing her with Riley just made it all the more painful.

Chapter 15

After the awards Riley and Des went away for a long weekend. Riley wanted to have Des to himself for a while, He was due to go on tour with his band and would be away for six mouths so they headed off to Beverley Hills where he had rented a beach house. The paparazzi, of course, found out were they were... They got shots of them rolling around on the beach kissing, all loved up.

Riley was very romantic and Des loved being with him, he made her so happy. She had fun with him and they relaxed together as they soaked up the sun. Riley would go for a jog every morning (with photographers hot on his heels) while Des would make breakfast. One morning she decided to get into the hot tub. When Riley got back from his jog expecting breakfast to be ready, she had other plans.

"Oh, Riley..." she called huskily.

Riley followed the sound of her voice and found her sitting naked in the hot tub, summoning him with her finger. Riley smiled at her and quickly took his shorts off. He got in the tub and moved over to Des, pulling her to him, kissing her neck. She moaned with pleasure and wrapped her legs around his waist, pulling him closer still.

"Oh Yeah… Oh Des…" he whispered as they made love in the hot tub.

Riley just wanted to stay there with Des but eventually they had to go back. Not wanting to leave Des while he was touring, he asked her if she could go with him but she couldn't. She had a busy schedule herself otherwise she would have gone with him, she said. To compensate, he told her he'd take her out for dinner before he left.

When they returned, it was back to work for the both of them. Riley had stuff to sort out before he went on tour – making sure that amps, *Lightning* rigs, special effects were all present and correct. A lot of careful planning goes into every tour and he liked to be involved with everything.

Des had a rock video to do with legendary rock group *Sharp Edge*. They had risen to fame in the mid-seventies and had been around a lot longer than *Eclipse, Dominance, Connections,* and *Lightning*. Des was really looking forward to it. She'd never done a video with this group and they were, after all, rock legends so she was really flattered when they asked her. The singer was only the legendary Paul Best and he'd not been performing for a while. He'd been working on new material and had changed his style. He still had long hair but he'd decided to go with the shaggy, permed, blonde look and he looked good…very good indeed….

Riley was a big fan and so were all the other band members. He couldn't believe it when Des told him whose video she was appearing in, so she was able to introduce Riley to Paul Best and the other guys from the band. When she started work on the *Sharp Edge* video, Paul had to do a lot of holding, kissing, and touching her. It all looked very real, very sexy. Unsurprisingly, he loved working with her. He thought she was fantastic to work with and a very beautiful woman.

Jake was really excited. He had met his favourite band. Even Lori was excited, She had just introduced them and she just had met Paul Best. This guy was so sexy. She was so flattered when he told her she was a very sexy girl.

"Oh God, Paul Best thinks I'm sexy… Fuck me!"

Des laughed. "I didn't know you were into Paul"

"Oh yeah, Des, he is sooo fit…. You are so lucky getting to roll around with him. I'll swap places with you anytime…" she said grinning.

"So you'd like to fool around with Paul would you?"

"God Yes!"

As promised, Riley took Des out for dinner the night before he left. He sat looking at her lovingly. He had fallen head over heels with Des and wanted to tell her exactly how he felt. When they had finished dinner they went back to his apartment and he poured them a drink. He sat down beside her and looked deep into her eyes.

"I've fallen in love with you, Des"

"Riley!" She took his face in her hands and kissed him.

"I have…. I really have…"

"Riley…."

Before he could say another word she kissed him again. He kissed her back lovingly.

"I'm so going to miss you while I'm away"

"When I get some free days I'll fly out to you"

"Oh yeah, Ripper! You beaut…"

He stood up and got hold of her hands. He led her to the bedroom and as she lay on the bed he stood over her gazing down at her, is eyes on fire. He crawled up the bed on all fours with a sexy look on his face. He unzipped her dress and peeled her out of it. Moving his mouth down her body, he could feel her rise to his touch.

"Oohh," she moaned with pleasure.

She pulled his T-shirt over his head and dug her long nails in his bare flesh. He tensed his body….

"Oh Des…Oohh fucking hell…"

She pulled him closer to her. He kissed and bit her neck softly as she pulled his hair gently to bring his head closer to her lips. They began to kiss passionately as she gently reached up and touched his face then moving her hands to the nape of his neck. Her touch sent shivers through his body as he eased out of his jeans, her lips brushing over his, biting his bottom lip.

"Umm… that's so sexy, Des…"

She ran her hands over his chest and down his body to his thighs. She was driving him mad. He eased between her thighs making love to her. He knew what he was doing alright. He definitely knew how to please.

The next morning he made her breakfast and shouted her. She sat at the breakfast bar and looked at him.

"Morning Des..."

"Riley...Do you have to be so cheerful?"

"Des..." he smiled as he kissed her.

"WHOA...Riley, you're hot and sweaty"

"Yeah baby, let me make you hot and sweaty too..." he said as he let out a loud sexy laugh.

"You're a rock star. You're not even supposed to be up at this time let alone be cheerful and making breakfast"

"Who said?"

"I did..."

"Well baby, I have been up for hours doing my workout while you have been snoring"

"I don't snore Riley..." she laughed, giving him a sexy look.

Riley laughed. "Hmm, yeah ya do, but I love you anyway," he said grabbing her. "Come on, make me more hot and sweaty...."

"Riley..."

She didn't need much persuading. Riley pulled her back into the bedroom and made love to her. The sex was hot and passionate... He took her breath away. He gripped her hips and pulled her towards him. She ran her hands over his shoulders down his chest. He looked her in the face, his eyes feverish, glittering with excitement. He moved down and used his tongue to please her

"Oh yes, yes, yes, Oh baby yes..."

He moved her legs apart. Gripping her inner thigh he pushed himself into her making her groan. She moved like a wild cat. He allowed himself to release then gently kissed her, before running bare assed across to the shower. Des followed him in, standing behind him. She wrapped her arms around him and kissed his back. He turned round and kissed her back and told her he was going to miss her so much while he was away. He made her promise that when she had some days free she would fly over to where he was.

"I love you Des ..."

Des didn't want that feeling again... It hurt too much when it went wrong and she wasn't letting herself get like that again. It would be so easy to fall in love with Riley but she wanted to avoid that feeling.

"Des, you're gonna love me..."

"I'll see you soon Riley…" she said as she kissed him.

"Des, I'll make you fall in love with me…" he said, pulling her back to him and kissing her harder.

Des looked at him with a warm expression on her face. Yes it would be very easy to love you, Riley she thought to herself. She smiled and then winked at him

"See ya…. You sexy, sexy man…"

Chapter 16

Des headed to meet Jake for lunch. They looked at the menu making small talk. Jake asked about Riley and how things were going with them.

"Great… Actually fantastic…"

"Good…. Have you fallen in love?"

"That's never happening again. I really love being with Riley and it would be so easy to fall in love with him but I just can't let myself feel like that again. I just can't…"

"Oh Des… I've got to say, I thought Staffan and you were for keeps, you can't let what happened stop you from falling for someone else.

"He shouldn't have slept with that girl. I loved him…" she said angrily.

"Do you really believe Staffan cheated on you? He's mad about you, Des"

"It's too late now," she said dismissing the question. "Now what are you buying me for lunch?"

"Hey, you're the big money earner now… I thought you were buying lunch," he grinned.

Jake had a list of her bookings for the next few months.

She had a lot of functions to attend, a commercial for ladies' eye make up to shoot and a grand opening of a designer shop introducing her own label. She was also booked to make another video. It was at this point she told him she wanted to go over and spend some time with Riley.

"Are you sure you're not in love?"

"Ha-ha no…."

By now, Riley had been away for three mouths and Des was missing him. They rang each other every night but she'd had such a busy time she'd not been able to fly out to see him. As she'd already said to Jake, this was really a big problem. She booked a couple of weeks and flew over to the UK. He had missed her so much and had written a song about how he felt about her. He'd called it *'YOU'*.

He'd just finished putting the music to it when she flew out to see him and so he sang it at one of the gigs while she was there. She thought it was a beautiful rock ballad. She took him sightseeing in London. Everywhere they went they were followed, fans would simply flock round them. Girls chanted Riley's name and men just stared at Desiree, amazed that one woman be so beautiful.

After two weeks were up she had to go back to New York. She had such a busy schedule she couldn't leave it any longer, she had photo shoots to do and a string of other engagements like opening a new Sports Centre. Riley would be away for another three months before he came back to New York.

When Des got back she was straight back to work and she met up with Lori for lunch at the Rock Joint restaurant. Lori had been touring Australia. Des asked about Scott. Lori said that she didn't know if he was cheating or not. She'd not found anything to suggest he had but she was watching him. She asked Des about her and Riley. Des told her things were great. Lori was happy for her. She told Des she'd been talking to Staffan.

"Have you?"

"Yeah… he still loves you Des"

"I can't think about Staffan. He hurt me so much."

"You know he wants to talk to you don't you?"

"No… I can't…"

"Why, Des?"

"I just can't"

Shortly after, Des was scheduled to go to back the UK. She was going over for promotional reasons and to attend a premiere of a Matt Adams film but he wouldn't be there having gone back to the states for a conference about his next film. When Desiree's limo pulled up there were hundreds of screaming fans all wanting her attention and in amongst the crowd was her mother.

Des stepped out of the limo revealing her beautiful shapely legs. The dress she had on had a side split and was extremely tight, hugging her figure beautifully. It was silvery grey and shimmered beautifully when she moved. She waved to all the screaming fans and started to sign autographs. At the front of the crowd there was her mother. She asked Desiree for her autograph. Des looked at her disbelievingly.

Carol had just wanted to see her beautiful daughter and thought this would be the perfect way.

"Please Desiree," she pleaded.

Des signed her autograph and walked away as if she didn't know her. To Des it was like signing any other autograph. She went into the film premiere and didn't see her again.

Chapter 17

Staffan and the guys had just come back from touring Tokyo and he knew that Riley was also due back in two days. He found out where Des was and he turned up. As usual, Des was surrounded by lots of people vying for her attention and, just as usual, she looked sexy in her very tight, short dress showing off her beautiful body. Staffan walked right through them as he had done the very first time he saw her.

"Hi Des"

"Staffan," she said looking very shocked to see him

She'd not really spoke to him since their divorce, the last time was at the RM Awards and she didn't really talk to him then. He looked so good, so sexy in his black jeans and black shirt.

"Will you join me for a drink?" He held his hand out.

"Hmm… OK, Yeah," she said taking his hand. She figured that she'd better talk to him as he obviously had something he needed to say.

They went and sat at a table in the corner. He had totally forgotten about Riley and getting back at him, all he saw was Des and realised how much he wanted her. They talked for hours before she realised what the time was. She had to be up early for an appointment in the morning.

Staffan asked her if she wanted to go back to his for a drink.

"That would be good but I have an early start. At least we're talking again"

"Please Des"

"Oh Staffan… I…"

"Please come back," he interrupted her.

Des looked at him and smiled.

"OK Staffan – one drink"

He took her hand and smiled at her again. All he could think about was getting her back to his apartment. He wanted her so much.

They took a cab back to Staffan's and whilst he fixed them both a drink Des went onto the balcony and looked at the view and sighed heavily.

"Beautiful view," Staffan said looking Des up and down.

"Yes it is," as she smiled

"I meant *you*"

"Oh" She smiled again, putting her head down.

Staffan moved towards her. He got up very close he leaned in and he kissed her, looking into her eyes at the same time. She wanted to kiss him back but moved instead – she felt very confused and thought, *'No… No…DESIREE!'*

He followed back into the lounge and sat on the couch next to her. He looked at her then went to kiss her again but she moved her head aside so he kissed her neck instead. She closed her eyes and sighed heavily, she was starting to feel how she used to when he touched her. She didn't want that feeling, it hurt too much.

"Oh God, my feet are killing me – do you mind if I take my shoes off?" trying to stop the feeling she was getting.

"No, here give me your feet"

She took her shoes off and Staffan pulled her legs across him and massaged her feet. She lay back and sighed yet again.

"Oh God, that feels so good," as she closed her eyes.

"Good, just relax" as he looked at her, wanting her even more.

He started to move his hands slowly up her legs as he watched her beautiful face he took her breath away. He slid down next to her. When she opened her eyes, he looked full into them.

"Bliv hos mig I aften..."

She looked at him. "What did you just say to me?"

"Stay with me tonight"

"Oh Staffan, don't do this to me"

She went to get up and he pulled her back Then he kissed her again.

"Du er sa smuk"

She looked at him again wondering what he'd said.

"I said that you are so beautiful"

He kissed her again slowly, but passionately. She couldn't help herself, she kissed him back, putting her fingers through his hair. He moved his hand up her legs, under her dress, unclipping her panties. He was so aroused, he slid his jeans down and eased himself between her thighs and made love to her. In their urgency they didn't even get undressed. She really wanted him and his talking Danish to her just turned her on even more. Afterwards, he got up, held his hand out to her and said, "Let's go to bed"

She looked at him and took his hand.

He led her to the bedroom and laid her on the bed. They undressed each other slowly as their kisses deepened, more passionately and they made love again, hot and very steamy. They really wanted each other, they couldn't get enough of each other. Having made love for some time they eventually drifted asleep holding each other, crumpled sheets wrapped round their legs.

Des woke up in the night, the lights shimmering in from the buildings across from Staffan's apartment. She lay there and watched him sleep. Quietly, she got out of bed. Wrapping the sheet around she got herself a drink of water and went out on to the balcony and looked at the view from the apartment, deep in thought. Staffan woke up feeling for her. Realising she wasn't there he jumped up and went to see where she was. He saw her out on the balcony, he stopped and stared at her for a moment before going out to ask what she was doing.

"Nothing, just admiring the view"

"So was I, before I walked out here."

He wrapped his arms tightly around her and started to kiss the back of her neck. As she turned, he swooped in, kissed her again then picked her up and took her to the bedroom. Her sheet fell to the floor then he made love to her again, tenderly and gently.

The next morning Staffan made some tea while Des showered and dressed.

"Can I see you tonight?"

"I can't. I've got a charity function to go to and it's going to be a late one"

"Tomorrow"

"No can't..."

"Then when? I really want to see you..."

"Staffan, we shouldn't be doing this"

"Why not?"

"Riley... I'm with Riley now"

Staffan shrugged his shoulders.

"He doesn't love you like I do, he doesn't touch you like I do, and he doesn't make you feel like I do. I don't give a shit about Riley... give me another reason."

Desiree couldn't give him another answer, but Riley *was* a good enough reason for the moment.

She and Staffan were divorced. What was happening, why did she feel like this? Why did she want him so much?

She started to think that they might have another chance, perhaps they could sometime get back together?

Chapter 18

Two days later Riley was back in town and, inevitably, the first person he saw was Staffan. He started to wind him up about Desiree.

"Can't wait to see Des tonight, Man. I'm sure she's missed me, you know what I mean," sniggering at Staffan. "I'm going to ask her to marry me."

This upset Staffan until he simply couldn't hold it in. He was sick of Riley rubbing his nose about Des.

"What make you think she's been on her own?"

"What? She wouldn't cheat on me… we're good together, she doesn't need any other man – I give her what she needs!"

"Oh is that right? Why was she in my bed two nights ago then? And man, she was hot, real hot – she couldn't get enough of me but I always had that effect on her

"You're fucking lying!" Riley was starting to feel sick inside.

"No, you ask her. She won't lie"

"Fuck off, you're lying!"

"No, it makes her go crazy when I speak to her in Danish"

"Fuck you. You're a fucking liar!"

Staffan smiled cockily. "Oh fucking hell, you *hope* I am a liar. Shit, it's gonna hurt when she admits that she slept with me, this is classic!"

"Fuck you!" Riley said through clenched teeth.

Angry and hurt, Riley went straight round to Desiree's. He had fallen for Des in a big way, she shown him his softer side, so loving and gentle. As he reached her door, his anger intensified. He banged violently on the door and when she opened it, he pushed past her with some force.

"Have you fucked Staffan?" He demanded

"What?"

"Tell me, did you fuck Staffan two nights ago?"

She put her hand to her mouth and looked at him. "Oh Riley. I'm so sorry. But how…?"

" You did, didn't you?" He put his head down and clenched his fists. Raising his eyes, he looked at her

"Look at me Des, I love you. Staffan took great fucking pleasure in telling me. He couldn't wait to tell me."

"Riley I'm sorry."

"Fuck you Des why? … Why?" Grinding his teeth.

"Riley, I'm so sorry"

"No, no, no…. fucking hell!" shaking his head. "Why… Why did you do that? Why didn't you just lie to me?"

"Riley, I don't want to lie to you"

"Now… he said you wouldn't lie. You should have lied, I would have believed you. I wanted you to say it didn't happen. I wanted you to say that because you've got me you don't need anyone else."

He put his head back and pushed his hands through his hair

"All I thought about when I was away was you"

"Riley…Riley"

He stormed out slamming the door. Devastated, he stood outside the door and put his hands to his head, tears rolling down his face.

Desiree hated herself for hurting him and she realised that her feelings for Riley were stronger than she thought. She understood why Riley was so angry and knew she deserved it. What hurt her most was that Staffan had used her to get one up on Riley.

Any hopes Staffan had about getting Des back had just gone. He'd hurt her again. He had hurt her twice and she never gave anyone the chance to hurt her once never mind twice. Staffan had and she would never let her guard down again. She rang Staffan and asked him to come to the apartment.

He thought she wanted to see him to tell him that she and Riley were finished and that she wanted him back. He couldn't have been more wrong

She let him in when he arrived. He put his arms round her and leaned in to kiss her but she pushed him away.

"Des, what's wrong. I've been waiting for you to ring me, ya know, to tell me that it was over between you and Riley.

"Why did you do that? Riley and I had a good thing going"

"Not that good – otherwise you wouldn't have ended up in my bed," and he moved in to her again.

He got hold of her and pulled her close and tried to kiss her but she pushed him away. She was so angry.

"You used me to get one up on Riley"

"I admit I wanted Riley out of your life. But I wouldn't *use* you. You know how much I wanted you that night, you felt it too…"

"I don't want to see you again Staffan"

"Des….come on, please. I'm sorry – but not sorry about you and him breaking up"

"I've hurt Riley and I understand him breaking up with me. I deserve that. But you using me to make it happen… Go, just go!"

Staffan tried to get hold of Desiree. "Des, I love you"

"I have got to make this right with Riley. Get out Staffan, get out!" She screamed, trying to hold back her tears.

"Man, you're the most infuriating and stubborn women I've ever met. You are not all fuckin' innocent, you enjoyed fuckin' me and you know it"

Staffan couldn't believe how stupid he'd been and he was also really angry with Des because she was so stubborn and just wouldn't listen. They were meant to be together, it was maddening that she wouldn't give in to it.

Riley hit the clubs that evening and was slowly getting drunk when a pretty young lady approached him. She had deep plum-coloured hair and looked really hot in the miniskirt she was almost wearing.

"Are you Riley Watson?

"Yep baby… and who are you?"

"Oh wow! I'm Annalise I'm such a big fan"

"Have you come over here to get laid Annalise?"

Annalise giggled as Riley grabbed her hand and led her to a cab to take her back to his apartment where they had hot, passionate, no strings sex for some considerable time. Annalise couldn't believe that she was in Riley Watson's bed having the kind of hot raunchy sex she had fantasized about for years.

"Fuck me like your life depends on it baby…"

When he started talking dirty to her she moaned and groaned with delight, she orgasmed time after time she was so excited.

Meanwhile, Lori was telling Staffan he was a total idiot.

"What on earth did you expect? What were you thinking of?"

"I wasn't thinking. Riley was getting on my fuckin' nerves banging on about Des and I wanted to shut him up. I wasn't even thinking about him when me and Des were together that night. It was just about her and how much I wanted her"

"Oh Staffan, now you've blown it"

"I've blown it, she's blown it. Well maybe its time to let go and move on"

"You don't mean that Staffan"

"Oh yeah I fucking do, maybe I've had it with Desiree fucking Beaumont."

"No Staffan, you love her"

"It's not enough – she's so fucking stubborn she makes me fucking angry"

"Staffan"

" Nah, Fuck it and Fuck *her*."

Next morning, Annalise was still at Riley's. She was asleep when he got up, he looked at her and thought, 'Oh Shit'. He made some coffee and sat on the couch.

Des had decided to go and see Riley. When she rang the doorbell he opened the door, saw Des and immediately slammed it shut.

She shouted, "Riley, hear me out!"

"No Des, please go away"

"I'm not going anywhere"

Riley opened the door even though he knew that if Des saw Annalise that really would be the end. Even though she had cheated on him and he was so angry he knew he would have forgiven Des – he still wanted to marry her.

"Riley please. I'm so sorry – it wasn't meant to happen"

Riley put his head down "I can't do this right now can we meet up later"

He really didn't want Des to see Annalise but then this beautiful, long-legged girl appeared from the bedroom wearing nothing but a sheet and asked Riley if he was coming back to bed. Sighing, Riley asked Annalise to go back into the bedroom while he spoke to Des.

"Do you mean *DESIREE BEAUMONT?* Oh wow, she's so beautiful – could I meet her?"

He shoved her back in the bedroom. Des could only look at him.

"Riley, I'm sorry. I'd better go"

"Des…Des… please meet me later"

"No…I understand, really I do. I hope you can forgive me one day"

She kissed him tenderly and left. Fighting back her tears she got in the lift. She just wanted to get out of the building and get home.

Riley closed the door and pressed his head against it. Annalise came back out of the bedroom.

"Is everything OK?

"No…no…" shaking his head.

"Have I done something wrong?

Riley told her to get dressed and leave.

"It's not you babe, it's me"

Annalise got dressed, thanked him for a great night and left, Riley sank back onto the couch and put his head in his hands.

"Fuck… Fuck… Fuck!"" He repeated.

Desiree had found a taxi and after giving the address settled back. The taxi driver looked at her quizzically.

"You are Desiree Beaumont?

Des smiled at him and said "Yes"

"Oh man. Wait till I tell the guys back at the depot that I had Desiree Beaumont in my cab!"

Des smiled again and he headed for the apartment where he dropped her off. She broke down, moving from room to room with streams of tears running down her face. There seemed no end to her tears but she knew this was her fault and she deserved it. She understood why Riley had slept with that girl. She had got hurt again – she would have to be harder from now on.

Down town, Johnny met up with Staffan for lunch to talk about the two bands doing a record together. Of course, Riley had to turn up at the restaurant. The dislike between them had only got worse since Des.

"Not with Des, Staffan?"

"Fuck off Riley"

"Why?"

"Just fuck off"

"Yeah Riley, fuck off – don't start this!" Johnny said.

Riley wasn't listening and carried on. Pretty soon, it came to breaking point for both of them.

"Not only have you her lost once, now you've lost her twice," he grinned. Couldn't keep your prick in your trousers and second you used her to get at me. What a fuckin' dick – you had the most beautiful woman in the palm of your hands but you couldn't keep her, could you?"

Riley hated Staffan even more now he was in love with Des and Staffan had ruined it for him.

"You didn't keep her neither did you… Now Fuck off Riley, just fuck off"

Staffan could feel himself getting to blowing point.

"I didn't fuck up, you fucked it up for me"

Staffan got up and hit Riley. He hit him so hard he winded him and Riley went down on the floor.

"That has been coming for a long time. Now stay out of my fucking way!"

"Fuck you!" as Riley got up and went to hit Staffan.

Johnny tried to break them up but he couldn't part them, their fists were flying everywhere. Finally, the police arrived and arrested them both. The Paparazzi loved it and the full blown fight in the restaurant made head line news

Jake read about it in the paper and told Des all about it. She told him she was finished with men. She was finished with getting hurt – it was time to concentrate on a new career in the movies – she wanted to be a *movie star*.

Chapter 19

1983

When Desiree went to lunch with Jake the press was all over her. Matt Adams, the big English film producer, was in the restaurant and wanted to know what all the fuss was about, so he went over.

"I should have known. The beautiful Desiree Beaumont. I've never had the pleasure"

He reached for her hand and gently kissed it He couldn't take his eyes off her, she took his breath away. Jake took the opportunity to mention that Desiree wanted to be actress.

"I've seen you in magazines and the rock vids… Can you act, darling?"

"I think so" she said quite flirtatiously.

"OK I'd like to see for myself. How about doing a screen test for me tomorrow?"

"Really?" She said with excitement. "Thank you."

"My pleasure. See you tomorrow, then. " He turned to Jake and said, "Bring her for 10"

"Thanks Matt – she won't disappoint."

"I don't doubt that for a second," as he smiled at her.

He had the most beautiful smile Des was very attracted to him. Jake couldn't help but notice.

"Oh, what is this"?

"What?".

"Are you eyeing up Matt?

"Well, he is very sexy," as she watched him walk away.

She noticed the number of women going over to him trying to grab his attention but he couldn't stop looking at Des. She had a lot of drive and ambition, she really wanted to be a movie star. Matt thought she was very beautiful and could be a big hit on the silver screen, but *could she act*?

The next morning Desiree went for her screen test. Matt watched her carefully, she captivated him. He couldn't keep his eyes off her. He told her she had great potential and mentioned that he had a small part that she would be perfect for her, if she was interested. Desiree jumped at the chance. She only have a few lines in the film but it was a start and she was grateful./

"Do I have to sleep with you now?" She said archly.

He looked at her, amazed at her directness, and asked why she thought that so she explained.

"We are not all like that, my darling"

A great smile spread across her face. "Thank you, Mr Adams, for this great opportunity."

"You're welcome. I see great things for you"

"Really?"

"Yes, I do"

She flirted with him a little and he discovered that he liked it. He liked *her*, he thought she was funny and so very beautiful.

Desiree worked hard on her lines. She didn't want to let Matt down and as time went on they formed a good relationship. He was very attracted to her but he didn't think she would be interested in him in that way as he was a little older than her. Finally, he managed to ask her to dinner one night and when she accepted he was shocked. He enquired if she liked dancing, and when she told him that she loved to, he smiled.

"Good! Would you like to go dancing?"

"Dancing with you?"

"Yes, with me."

"Yes I would"

"Tonight then?"

"Yes… that would be nice"

He was so charming, such a gentleman. Desiree really liked Matt and the way he made her feel so good about herself.

He picked her up at seven thirty. He looked really handsome in a black shirt with black trousers, his silky black hair flicked back and he smelt of a woody scent. So nice… so sexy…

He took her to dinner at an exclusive club where The Ralph Dallas Band was playing, one of the biggest swing bands of all time. Des had never been to a club like this before. She found it really enjoyable.

"Do you want to dance, Des?"

"Yeah, but I don't know how to dance to this sort of music"

"Come on, just follow me"

Matt took her hand and led her to the dance floor. Everybody in the club knew him and were very interested in Des. Everyone's eyes followed them as they made their way to the dance floor. He was the envy of all his friends as he wrapped his arms round her waist and she placed her arms round his neck.

"You're so beautiful"

Des smiled at him and moved her hand to the back of his neck, running her fingers though his hair, looking straight into his eyes.

"And you are a very good looking man"

He smiled at her, showing his beautiful white teeth. He kissed her cheek and asked what she wanted to do next.

"Anything?"

"Let's go for some pizza."

"Pizza? I have a figure to look after, Mr Adams"

"I'm hungry, Miss Beaumont, and besides – you are perfect!"

"You're hungry? You've just had a huge meal… where do you put it?"

"I'm a growing boy," he smirked.

They got in the limo and headed to Planet Pizza. Matt's bodyguard was waiting close by as the paparazzi had got wind of their date. Anything that Desiree Beaumont did was big news and they wanted everything. As they went in, flashbulbs started flashing and Matt's bodyguard had to push some of them back as they got a little too close for comfort. Des sat on a high swivel stool, swinging her legs back and forth. Matt couldn't take his eyes off her. Her dress had a split up the front showing a great deal of her beautiful legs. He just looked intensely at them.

"You need to put them away," he said, smiling his sexy smile.

"Why?" She asked, swinging them even more.

"They're very distracting."

"Really?" as a cheeky grin crept across her face.

"Are you flirting with me, Desiree?"

"Could be…"

Matt laughed. "You're a bad girl"

They got their pizza and ate it in the limo going back to Des's. Matt dropped her off at home and asked he if had enjoyed herself.

"Oh Matt *Yes*, I don't know what to say apart from thank you for such a lovely night."

"Say you'll see me again."

"I'd love to"

"I'll call you tomorrow."

He couldn't get Des out of his head, she'd really turned him on swinging her legs like that and he couldn't sleep for thinking about her. It was all over the paper about Matt and Des the next morning.

Matt called Des to ask if she was free that night and whether he could see her and, of course, she accepted. He told her he would be there at eight and to wear something warm. She was very intrigued so decided to wear a figure-hugging knitted dress, after all she still wanted him to see her figure. When Matt arrived at her apartment she opened the door and kissed his cheek. He handed her a shawl.

"You'll need this"

Des looked at him. He still wasn't giving anything away.

When they got outside there was a horse-drawn carriage, with the most beautiful black horses she had ever seen.

"Oh Matt, this is so lovely," as she went over to the horses and petted them.

"I'm glad you like it"

He took her hand and led her to the carriage. She smiled at him as he helped her in, he looked so handsome in his black polo neck jumper, black trousers and black zip-up jacket.

They trotted leisurely through the park then suddenly pulled at a table. He got out and held his hand out to Des. He had certainly picked the most romantic spot. They were on the edge of a lake surrounded by weeping willow and cherry trees. He had candles placed all around the table, it was beautiful. The food was delivered and served by a uniformed waiter. A brass band played romantic music in the background while he wined and dined her. He had thought of everything.

When Des arrived on set the next day she was greeted with a dressing room full of flowers and balloons, all from Matt.

"Some one likes you!" Jake laughed.

Des smiled. "They're all from Matt."

"Matt hey? You've been seeing a lot of Matt lately"

"I like him, he's so nice."

Over the water at Staten Island Matt had a business meeting with actor Trent Douglas. Matt had got there early so decided to have a drink at the bar. While he was waiting who should see him and make her way over but English actress Millicent Lee.

"Oh Matt Darling, how nice to see you," as she kissed his cheek.

"Hi Milly"

"I hear you are seeing that rock chic video Desiree woman"

"Yes Milly, I'm seeing Desiree."

"A little young don't you think? You are making a fool out of yourself, Matt."

"I beg your pardon?"

"Well she's only 20 something… and you're what, 45?"

"What does that matter?"

Millicent had always wanted to be the main woman in Matt's life but it was Vivian who had stolen his heart all those years ago. She had always been in love with Matt and was very jealous of Desiree.

"I didn't take you for someone so bitter, Milly, it seems like you're just jealous of Des."

"Why the hell would I be jealous of her?"

"Because she is beautiful, she has it all, everything I want"

Millicent narrowed her eyes and gave Matt a frosty look and marched away, snapping at the waitress that had got in her way.

Chapter 20

Lori was growing increasingly suspicious. She *knew* Scott was cheating on her but didn't have any proof. She arranged a girls night out with Des, Jenny, Judy and Ellen. They were having a fantastic night when Lori told Des she thought she wanted a divorce. Enough was enough. She'd had it with Scott. Des asked if she was sure.

"Yes. Anyway, I want to know all about Matt Adams"

"I like him, I like him a lot, Lori, he's so nice."

Lori smiled at her friend and mentioned the fact that they were both crap at choosing men. Des laughed and agreed. Just then a very handsome rugby player, Ethan August, came over.

"Hi Ladies"

"Hi sexy" Lori said

They got talking. Des was watching her with Ethan. She was quite drunk and started heading out of the club with him. Des grabbed her arm and pulled her to one side.

"What do you think you're doing?"

"Having some fun, Des"

"What about Scott?"

"What about him? Fuck him," and shrugged her shoulders.

"Are you sure you know what you're doing?"

"Yeah babe, I'm not that drunk I don't know what I'm doing. Come look at him, he is *so* sexy, Des"

Ethan was very sexy, there was no doubt about that. Standing six foot with short, spiked brown hair, brown eyes, and what a body – all six pack and rippling biceps.

Ethan grabbed Lori's hand and led her away. Lori looked back at Des and waved. Des continued to party with the girlfriends on the dance floor when Dale Tanner spotted her. He made his way over to her and made small talk for a while before he asked her if she would like to do a commercial for endangered animals. Maybe she would like to do a tour of the rescue shelters in Africa, Asia and the Mediterranean. She got extremely excited about this offer and told Dale she would love to do it. He was really pleased and told her he would be in touch to work out all the details with Jake. She said she would look forward to hearing from him.

The following morning, Lori had made the headlines with her antics with Ethan, making headlines in Britain and America. Furthermore, Scott had seen it. He woke up to an empty space in their bed then saw the paper. He was livid.

When she eventually arrived back home Scott was waiting for her.

"Where the fuck have you been?" He hissed and threw the paper at her. "Is this true?" He raged. She had never seen him so angry.

She looked down at the paper by her feet. "Yeah, we can both play that fucking game."

"Why, Lori, why?"

"I know you've cheated on me again, just fuckin' admit it"

"OK… OK I have cheated on you, Is that why you've cheated on me with the fucking rugby player?"

"You bet your sorry arse that's why! He was fantastic too!"

"You fucking bitch!"

Scott lunged at her, shoving against the wall

"You're a fuckin tart!"

He raised his hand and was about to hit her then lowered it and decided against it. His eyes narrowed, they were cold and angry and she knew she had got to him.

"Don't like it, do you Scott?"

"Lori ,shut the fuck up. I swear I'll…"

"You hated it when I was with Riley and you swore to me you would never cheat on me again – but you still did."

Lori kept pushing him and pushing him; she told him she didn't love him anymore, she wanted out of the marriage. She'd had enough of him and his cheating. He marched over to her, stared straight at her and told her he was leaving. He packed some of his stuff and told her the rest would be collected. He was going.

"Good… the sooner you're out of my life the fuckin' better… I want a divorce"

"Over my dead body! No fucking divorce, Baby" he slammed the door as he left

Over the coming weeks, Ethan and Lori saw a lot of each other, she even went to some of his games and he went to a couple of her concerts. They seemed a good match. She had once wanted Scott so much but his cheating ways were more than she could deal with.

Matt and Jake had met up for lunch and talked about how Desiree was doing. Matt told him she was doing fantastically well, great potential.

"I told you, Matt"

"She's so beautiful, sweet and vulnerable"

"She's been hurt in the past and is very wary"

"I think I'm in love with her"

"Yeah, everyone loves Des"

"No Jake – I mean it. I'm in love with her, I want to be with her. She's intoxicating, she takes my breath away"

"Oh, I see"

Matt then mentioned his age and told Jake that he knew he was twenty two years older than her and he knew she'd been married to the very sexy Staffan Templeton but he wanted her and asked Jake what he thought.

"If that's how you feel, Matt, then all you can do is take the chance"

Shortly after, when Desiree was to accompany him to a film awards night, he decided to tell her how he felt. Desiree had already realised she was falling for him too, a feeling she was desperately trying not to have had just suddenly crept up on her. When they left the awards that evening for Desiree's, she leaned in and kissed him. When Matt asked what she was doing, she told him she just wanted to kiss him

"Why?" He asked, stunned but pleased.

"I wanted to"

"Did you feel you *had* to kiss me?"

"No, I just wanted to."

"Really?"

He thought this was his chance to tell her how he felt. He leant in and kissed her back, staring at her intensely. The limo came to a standstill at the entrance to her apartment block. She looked him in the eyes and asked if he would like to come in. He asked if she was sure, Desiree told him she was very sure.

Matt told his driver to go home and to just come back to pick him up in the morning. He looking questioningly at Des, unsure they were on the same wavelength. Des nodded to reassure him. The driver said, "OK, Mr Adams" thinking 'You lucky bastard'.

As Matt followed Desiree into the elevator, she turned and kissed him. He kissed her back very passionately. As she opened her apartment door, he pulled her back in to his arms.

"Are you sure about this, Des?"

"Matt come in"

She took his hand and smiled at him, leading him to the bedroom. He leaned over her and began to kiss her tenderly. Lost in the kiss, she relaxed completely. He ran his hands over her breasts, moving them down her body He was very gentle, the warmth of his breath on her neck exciting her. It wasn't like she had with Staffan or Riley, for that matter. This was very different – he was making love to her very gently and tenderly and she was enjoying it.

As morning approached, the sun appeared through the drapes. She woke him gently, smothering him with butterfly kisses until he opened his eyes and gazed at her, still not believing that this was real, that somehow he was still dreaming

"She smiled at him. "Good morning"

"Wow, you even look beautiful in the morning, Desiree"

"Thank you – but I think your eyes must be playing tricks on you. I'm not good in the morning"

"Des, I want to see you again and again and again."

"Really? Even after seeing me in the morning?" She gave a playful laugh.

"Yeah," he laughed. "Did you enjoy last night?" He asked nervously.

"Yes – the awards were really great."

"No… Des, I meant…"

"Oh… " she giggled.

"You were married to Staffan – I'm not a young stud like him…"

"Oh Matt you don't give yourself enough credit. You were fantastic… really fantastic" and she kissed him.

Matt pulled her to him and kissed her back.

"Really, did I satisfy you?"

He wasn't normally that worried about how he'd performed in bed, but he wanted to keep Des. He decided to hold off telling her how he felt just for the moment, thinking he would see how this goes.

"Yeah, you are very sexy man, you made me feel fantastic"

"Come here Des, and I will make you feel like that all over again"

He pulled her back into bed and this time they made love slowly and tenderly, both of them taking their time. Matt had been with a lot of women in his time but Des was the one he wanted most to impress.

"Des, I'm going to have to leave you"

"Yeah… that's a shame, we could have stayed in bed all day"

"Hey… don't tease me!"

When his car came for him he asked Desiree if he would see her later

"Yes, if you want to see me…"

"Oh darling, I do… very much so"

"I'll see you later, then"

Matt kissed her, "Oh yes, definitely!" throwing her that sexy smile.

"Good, I'm glad" as she winked at him.

That evening, Matt flew Desiree over to Italy in his privet plane to an exclusive restaurant. D'Angelo was an old friend of Matt's, so when Matt said he was bringing Desiree Beaumont as his date D'Angelo was very impressed, not to say excited. D'Angelo made sure they had the best seat in the restaurant with lights draped round a big umbrella out by a pond. Swans, among other birds, were just drifting along minding their own business. Des was very impressed. D'Angelo made them his speciality. It was spectacular, her mouth watering as she took her first taste.

"Hmm, this is beautiful" she complimented him.

"Thank you, *sei un Angelo!*"

She smiled and looked at Matt who told her that D'Angelo had said she was an angel. D'Angelo took her hand and kissed it gently and told his friend he was a very lucky man. Matt quickly agreed.

While Matt was wining and dining Des, it was lunch time in New York. Vivian was having lunch with her friends Sally Crossley, Jess Lang and Loretta Jennings. Millicent Lee was also joining them. They were all bitching and trying to outdo each other. Vivian was telling them about a new lover who was ten years younger than her when Jess brought Matt into the conversation.

"Oh by the way, have you heard who Matt's seeing?"

"Who?" Viv asked.

"Only Desiree Beaumont" Millicent chirped in.

"Desiree Beaumont? She's…"

"…Only twenty two," Loretta finished for her.

"…Only after his money," Millicent chipped in, showing her green-eyed monster.

"She has her own money – besides Matt is still very attractive," Vivian pointed out.

"Yes he is – and you Millicent are just jealous" smirked Sally.

Millicent snorted. "Can we talk about something else?" She snapped.

Sally knew she had put Millicent's nose out of joint and she was glad she'd got her back for a remark about her facelift last month.

Soon, everyone was talking about Desiree and Matt. There was a lot of speculation about their relationship, some were saying she was only interested in his money, others said Matt just wanted a young, hot woman on his arm.

He had taken her to a friend's birthday party the week before, where she had met Millicent. For most of the evening Millicent had stared at Des. It was only when Matt left her to get them some drinks that Millicent went over.

"So you are Desiree Beaumont, Matt's new playmate. You won't last long – they never do"

Des didn't care too much for Millicent and was ready for her. Millicent couldn't help herself. She had asked Des what she saw in Matt apart from his money. Des was just about to give her a piece of her mind when Millicent spotted Matt heading back so she made a quick departure.

"What was that all about?" Matt asked.

"Nothing I can't handle, have you slept with her?"

Matt shook his head. "Why?"

"No reason"

"Let's get out of here – I just want to be alone with you"

As they made their way to the door she said, "Just one minute Matt" and walked straight over to Millicent and tapped her on the shoulder.

"You want to know what I like about Matt – well, he's a fantastic fuck."

With that she turned on her heels and headed back to Matt leaving Millicent with her mouth wide open. Sally stood with her shoulders shaking silently laughing at Millicent's embarrassment.

"What on earth did you say?"

"I told her you were a good fuck."

"You didn't!" He said laughing a warm but hearty laugh.

Matt and Des had been seeing such a lot of each other, he even whisked her off to Texas for a rodeo show at White Rock Lake and bought her a stetson and proper cowboy boots to wear with her jeans and T-shirt. She was so excited, she'd never been to anything like this before. She was really thrilled by the riding, riding with real bucking bulls and horses, barrel racing and calf roping, she wanted to see it all. Matt was amazed at her excitement.

"Do you want something to eat?"

"Yes, I'm a little hungry now"

"Come on"

He put his arm around her and took her over to the trolley rides and on to the Chicken Dance diner.

"Wow, you must have been hungry, I've never seen you each that much.

"All this rodeo activity certainly gives you an appetite!"

Matt laughed. "What would you like to do now – there's a country music band on"

"Yes that would great, let's do it!"

When they got to the bar, the *City Night Cowboys* were already on and they pointed out to the crowds that they had a couple of celebs in the audience and got them up to do a little line dancing. Des had such fun. She loved being with Matt he was so funny and he really knew how to show a lady a good time.

Chapter 21

Matt wanted Desiree more and more but he wasn't sure that she felt the same way. As it happened, she was she truly falling in love with him as well. He made her very happy, the happiest she'd been for a while. Matt had been married before to the very beautiful actress Vivian Towers but it didn't work out. They agreed that the marriage wasn't working and decided to divorce for the sake of their son, Luke, before they ended up hating each other.

Luke was not much older than Desiree. He was a budding artist and travelled a lot. He looked very much like his father and, after all, Matt was a very attractive man. About six foot tall with short black hair and beautiful piecing blue eyes he had a beautiful muscular tanned body. Many women found Matt very appealing and would love to be in Desiree's shoes – Millicent for one.

Matt was think of asking Des to marry him and thought that he should find out how she felt about him before he asked her.

"Des, I want to ask you something"

"Go ahead"

"Will you answer me truthfully?"

"Yes… I don't like lies"

"OK – how do… hmm how do you feel about me? There, I said it!" He said nervously but straight to the point.

"You want to know how I feel about you?"

Matt nodded. He thought it was going to be something he didn't want to hear.

"Well Mr Adams…. I love you"

Matt smiled that sexy smile and winked at her

"Well Miss Beaumont, I can tell you that I'm in love with *you*"

"Oh Matt…" throwing her arms round him, "Do you know how that makes me feel?" giving him a big grin.

"You can show me if you want"

Des moved closer and kissed him slowly and grabbed his lip with her teeth. She made him feel very horny and she knew it.

Having decided he was going to ask Des to marry him, Matt had the best jeweller in New York come to his house so he could pick the perfect ring. After hours of looking, he found a cushion solitaire enhanced on each shoulder with ten side stones, this was the one. He had rented a luxury yacht and had set up dinner to be served shortly after they had arrived He picked Des up and couldn't believe how beautiful she looked. The sparkling red dress she was wearing looked stunning, her hair swept away from her beautiful face cascading into vintage curls down her back just sitting on her hips. She blew Matt away when he saw her.

They sat back in the limo and stared into each other's eyes, smiling at one another. As they approached the yacht he held his hand out to her and led her to the lounge. As they set sail he poured them both a glass of champagne, then took her outside onto the deck, the water quietly rushing by. It couldn't have been more romantic, the stars were out and the moon was *Lightning* up the sky.

The steward came out to tell Matt that dinner was served. They went back inside and, while they were enjoying dinner Matt, pulled out the box containing the ring. Desiree looked at Matt – she knew what it was but she wanted to make him say the words.

"More gifts? You spoil me."

"Sort of …"

Matt opened the box and took the ring out. Desiree's eyes widened. There before her was an enormous diamond, sparkling for her.

"Oh, Matt"

"Marry me Desiree"

"Yes... yes... yes ...I will," she said excitedly, crinkling her nose up

"I love you, Desiree Beaumont."

"I love you too"

"I can't wait to announce this to the world" Matt said.

"Matt, before we do I would like to tell Staffan. I feel I owe him that much, I don't want him to read about this in the papers."

"OK yeah... " At the back of his mind was Staffan again and how he was still very much in her thoughts.

Unfortunately, the press managed to get hold of the story first and broke it to the world and his dog. There it was right on the front page in big bold letters. Desiree hadn't wanted the announcement out until after she had told Staffan but it was too late.

Everyone thought that Desiree was marring Matt for his money. After all, why would a twenty-three year old beautiful woman marry a forty-five year old man if it *wasn't* for money. Desiree, however, had enough money of her own – she loved Matt for himself, he made her happy.

When Staffan saw the news, he was devastated and then angry. He had hoped that she would change her mind – he still hoped that they would get back together. This had made it final.

After it all blew up in the papers, Des felt she needed to talk to Staffan to explain. She rang him about their apartment which she had got in their divorce settlement. She wanted to know if he wanted it back after she married Matt. He said he would come round to see her, never mentioning her engagement. He wanted to see her in person – to hurt her, like she had just hurt him. When he came round, he was really cold with her.

"Staffan I wanted to ask if you wanted the apartment back"

"Why would I?"

"Well I'm..." she was just about to tell him, when he interrupted her.

"When were you going to fucking tell me about getting married?"

"I was going to tell you"

"Oh I see. You were *going* to tell me! But you thought it would be fucking better if I read it in the fucking paper first, yeah!"

He was pointing his finger at her aggressively. He was so angry he shouted at her, he was so brutal and cold. She had never seen Staffan like this before.

"I didn't have tell you anything, I don't have to explain myself to you."

"No you don't... well fuck you Des, you fucking bitch!"

Staffan had never spoke to her like that before and it shocked her.

"Sell the fucking place! I don't fucking want it! I shared this with you – I don't want to be reminded of it, thank you very fucking much!"

"OK... I'll sort everything out and sort your half out"

"Just fucking send it to me," he said through clenched teeth and poking her chest with his finger"

"OK," she said quietly trying to keep things calm.

"See ya baby" and he walked away.

"Staffan" she shouted, running after him, grabbing him by the arm. He turned round

"What do you want? Do you want me to fuck you one last time before I leave your life forever?"He said coldly, pushing her against the wall?

She slapped his face as hard as she could. He just looked at her icily and then pushed past her.

"Staffan, please..."

She got in front of him. He pushed her against the door and stared into her eyes. More than anything he wanted to kiss her and make her realise it was him she really wanted – but he also really wanted to hurt her for doing this to him.

"Get out of my way, Des"

"Staffan..."

"Get out of my way, Desiree! " grinding his teeth

She moved turning her back to open the door, he grabbed her arms pulling her back close to him and whispered in her ear.

"The old man ain't going to keep you satisfied baby, he ain't gonna be able keep up with you. I'm the one who knows how to keep you happy"

"Staffan, don't be so disgusting"

"Oh Baby, you're gonna to miss me in your bed... you can't get enough of me, that's why you cheated on Riley!" He was so arrogant, his tone was so hard.

She could feel him so close, his breath on her neck. She always felt dizzy when he was so close but why was he making her like this again? She loved Matt, she was over Staffan. Des turned her head round and just looked at him. He just gave her another frosty look.

"See ya around, Baby!" He stormed off

In the lift, he fell back against the lift wall and closed his eyes, fighting back his tears. Desiree had hurt him so deeply, she would never know just how deeply. He wiped his eyes, took a deep breath, and stepped out of the lift. He made his way to his car and drove away.

Des stood with her back to the door shaking, she couldn't catch her breath as tears started to roll down her face.

'What's wrong with you? Stop it!' She said to herself. 'You don't want Staffan, you don't love him anymore!'

Later that day when she met Matt for lunch she was really quiet, so quiet that Matt asked if she was alright.

"Oh yeah, I'm fine"

"How did it go with Staffan? Everything sorted?" pushing her to tell him.

"Yeah… I'm selling the apartment and Staffan will get his half when it's sold"

"Good, now we can get on with our wedding"

"Yeah" she said, touching his face, smiling at him.

Des watched Matt all through lunch, watching his lips when he spoke, when he smiled.

"Des?"

"Yeah?"

"What's wrong?"

"Nothing, I'm just looking at you"

"Why?"

"I love you Matt"

"As much as I love you, I hope" He gave her a gentle smile.

Matt knew that there *was* something wrong and he knew it was to do with Staffan.

Chapter 22

Staffan decided he had to leave New York. He told the guys he was heading out west and needed some time out. As it happened, they agreed – he did need some time out, in fact they all did. He told them that while he was away he would start writing some new material.

"Yeah that'll be great. We'll join you later – relax for a while" Delmar said.

"Yeah... going to"

"It'll get easier"

"Yep... time to move on, to forget Desiree fucking Beaumont"

Staffan moved to California and spent some time on own to get his head back on track, put Des behind him or at least try. He even started dating again, he was romantically linked with Nadine Turner, a model he met on a photoshoot.

They guys left him alone for a while then joined him. A little later they got stuck in to getting some new stuff written. Johnny also got hold of him about the record so Johnny, Staffan and both bands sat down wrote *Rip it Down* and then recorded it. The tone was full and rich as the music filled the air. The full bass guitar spoke a language of the soul – a real heavy tempo, real rock 'n roll. Delmar and Hadley got lost in the riff. They shot some video at the same time.

The song got a lot of airplay. As a result, it did well in the charts and reached number 5, they were really pleased.

Johnny's marriage had started to show signs of cracking, but they were hanging on in there. After all, they had a child and one on the way, so they were trying to make it work although it wasn't going to be easy as both bands were doing world tours. They would be away for eighteen mouths which would place a strain on any relationship.

Desiree on the other hand was very happy. She went wedding dress shopping with Lori and they found the most beautiful dress – a strapless, long ivory chiffon dress with diamanté under the bust line and she was going to wear her hair up with diamantés scattered in her hair. Later, they met up with Ellen, Judy and Jenny for lunch and talked about the wedding and the film that Desiree was co-starring in with Jenny. Des and Jenny were cast alongside actors Martin Laurence and Steven Russell. Lori also had a new single out which was climbing the charts nicely. However, what the ladies really wanted to know was how she could be with a man like Staffan then go for an older man like Matt.

"Easy. Matt is a very sexy man"

"Well you and Staffan were very erm… 'full on' shall we say?" Jenny giggled.

"I know what you're saying, Staffan was fantastic and how he made me feel in bed… well, let's just say he could take me to a place I didn't think I could reach"

"Des, you sound as if you are still in love with him." Lori said.

"I love Matt" she quickly came back.

"I just want you to be happy"

Lori was not convinced Des was really over Staffan. None of them were and thought that Des was making a mistake. Des, however, genuinely loved Matt and she didn't understand what everyone's problem was.

A few weeks later Matt and Des attended a film festival. Des was dressed in a beautiful black, floor-length sparkling dress with a high split up the side. With her beautiful black hair flowing down her back she looked absolutely stunning. The film star Brett Gregson had seen Des and instantly made his way over to her. He was, after all, a young stud and liked the ladies. He obviously thought he was in with a chance with Des.

"Hi there, gorgeous," and he moved his hand to her waist.

"Hi, Mr Gregson"

"Call me Brett… Now tell me what a beautiful woman like you is doin' with Matt"

"What do ya mean?"

"What I mean is, I think he might be too… Let's just say I think I could give you what you need, if you get my meaning"

"Really? Well let me tell you Matt is all the man I need"

Matt had been cornered by Millicent Lee.

"How are you Milly"?

"I'm just fine Matt. I see you are hell bent on making yourself look stupid.

"What?"

"Your *marrying* her now, she's in all those rock videos with all those long-haired men gawping at her and touching her. How do you stand it?"

"It's just a job, Milly"

"Oh Matt you need a woman that can please you"

Matt told her he had a woman that pleases him.

"She'll cheat on you. Men flock round her like bees to a honey pot…. Oh and look there's Brett"

"So you don't think I can please her then?"

"I didn't mean that, darling.

"No… you are a bitter cow because I knocked you back"

Millicent turned and walked away giving Matt a cold look, a very cold look indeed. Matt had already seen Brett go over to Des, so he made his way over to her. Des took Matt's hand and he pulled her to him, forcing Brett to release his grip on her. Matt immediately put his hands round her. He knew that Brett was interested in Des but she wasn't going to be another notch on his bedpost if he could help it.

"Brett"

"This woman is beautiful"

"Yeah she is, and she's all mine!" Matt pulled her closer to him.

"You're a lucky bastard Matt"

Matt gave Brett an arrogant smirk as if to say 'yeah stay away'.

He led Des away to the dance floor and pulled her close.

"I love you, Des," he whispered.

He wasn't an idiot, he knew lots of men wanted Des and it did cross his mind that he could lose her to a younger man. However, the man he was most worried about was *Staffan*, because he knew she still felt something for him.

September 1983

Desiree and Matt got married. They had a lovely wedding, setting pearly white balloons off in the sky. They fed each other wedding cake and spent the whole time gazing into each other's eyes. Lori could see that Desiree was happy. Just maybe she had got it wrong, maybe Des had got over Staffan, she looked so in love. The couple headed off to the beautiful island of Bali for their honeymoon, staying in a small but quaint hotel in a private cove. Every day started with freshly baked bread or cinnamon rolls for breakfast. They went snorkelling in the bay every morning, then enjoyed the wonderful view of blue lagoon sea and the white sandy beaches. They only had eyes for each other.

"Matt, you are beautiful"

"Beautiful? I've never been called beautiful before"

"Well you are. You're perfect"

Matt laughed and pulled her to him before kissing her.

"You are beautiful, Desiree. Many men would so love to be in my place right now"

"They don't interest me… just you"

It was true. Desiree could have her pick of men but Matt was the only one she wanted.

Whilst Des and Matt enjoyed their honeymoon, Jake went to California to check out a model Glen Price suggested that he take a look at. While he was there he met up with Staffan and Nadine for lunch.

"Staffan! Hey, great to see you"

"Yeah, good to see you too – I read about Des's wedding and saw the photos – she looked great"

"Yeah, she was stunning"

"This is Nadine, my girlfriend"

"Pleased to meet you, you are a very beautiful girl"

She smiled and thanked him and excused herself while she went to the powder room.

"So, what are you doing Staffan?"

"Writing some new stuff"

"Great… can't wait to hear it"

"Des looked very happy"

"*You* look happy Staffan, Nadine must agree with you, mate"

"Yeah… she's a nice girl"

Jake knew Staffan was still in love with Desiree but at least he was dating again. Maybe he could finally move on and fall in love with someone else.

Nadine came back and they had lunch. Over coffee she asked Jake about Desiree, Staffan had talked about her so often.

"What is she like?"

Jake felt a little uncomfortable talking about Des to Staffan's girlfriend, especially in front of Staffan.

"Desiree? She's beautiful, funny… she's Desiree"

"Oh, I know she's beautiful– but what is she *like?*"

"She's Desiree, OK? Now can we change the subject?" Staffan snapped.

So Jake asked Staffan when he was on tour.

"We have just done one tour with *Connection* and *Eclipse*. We've got a couple of months off then we are back on tour with *Sharp Edge"*

"Fantastic, send me some tickets and I'll be there"

"No probs"

"I've gotta go – meeting with Glen. I'll see you at the gig"

Staffan gives him the thumbs up and told him his ticket would be in the post.

Chapter 23

1984

Matt started work on his new film. He'd cast Desiree as the leading lady alongside Darrel Rawlins. The film, *Love So Strong,* was about two people who met and fell in love but lost each other before finding each other in the end. It was set to a big hit and would to go on to win several awards, with Desiree getting a nomination for Best Actress. The film really put her on the map and now she started getting offers from everywhere..She began to get a very heavy work schedule and would be working away from home for long periods of time, making her very tired Matt insisted she took a break.

"I can't Matt, I'm in the middle of a film"

"OK finish – but then break"

"OK, Matt"

"Promise me, Des"

"I promise…"

"Good. I need to have some quality time, darling I'm beginning to think I've gone celibate"

Desiree laughed and leaned in to kiss him.

"Come on babe, take me upstairs and prove that I'm not celibate"

Desiree took hold of his hand tightly and smiled raising her eyebrows.

"Have I been neglecting you?"

"Yes you have. Now take me to bed"

As they reached the bed Des pushed him down, opening his shirt. He reached out to her and pulled her to him. She moved her hands down his body, kissing him at the same time, moving down his body as he moaned with pleasure, pulling her even closer. His mouth brushed against her slowly, sensuously, her body immediately responding to his touch. He started undressing her until she was completely naked. Her breath quickened.

"You have an exquisite body," he said as he trailed his fingers from her neck, between her breasts down to her navel.

He was rising to the occasion fast, her body spasmed as he kissed the inside of her thighs. She gripped the sheets, her head went back, her mouth opened and she gave out a long, drawn-out moan of pleasure. He thrust himself into her. As he moved between her thighs, they pushed against each other, trapped in rhythm. Their mouths were locked together, their sweat mingled as they moved faster. Finally, he allowed himself to release and he withdrew, panting as he rolled off her, clearly out of breath. He smiled at her. "Oh, Baby." Desiree was like a drug and Matt couldn't get enough of it.

A few months later they took that well-deserved break. They had both been on really heavy schedules so they took the yacht and went off to a beautiful tropical island and just relaxed for a while. When they had been there for a few days, Desiree began to feel unwell and eventually she fainted. Worried, Matt got her to the local doctors.

There, they were told that Desiree was, in fact, pregnant. They were both over the moon, Desiree couldn't wait to be a mum. She was determined to be the best mum ever, she didn't want her baby to have a mum like hers. She made so many plans, this baby would have the best of everything.

It wasn't to be. A few weeks into her pregnancy she was rushed to hospital with abdominal pain and uncontrollable bleeding. Nearly hysterical, she was also being sick and was in severe pain. As she kept drifting in and out of consciousness, the doctor informed Matt she was having an ectopic pregnancy and need to go her down to theatre straight away to terminate.

Matt told the doctor to do whatever they needed to do. When Des came to from the anaesthetic Matt had to tell her the news. She was devastated.

After Desiree came home she took a few more weeks off then she started work on her new film, *Boomerang!* which was being filmed in England. Matt had a house in London so Des moved back to the UK. She was soon back into a heavy schedule Matt missed her terribly, but he also had a busy schedule himself, he was going to join her as soon as he'd finished the film he was producing. Weeks in to the filming Jake had gone to meet Matt at the airport. Things were going well. Des was sat in her trailer when Julie the wardrobe girl came in.

"There's someone to see you, Des"

"Oh hmm… send them in"

Des was putting her hair up ready for the make-up artist, when her father walked in.

"Desiree"

She knew that voice. It sent cold shivers down her spine. She turned round in sheer panic to find him leering at her, drunk and aggressive.

"How did you get in here?"

"Desiree, I'm your dad… it was easy. I want money"

"Get out!"

"Don't you start fucking with me, you little bitch!"

"Get out!"

He slammed his hands on the side of the trailer wall in drunken anger. Des started shaking. He was demanding money from her, he started to move towards her and grabbed her by the arm. Des pulled away knocking him over as she did so. He got unsteadily to his feet he then grabbed her by the neck and hit her with his other hand, cutting her lip open. She pushed him again but his grip on her neck got tighter and it just made him angrier. He hit her again and again. She did try to hit him back but he was just too strong.

"Money, Desiree!"

"Fuck off!"

"Fuck off?… You're telling your old man to fuck off? You little bitch"

By now Matt and Jake had arrived on set.

Matt asked Julie where his wife was and she told him she was in her trailer.

"Thanks"

"Matt, she's got someone with her"

When Matt asked who, Julie told him the man had said he was family, a David Louis.

Jake looked at Matt. "It's her dad – he's a nasty bastard. Come on!"

Matt told Julie to call security then they rushed to Des's trailer. When they got there she was barely conscious, her eye was black and blue, there was blood everywhere. David still towered over her. He had slammed her into the wall, banging her head. Matt grabbed David and pulled him away from her while Jake rushed straight over to Des.

"Jake, tell me she's alright!" He still held David against the wall.

"We need to get her to the hospital – someone ring for a fuckin' ambulance and make it quick!"

"She's just a little tramp like her fucking mother." David shouted.

Security come and got hold of David, but not before Matt had taken a swing at him, hitting him on the jaw and knocking him for six.

"You stay the fuck away from my wife or I'll kill you!"

Matt got on the floor and sat with Des till the ambulance came.

"Come on, baby. Please…please!"

Matt was covered in Desiree's blood. He couldn't tell where it was coming from and he truly thought he was going to lose her. They rushed to the hospital with the paramedics working on her furiously. She was in such a bad way.

David was arrested and charged with Intent to Harm. He was not allowed anywhere near Des. Matt made sure that he could never go near her again. Whilst Des was unconscious, her mother went to the hospital. She had read about the attack on her daughter in the paper. While Matt was stood outside, Carol approached him. She told him who she was and asked if she could see Des, just for a short time. Matt asked what she wanted to say.

"Nothing, Mr Adams, I just want to see her. I can't believe he would do this to her"

"Well he did… take a good look at what he did to her"

He showed Carol in to the room. She looked at Des and then she gasped as the tears started to roll down her face.

"I'm so sorry Desiree, my beautiful girl," she said, stroking her hair gently. "What did I do to you? I loved you so much." Then she left.

Matt watched Carol and felt more than a little sorry for her. She honestly though Des would be safe with David but now she hated herself, seeing what he had done to her

Matt sat with Des when she came round.

"Matt" Des called, sounding very groggy.

"Hi Darlin'" and kissed the top of her head, the only place that wasn't black and blue.

He told her that her mother had been to see her.

"What did she want?"

Matt told her how upset she had been but it didn't seem to interest Desiree at all. Her only response was to tell him not to let her in again. By the time Lori arrived Des was sitting up in bed.

"Hi, Babe... The things you'll do to get some time off!"

Des tried to laugh but it hurt too much.

"ARRR... don't make me laugh"

"I'm sorry Babe. How're you feeling?... I know how you look"

"Shit on both counts"

When Des came out of hospital she had to rest. Her film was well and truly over schedule but they filmed the bits they could while Des slowly recuperated. She couldn't wait to get back to work.

Chapter 24

Diamond Rock Weekend

Diamond Rock Weekend was upon us again and what a line up they had this year: *Sharp Edge, Eclipse, Dominance, Connections, Lightning* and all the support groups that were up and coming. Staffan was chilling in the beer tent when Riley backed in to him, knocking his beer out of his hand all over his jeans, which, luckily, were leather.

"What the fuck, watch what you're fucking doin'!" Staffan spewed and they both swung round.

"Sorry mate… Oh, Staffan"

"Riley…" he said wiping himself down.

Riley handed him another beer.

"How ya doin?"

"Good – what about you?" Staffan turned to walk away when Riley shouted him back.

"Look Staffan, I know we've have had our differences' but why don't we actually get on?"

"Ya know what… I don't know…. how did this fuckin' start anyway"

"This started well before Des"

Staffan nodded in agreement. They hadn't really seen each other since the incident in the restaurant. They both laughed and shook hands and gradually started to get on. OK, they were never going to be best buddies but there was no sniping or snarling All the bands at the rock weekend had a great time: partying, getting drunk, smoking dope and doing some not so tasteful things with a blow up doll. Andy, Delmar, Hadley and Riley flashed their asses off at one of the film crew – a picture that would find its self going in the rock mags.

Staffan's relationship with Nadine came to a close, he decided he was too young to get tied down with one woman when there were so many out there. Staffan and Riley had a great weekend with all the girls they were surrounded with, draping themselves over them, they made sure that they lapped it up. One group of girls surrounded the stars' trailers to get a glimpse of their favourite rock singers. When Johnny, Staffan and Riley appeared they all pulled their T-shirts up over their breasts and flashed them.

"Nice tits, darlin!" Johnny shouted.

"Want to feel em?"

Riley went over. "I surely do"

Riley, Staffan and Johnny worked their way through the line, then Hadley and Delmar appeared and wanted to know what they were missing out on. When they found out they joined in the fun. Delmar even took one of the ladies back to his trailer. Johnny and the rest of the bands were shocked to see Staffan and Riley getting along as it was well known that they hated each other.

Meanwhile, it was Des's 24th birthday and Matt had arranged a big surprise party for her. She thought they would just be having a romantic dinner together. He told her that they were going to the Beckondy Hotel for her birthday. He had bought her a beautiful, white gold necklace and a bracelet to match for her birthday so she decided to put on a white glittery dress, cut out in random places revealing her body. She looked ravishing with her hair messily on top of her head, so that it just fell randomly. When they got to the hotel, Desiree started towards to the restaurant but Matt led her to a big function room. When he opened the doors, all her friends were there waiting for her. Lori and Ethan were there, Paul Best was there as well – so many people. At one end of the room was a big band and Matt had arranged to sing a romantic song to her, as well as *Happy Birthday*.

Des was really quite shocked he was such an accomplished singer. His voice was so romantic and matched the song. He got her up to dance while he sang.

"I love you, Mrs Adams"

"I love you. Thank you for this"

"The pleasure is all mine"

"I didn't know you could sing, baby.

"Well… *surprise*"

Everyone joined him in singing *Happy Birthday*. Des smiled then a made a brief speech, telling everyone that this was the best birthday she had ever had and thanked them for coming. Paul Best came over and asked Matt if he could steal his wife for a dance.

"Yeah, just bring her back"

"Oh man, don't know about that one"

Des and Paul headed off to the dance floor.

"Des… Des… you are stunning"

"Why thank you, Paul"

"I've flown back from the rock weekend just for you, I hope you know. I'd love you do another video with me"

"Anytime Paul, just tell me when"

"Well, it's funny you should say that…"

They headed back to Matt discussing the video. Des told Paul she would do it and told him to have his people get in touch and they would arrange it. Lori appeared from nowhere and gave Des a big hug.

"Happy?"

"Yeah, very happy"

Paul smiled at Lori. "Wow, sexy lady"

A smile swept across Lori's face.

"Would you like to go for dinner some time Lori?"

"Yeah, that would great"

"I'll call you"Then he went off to mingle

"Oh fucking hell, Des, Paul Best asked me out!"

"What about Ethan?"

"Not married to him… besides I'm getting bored"

"Well, OK then" Lori and Des laughed in unison.

They were still laughing when they reached Matt who wrapped his arms round Des and kissed her asking what they were laughing at. Des told him about Lori having the hots for Paul.

A few days later Des and Matt were at the Marina restaurant. Matt was telling Des about an idea he had about filming something totally different but he wasn't sure what, when Staffan and Edvin turned up. Staffan had seen Des and walked straight past as if she wasn't there but Edvin stopped to say 'Hi' and ask how she was. She told him she was good then introduced him to Matt.

"Pleased to meet you, Mr Adams"

"Likewise," as he shook Edvin's hand.

Edvin made his way to his table.

"Wow, Staffan, that was cold"

"I can't talk to her"

"She knows you've seen her"

"I don't give a shit"

"Will you ever forgive her?"

"No… now let's eat"

He looked over at her. She was so beautiful, he had never loved any women like he loved her. In the end, he had to look away and put his head down. Edvin saw his face, now and when had walked past her, he knew Staffan was still in love with her. Meantime, seeing Staffan and Edvin together had given Matt the idea he had been looking for. He wanted to do something different and came up with the idea of a *documentary* – what could be better than doing a documentary on rock stars?

He went to see Paul Best first, then Riley and Johnny, he also wanted Andy Marsh and Staffan. Paul, Riley and Johnny's bands had said they would love to do it, as did Andy and the band. The only one he hadn't seen was Staffan's band. He was wasn't sure about Staffan, he didn't know if he would agree although he thought perhaps the rest of the band would.

He called in personally to the studio and was talking to Edvin and Delmar when Lucas and Barny walked in. They wanted to do it but they told Matt they didn't think Staffan would. Matt asked when he was coming in and Delmar told him he would be there any time now.

Half an hour later Staffan appeared wearing sunglasses, severely hung over.

"Staffan – Matt wants us to do a documentary with *Connections, Lightning, Sharp Edge* and *Eclipse.* What do ya think?"

"No"

Edvin said, "Staffan, come on – it'll be great"

Matt looked at Staffan and said, "Staffan I didn't marry Des to get at you"

"Fuck you, Matt"

"Staffan, I really want your band to do this. I picked my five favourite bands. Come on, don't blow this"

The guys looked at Staffan. "Yeah,come on Staffan"

"No..." and he walked away. He wouldn't even entertain the idea.

Delmar and Edvin told Matt they would talk to him and to leave it with them. Matt said 'OK' and they told him they would be in touch. After Matt had left Delmar and Edvin talked to Staffan and told him if it had been any other producer he would have jumped at it. Staffan hummed and hahhed. They repeated that Matt had not taken Des from him, they were already divorced. Barny shouted it was such a great opportunity and Staffan was going to fuck it up if he wasn't careful. After some hard thinking, Staffan eventually came round so Delmar called Matt. Matt was delighted and told him that he would come in the next day to discuss everything with them.

"Morning guys"

The very first words out of Staffan's mouth were, "Des isn't going to be there is she?"

Matt said, "No" and shook his head.

"Cos' the minute she appears I'll fuck off – I don't want to be anywhere near her... understand?"

"OK"

"OK... then we'll do it"

Matt shook their hands and said 'Great'. He went over a few things with them then told them to stay in touch. He turned to Staffan and told him he knew he still loved Des. Staffan just looked, put his head down and walked away.

Desiree started work on her new calendar. Marcus had some great poses for her – one a close up of her face, another naked with just a towel draped over her. He insisted she was pictured with two big tigers as well! Des loved it.

"You're going to make men go insane with these, Des"

"I'm going to lose all this one day, Marcus"

"Never Babe"

Des laughed. "You do so much for my ego"

After the calendar shoot, Desiree started some work on a charity for children in children's homes which was close to her heart, she knew all about this. She visited a number of homes to see the children, taking them treats and sitting and talking to them. Kids loved her, they all wanted to have their photos taken with her and Des tried to pack as many in as she could.

She also worked for a charity for animals, something else she loved and equally close to her heart. She had always wanted a pet as a child but sadly never had one. She did a sponsored kiss – each kiss costing a $1 – and raised thousands. She took part in a sponsored walk and again she raised thousands. People would pay to see her never mind whether she did the walk or not, they flocked to see Desiree Beaumont. She had planned some events that she wanted to get started but, unfortunately, her busy schedule prevented this for the moment.

Lori was also involved in a lot of charities and Des wanted to get her involved with hers. Another one with a busy schedule, Lori was already back on tour. When she was in full swing of the tour, she fell over in rehearsals. Her ankle came up like a balloon and started to bruise straight away. They took her to the hospital in an ambulance and checked her out. She had some x rays that confirmed she had broken it. She still carried on with the tour but now with the ankle in plaster. Des met up with her one night and sang a couple of songs. They had a great time. Des took the mickey out of Lori hobbling about in her plaster.

"I want you sign my cast, Des"

"It'll be worth thousands for charity"

"Yeah, they could put it up for auction"

"Yeah, what do ya think?"

"Great idea – you're not just a sex symbol are you honey bun?" Des said laughing.

"No Babe, I'm not" Lori laughed with her. She carried on.

"Des, I've been thinking"

Des looked at Lori. "Yeah? What do you want me to do?"

Lori gave her a wide beaming grin and cuddled her. She told her about her new single and asked her to be in her video. Des wasn't sure what she would do in the video – her normal videos involved touching, kissing and generally looking sexy. Lori told her that the song was called *Count on Me* and was about them and their friendship. Des smiled and told her she would love to be in it.

After the show, she flew back home to Matt. He'd missed her and wanted to show her how much so he had cooked special meal for her. She took a bath and came straight down, her bathrobe slightly open, revealing a little flesh.

"Oh darlin, you look so very sexy"

"Do I?" running her tongue over her lips, sliding her fingers over her breast making sure he could see her nipples stand up.

"Oh Yeah… wet hair and nothing under on that robe. You are a real turn on!"

Des let the robe fall casually to the floor. Matt looked at her, wide-eyed. He moved over to her and kissed her. She kissed him back very passionately, ripping his shirt open, his buttons flying everywhere. She moved her mouth down his body, opening his jeans. She wanted dirty sex on the floor right then and there, there was no stopping her She was quite rough, digging her nails in his skin.

"Ahh, darlin" Matt had never seen this side of her.

"I want you Matt and I want you *now*" she demanded.

"Wow, what's got into you? You're *wild*, darlin"

"You've seen nothing yet," she said seductively as she pulled him down to the floor.

Matt couldn't get his jeans off quick enough. He liked this side of Des. She sat on top him and grabbed his lips with her teeth, kissing his neck, moving her hands down his body taking full grip of his manhood. His erection was hot and throbbing as she thrust against him. His hands dropped to her hips to keep up with her rhythm. He traced his fingers slowly down her throat. She licked them, taking his index finger and sucking on it sexily, making him moan with pleasure.

"Oh yessss, oh Man!"

Her orgasm shook her body as she made love to him. He couldn't hold out any longer he just had to come otherwise he would of exploded.

"Is that good baby?"

"Oh, fucking hell, Des…"

Dinner was burnt and they ended up going out to dinner. When they came back she took him upstairs and pushed him on the bed and stripped him. His manhood hardened as she licked her lips. He could feel her breasts pressing against him as her mouth moved slowly down his body. She was sending him in to a frenzy.

He brushed his fingers over her nipples. Between the groans and sighs he managed to reverse the position. He moved over her, kissing her hard, moving down her neck to her belly, tracing his tongue round her navel. Her heart was racing and he moved his hips between her thighs, her body immediately responding as he thrust back and forth, her breathing muffled and ragged.

"Have you missed me, Des?"

"Oh Yeah, baby"

"You are very horny, Des"

"And you are a very sexy man. You're in for a long night baby"

"Oh Yessss!" as he got more turned on by her.

Chapter 25

Matt had got all guys together for his documentary and they had a great time. He filmed them together and asked how they all got started, who influenced them in their childhood, how they discovered their style and sounds. They shot short videos of their rock 'n' roll heroes, their guitar Gods sang some of their songs. They all loved working with Matt, they all thought he was really cool to work with, even Staffan. While Matt was away filming with the bands, Des attended a gala with Lori. Unfortunately, Millicent was there with Vivian. Millicent was in fine form and went over to Des.

"Now you have your claws into him, you can have all his money"

"Go away" Des said, dismissing her.

"Don't tell me to go away, do you know who you are talking to?"

"Yes, *a bitter cow*"

"I beg your pardon"

Desiree gave Millicent as good as she got. Vivian did try to stop Millicent making a fool of herself but she wasn't listening and continued to insult Desiree. Lori told her to go away because she was causing a scene and it was embarrassing. Millicent, however, had had a little too much to drink and she wanted to let Desiree know exactly what she thought of her.

"You are a little tart"

"And you are a has been who could not make it into Matt's bed – and you don't like that, do you?"

Desiree began to walk away when Millicent grabbed by her hair and yanked her back. Des turned and slapped her across the face, telling her that if she ever put her hands on her again she would get more a lot more than a slap. Vivian shook her head. She couldn't believe Millicent had done that and she understood why Des had slapped her. When Matt had finished his documentary and made his way back home, he ran into Vivian, his ex-wife, and she told him all about Millicent making a scene at the gala. Matt was furious and went round to Millicent's and demanded to know what she was playing at.

"Oh dear, did she come running to you with her tail between her legs?"

"Why did you attack Des like that?"

"What do you mean attack *her*, she attacked *me!*" She moved over to Matt and pushed herself against him, trying to kiss him.

Matt pushed away forcefully.

"What do you think you're doing?"

"I love you… I've always loved you"

"This has to stop, Milly. We were never going to happen – not then, not now!"

"But…"

"But *nothing*"

"Matt…"

"No… this stops now, let this be an end to it" He left, slamming the door shut.

He had rejected her once again. She slumped to the floor and sobbed bitterly. His words packed a powerful punch, she felt so humiliated.

Globe Music Awards

Anyone who was anyone was at the music awards night and Des, Matt, Lori, *Dominance*, *Connections* and *Lightning* were all there. All three bands were nominated for awards. Staffan had seen Des. She was more beautiful than he remembered but he was cold towards her.

She had hurt him more than any other woman could ever do when she married Matt and he wasn't about to forgive her any time soon. He'd tried desperately to avoid her but that didn't work. They bumped straight in to each other at the bar and looked at each other intensely.

"Des…" he didn't know what to say he didn't want to be that close to her he felt angry and excited at the same time.

"Staffan" she said with a sigh.

Saved by the bell. Barny came over and grabbed Staffan.

"Staffan …Staffan … Oh, hiya Des," Barny said, throwing his arms round her.

"Hey Barny"

"Staffan, come on – there's someone at our table that we need to meet"

It never occurred to Barny that maybe they were talking, he just dragged Staffan off back to the table to meet Gary Jacobs, a record producer.

"Bye" he threw over his shoulder.

"Yeah, see ya Staffan"

He turned and looked back at her she stared at him. When Lori broke her stare, she took a sharp intake of breath.

"Des… What was that about?"

"What?"

"You and Staffan"

"I don't know, he's so cold. He hates me"

"Oh no he doesn't… Hey, guess who's here – just to complicate things a bit more"

"Who?"

"Riley. I've just been talking to him – and he asked if you were here"

"Oh shit, another one who hates me. Lets pack 'em all in tonight," she said solemnly, shaking her in disbelief.

They headed back to their table and Matt asked her where she'd been.

"At the bar"

"Oh, doing what? You've no drink darlin"

"Shit, I must have left it"

She totally forgot what she was doing after bumping in to Staffan, he completely threw her.

"I saw Staffan earlier, Des"

"Yeah?"

Matt looked at her, confused by her lack of concentration. She seemed very far away. Des and Staffan didn't speak to each other again that night but he kept glancing over at her and, when she spotted him at one point, they caught each other's eyes. They both quickly looked away.

"Des, darlin?"

"Yeah…"

"Come and dance with me"

"OK" she held her hand out.

Matt took her hand and they went to the dance floor. He put his arms round her and pulled her close, really tight.

"Tell me you love me, Des"

"I do love you, Matt"

"You seem a little distracted"

She touched his face smiling at him. He leant in to kiss her. She kissed him back very tenderly.

"I love you very much Matt"

"Des, you've no idea just how much I love you"

"Yes I do," as she kissed him again.

Just then Lori came over and joined them. Matt put his arm round Lori.

"Oh, fuck me… two beautiful women in one night and at the same time – how lucky can one man get?"

Des mentioned that she'd seen Scott and he was looking very drunk.

"Yeah, he's over talking to Paul Best"

Lori Des and Matt just carried on dancing and having a good time together. Matt had his hands full with the two of them but he didn't mind. Besides, he was the only man there with two beautiful women on his arm. Then Scott appeared.

"I want to talk to you" pulling Lori by the arm. He'd had a few too many drinks and was a bit rough.

"Scott, mate…" Matt said.

Des looked at Scott and told him that Lori was with them.

Lori shrugged and said she was going to go and talk to him. She was going to tell him she had filed for divorce and that she was going to see her lawyer the following week to sign some papers. She wanted to get the ball rolling and get this divorce done with. When she told Scott, he went mad and shook her.

"No… no-one leaves me – *you* don't leave me!"

"Scott, we are never getting back together"

"You fucking bitch"

Scott grabbed Lori really tight, he was hurting her. She asked him to let go but he wouldn't. Hadley had seen Scott with Lori, he saw how rough he had been and how aggressive he was becoming,. He went over and asked Lori if she was OK. Lori shook her head nervously.

"Let her go, Scott"

"Fuck off, she's my wife"

Hadley grabbed Scott's arm in order to make him release Lori, but instead he gripped her tighter still.

"Let go Scott!" Hadley insisted

Johnny had noticed Scott and Hadley facing up to each other and made his way over.

"What the fuck is going on?"

Hadley told him. "The fucking prick is scaring her, he won't let her go"

"Let go of her, Scott. She's fucked you off… get over it"

"Fuck off!"" Scott pushed Johnny away with his free hand.

Just at that moment, Hadley hit him and he stumbled back, letting go of Lori.

"Fuck off Scott – just leave Lori alone, she doesn't want you so piss off!"

"Oh fucking hell, it makes perfect sense now. You after getting in her knickers, Hadley?"

"Fuck off, you fucking prick. Come on, Lori."

Hadley took her hand and led her to the bar for a drink to calm her nerves, Scott had really shaken her up. Meanwhile Des had headed for the bar. She bumped into Johnny Barren, falling straight into his arms.

"Oh, I'm so sorry"

"That's OK," Johnny said looking straight into her eyes. "You've just made my night"

Des smiled as Johnny released her from his arms and said "Any time" He headed back over to the guys.

"Oh man, Desiree Beaumont is one hot woman. Staffan was one lucky bastard"

Staffan only heard the last bit.

"And why am I a lucky bastard?"

Lance said, "Johnny has just bumped in to your ex-wife, she went straight into his arms"

"Yeah I saw you with her"

"She's so beautiful –and she smells so fucking good"

Staffan laughed. "She's addictive isn't she. First time I saw her I got a hard on"

"Oh man… understandable!"

Des was still at the bar when Riley appeared.

"Hi Des"

"Riley, it's nice to see you"

"It's nice to see you," as he looked at her. "You are so hot, you never change"

Des moved closer to him and whispered, "I'm sorry"

"Des please don't. Why couldn't you've just fallen in love with me?"

"Riley you weren't the problem… I was stupid, didn't know what I had"

"What? Des?"

"I didn't deserve you after what happened" Des kissed him lightly. "I better go".

As she walked away he grabbed her arm.

"Des"

"See you later, Riley," and kissed him again.

Riley couldn't believe what he was hearing. Was she telling him that she had fallen in love with him? He would have forgiven anything. He had loved her, even wanted to marry her. He would still have married her.

Just then the host, Dale Tanner, announced that the awards were about to start and asked everyone to take their seats. Everyone settled down and waited anxiously to see if their name would be announced. Lori had a good night. She won three awards, *Dominance* won two and *Connections* won two as well.

Everyone had had a good night. They were all in high spirits, as you can imagine, plenty of food to eat and the booze was flowing nicely round the room, they partied all night.

Chapter 26

Matt and Des took a vacation before Des was scheduled to go on location for her next film. They wanted to spend some time together before she left. They went back to Bali where they had been on honeymoon. While they were away they talked about trying for another baby.

"I'm not sure Matt"

"You fill up with work, charities, films, interviews, and rock vids," he countered. "I'm tired of having a marriage over the phone"

"You of all people know how this business works"

"Desiree I want to spend time with my wife, I want us to have a baby… maybe you just don't want a baby with *me*"

Matt started to shout at her. She shouted back at him and told him he was being stupid – she loved him and she *did* want his baby but she was scared of losing it. Matt looked her and told her he was sorry, it hadn't occurred to him that she was worried about losing another baby. He reassured her, she would be fine getting pregnant, everything would be fine this time. They agreed that after this film was finished, they would try again for a baby

Staffan was dating another stunning model, Fallon Mathews. They had become quite an item. Staffan liked her and they got on really well. Could he have finally got over Desiree?

Matt was sat having breakfast, reading the paper and there was Staffan pictured with his new girlfriend. He handed the paper to Des to see her reaction. She was a bit puzzled at first as he knew she didn't read the paper but then she realised why he had given it to her.

Matt was still having a bit of self-doubt about things. Maybe it was losing the baby and Desiree not wanting to try again for so long or could it be the dirty sex she wanted not so long ago and then seeing Staffan at the awards?

"Does it bother you?"

"What?" She knew what he meant but she wasn't giving him the satisfaction.

"Seeing Staffan with that girl"

"No, why should it?

"I think it does"

"Don't be stupid"

"Why is it stupid. I think that, deep down, you still love him"

"I love *you*"

"Do you Des? Really, do you?"

"Yes. Stop it Matt. Staffan can see who he wants"

By now, Desiree was really big in the film industry and started playing more leading parts. The world couldn't get enough of her. Lori went back on tour again and she was also going on the Cara Jakes talkshow for an interview. Desiree and Lori had come a long way since they did their first photoshoots with Marcus.

The Cara Jakes Talkshow

"Welcome, Lori"

"Hi Cara"

"You've have sold over 100 million albums"

"Yeah, Wow!"

"You and Desiree Beaumont have also been on a tour of children's homes all around the world. How did that go?"

"Oh… it was fantastic. The kids were fantastic – we went to see them and what great kids. We had them dancing with us, singing with us – we had a great time with them and I would just like to say, *HEY GUYS IF YOU'RE WATCHING! Love and kisses!*"

"Do you think you and Desiree will ever go back?"

"Yeah, definitely"

"You're on tour at the moment and your new single is coming out"

"Yeah, it comes out tomorrow"

"You are going to sing it for us now aren't you?"

"Yeah!"

"Great we will let you go and get ready– *Lori Miller everyone"*

Desiree took a few months break although Matt was still having to work. He had to take a trip to Acapulco. Des told him she would go with him to spend some quality time with him. When they arrived in Acapulco they were shown to their penthouse suite. It was beautiful, with a four poster bed big enough to fit four in it and it had a rooftop pool. Des loved it.

While Matt went to his meeting, Des went shopping. She bought loads of stuff: dresses, shoes, bags you name it she bought it. It didn't take long before people spotted her and started flocking around her. The paparazzi had also found her, flash bulbs flashing everywhere. She certainly knew how to work the camera and charm the crowds. She waved happily and signed autographs She had bodyguards round her because she never tried to hide her identity. More and more people crowded round her. As she came out of one shop a man grabbed her so her bodyguard had to wrestle him away.

"DESIREE! DESIREE! I LOVE YOU!" He shouted and her bodyguard bundled her in to the car.

The fan tried to get to the car but the bodyguard pushed him aside forcefully.

"Back off!" He shouted.

When she got back to the suite, she noticed Matt in the pool relaxing with a bottle of chilled champagne. She dumped her bags in the bedroom, took her clothes off, put her robe on and went out to him.

"Hi darling. Good shopping trip?"

"Matt… tell me, have you ever had sex in the pool?"

"In a Jacuzzi… not the pool, though. Why don't you get in here and show me what it's like"

Des smiled. "Maybe…"

"Don't tease me Des, get your sexy arse in here!"

Des smiled again and walked slowly over to the pool, slipped her robe off revealing her beautiful naked body. She moved seductively down the steps and over to him. Matt's eyes lit up with passion.

"Desiree, you are just perfect"

He pulled her closer to him. As he turned her round he begin to gently kiss butterfly kisses all the way down her neck, down over her shoulders, moving his lips down her back. She sighed with pleasure, quickly turnings back around and wrapping her legs round his waist. He moved her back towards the side of the pool, gliding his hands over her breasts. His kisses were deep as he eased himself into her. Back and forth they drifted slowly then the rhythm became faster as he made love to her.

"Oh fucking hell, Des! Hmm baby!" He moaned with excitement.

"Arrrrgh!! Matt… Oh! Oh!"

After making love in the pool, Matt took her by the hand, grabbed the champagne and led her to the bedroom to the four poster bed. He laid her down, kissing her passionately moving his hands down her body making her move to his touch. He brushed his lips over hers, making her want him more. She gazed at him breathlessly as he brushed his lips over her breasts, moving his mouth down her body, flicking his tongue over her soft skin, moving down to her legs. She groaned with excitement as he moved between her thighs and again made love to her for it seemed like an age. They moved their hips together, both breathing heavily. His eyes rolled back as he climaxed. Both panting heavily, they lay back and relaxed. As Matt struggled to get his breath back, he got up and ordered room service. The plan was to stay in bed and make love all night.

"Stay there don't move, Mrs Adams. I'll be right back"

Des lay back in bed and relaxed while Matt went to the bathroom. He was washing his hands when he suddenly felt a sharp pain in his arm and stumbled backwards, howling with the pain. Des heard a crashing sound and jumped up.

"Matt!"

"Yeah?"

"Are you OK?"

"Yeah… I dropped something that's all"

When Matt came out of the bathroom Des looked at him.

"Baby, you're as white as sheet"

"I'm fine … has room service not come yet?"

"No you only just ordered it"

Des looked more closely. He was clammy and white. He didn't look at all well.

"Baby, are you sure you're alright?"

"Yeah, I'm fine"

Des wasn't convinced. She wanted him to see a doctor but he insisted he was fine. Matt didn't tell Des about the pain in his arm, he didn't want her to worry her. He knew if she knew about it she would make him see the doctor and he was just fine. After all, it was just a little cramp, wasn't it?

Chapter 27

1985

Desiree was on the film set, shooting scenes for her new film when she got an urgent call from Jake. Matt had been rushed in to hospital with a suspected heart attack. He had been having lunch with Jake when he suddenly grabbed his arm and fell to the floor. As they waited for the ambulance, he told Jake about all the pains he'd been having. Des didn't know anything about them.

She told the director she had to get back to England and took the next UK flight. A car was waiting for her as soon as her plane landed and rushed her to the hospital. Jake met her outside Matt's room with a terrible look on his face.

"Jake, what's wrong?"

He didn't know how he was going to break the awful news that Matt had died When he did, she screamed a blood-curdling scream, the colour draining from her face. She dropped to her knees, fighting for her breath.

"No… no… NO!"

"Come on Des, let's take you home"

"No Jake… I want to see him"

"No babes, come on"

"No.... Jake let me be with him for a while"

Jake led Des in to see Matt. It was just like he was asleep, she kissed his lips gently and put her head on his chest. She just sat there and told him she loved him over and over again and begged him not to leave her.

"Please don't leave me... Matt, please don't leave me"

Jake gently took hold of her, putting his arms round her and felt her shudder. When the tears eventually came they wouldn't stop, she was crying uncontrollably. She was having trouble breathing, she kept hyperventilating. Finally, Jake took her home and called the doctor. Lori was flying over to be with her and she arrived at the same time as the doctor.

"I've given her a sedative. That should calm her down and hopefully make her sleep"

"I'll check on her later," said Lori.

"The press are congregating out there"

Jake made his way outside to the reporters and gave a statement.

"It's with deep regret that I have to tell you that Matt Adams died early today. Miss Beaumont is in a very distressed state at this time"

"Is it true that Mr Adams suffered *two* heart attracts?"

"Yes, that is true"

"Where was he at the time?"

"He was having lunch with me"

"You were with him?"

"Yes, I was. That's it guys – I hope you will respect Desiree's privacy at this sad time and let her grieve for her husband"

Next morning, Lori made eggs and bacon in the hope she could get Des to eat something Jake was just finishing his when Des appeared, her eyes red and puffy, looking dreadfully groggy from the sedative.

"Des come and sit down"

Des sat down tears rolling down her face. Lori wanted to help but she didn't know how to.

"I've made some breakfast"

"I don't want any"

"Honey, you've got to eat"

"No"

When Lori handed her a cup of freshly-made coffee, she just stared at it.

"Drink some coffee Des" Jake said, taking her hand,

Des lifted her head.

"What am I going to do without him?"

Lori turned to the window, putting her hands over her mouth to stop herself from crying out loud, her tears falling over her hands. Jake took Des in his arms and held her tight.

"Oh Des, I'm so sorry"

Matt's son, Luke, flew over with Vivian and they went straight over to Des's. Vivian could see how deeply Des was hurting. Staffan had called to see how Des was. He couldn't get back for the funeral as he was on tour on the other side of the world. Riley and Johnny couldn't get back either. Andy Marsh and Paul Best let Jake know that they would be there. Even Millicent was there. Lori told her to leave her alone but she told Lori she just wanted to say how sorry she was.

The whole world was in mourning for Matt, the funeral was on every channel and all over the news. Matt Adams was loved by millions. As the casket was removed from the hearse, Des broke down, blinded by her tears. It was like she'd had her heart torn out leaving a big hole. As they lowered the casket into the grave, she sank to her knees with a heart-wrenching wail.

"Noooooo, Matt, Noooooo don't leave me!"

Jake and Paul helped her to the Limo to take her back home. She walked into the house in a daze, with everything going in slow motion. After a while, people had started to leave the wake. Lori told Des she would go back home and get some clean clothes and come straight back. Des told her she didn't have to do that, she would be fine.

"I have to get used to being here on my own so I might as well start tonight"

"Are you sure?"

"Yes"

"If you need me, call me – no matter what time it is, just call"

Des hugged her friend and thanked her and Jake for being there when she needed them most.

The house felt so empty after everyone had left. At every step she made she could hear her stilettos echoing on the wooden floor as she walked through the hall. It sounded so loud. She looked around – she had never felt so alone. She slid down the wall, her tears fell down her face, she just wanted Matt to be there.

As the weeks passed, nobody had seen Des. Lori had called her to make sure she was alright, to discover she didn't want to go back to finish the film. She just wanted to be on her own. The studio were threatening to sue Desiree and her response was to tell them to go ahead. Jake managed to sort it out and buy her some time. Desiree's world had fallen apart, she was devastated, she was slowly getting more and more depressed.

She realised she couldn't live in the house with so many memories of Matt, it was just too painful. She need to move on so she had her lawyer come round for a meeting. She wanted to give both houses to Luke, indeed, she made sure that Matt's son got all of his estate. Luke was shocked that Desiree gave him everything. She was his dad's wife and he had left her everything. She pointed out that she loved his dad for himself, not his money.

Back in America

Desiree asked Jake to help her find a new house and he brought her some photographs. She flicked through them then finally spotted the one she liked the look of.

"This one, *Silver Stone Way*"

It was a bungalow with four bedrooms, walk-in closets and en-suite bathrooms, a big lounge leading into the kitchen, lots of grounds and a swimming pool.

"Hmm Des I wouldn't bother with that one… I thought I'd took that out of the pile"

"Why it's perfect it isolated and it's empty"

"And it's derelict"

"I'd like to see it, will you take me"

Jake wasn't sure about the house. It had been empty for years. He drove through the rusty gates which were hanging off the gateposts and up what had once been a gravelled drive, but was now was overgrown with weeds and grass. All the trees and shrubs were overgrown too.

"Oh fuck me, Des. You don't want this place"

"Come on Jake, let's have a look inside"

"Really, do I have to?"

The floors were rotten, the roof had a hole in it with moss covering the inside and outside and there was dust everywhere. Jake opened the lounge door and it fell off.

"No! You've see enough"

"Jake, I've not see the pool yet"

"Des, you're not serious!"

When Jake saw the pool he just wanted to get out of there, it was empty and the bottom was strewn with mould, leaves and heaven knows what else.

"This the one"

"No way… Des"

"It will keep me busy"

"You have a film to finish – that will keep you busy"

Des told him that she would work on the film until the house was ready. He shook his head in disbelief that this was the house she wanted.

As it was, she finished the film and then took some time out while the house was finally finished to her standards. The floors were tiled in black marble and she had black wooden shutters put up at all the windows. With two white leather couches in the lounge it looked fantastic. The pool was cleaned and working and all the gardens had been transformed into lush green lawns – oh, and the path was gravelled again. She had security gates installed and she even got herself a housekeeper. Mae she was a lovely lady, the type of woman Desiree would have loved as a mum. All in all, she had turned this run down house in a beautiful home.

Even though she had done all this, her thoughts kept turning back to Matt. Renovating the house had taken a little of the pain away but it didn't stop her from getting more and more depressed. She would just sit at the window most of the time, staring into space, telling Matt how much she missed him.

One night she sat there as a storm raged overhead, just watching and clutching her usual bottle of wine. As the dark haze started to descend, the rain started to fall. Massive raindrops went splat as they hit the windows, lightning lit up the sky and a violent wind was bending the trees wildly.

Mae grew very fond of Des and tried to look after the best she could but Des's friends still worried about her. She was drinking far too much and she had started taking pills to sleep and pills to keep her going during the day.

She was out of her head most of the time. When she went back to work on a new picture, she was starting to become a director's nightmare. She was awkward, refused to do the simplest things and was always late.

One morning it was all too much and she didn't show at all. Lori tried to get hold of her for hours but she couldn't get any answer so she called Mae. When Mae let Lori in they found Des unconscious. She had overdosed on barbiturates loaded with alcohol. Lori thought she could have done this on purpose but wasn't sure.

"Des! Oh shit, Des!"

She called the paramedics and Des was admitted to hospital to have her stomach pumped. The medics said she'd have to stay in for a few days. When Lori went in to visit her, Des told her she felt like shit.

"Yeah, bet you do. You really scared Mae and me, I can tell ya. Des, did you do this on purpose?"

"No…" she said, shaking her head.

"You can tell me if you did. I know you're hurting and you miss Matt"

"No!… "

"Oh Des, you've got to stop drinking"

"Now you're my fuckin' mother?"

"No – I'm worried about you"

"Get off my fuckin' back!"

"OK Des, do what the fuck you want!" Lori was so angry, she just walked out and left Des in the bleak hospital room.

It didn't get any better. When she left hospital, she was straight back on the booze and the pills, with a really terrible effect on her acting. Directors didn't want to work with her, she was getting more and more difficult. She was never on time, if she even turned up at all, or they had to send her home because she was so out of it. The brutal fact was that Desiree was losing it.

She didn't know what she was doing one day to the next. She was filming and the director asked her to say a line again.

"*Cut*… Let's do that again, Des"

"Fuck off! There was nothing wrong with that fuckin' line"

"I want the line doing again, OK? and… *action.* Cut! No…no…no! for fucks sake, Des!"

"What *now*? Fuck you"

"It's a wrap guys. Let's start again tomorrow. Desiree, get yourself fucking sorted out"

"I'm the fucking star so fuck off, you need me – I make you your money"

"Yeah and I'm the fucking director. Fuck off back to your trailer and sort your head out"

"Fuck you!" She said aggressively, kicking the lighting stands over as she stomped off the set.

"Des come on. This is not *you*"

The director called Jake to come on the set to see Des. She had gone back to her trailer and was systematically trashing it, swigging vodka and being very loud. Jake banged on the trailer door.

"Des!" He shouted.

"What? Fuck off!"

"Des, what the fuck are you doing? Let me in"

"Jake… Jakey… Jakey…" she opened the door and threw her arms round him.

"Put the bottle down"

She took another swig of vodka and Jake grabbed the bottle. "No more"

"Jake…"

"No Des, stop"

She moved closer to him. "Do you want to screw me, Jake?"

She kissed him and started to undo the buttons on his shirt, moving her hands down his body.

"Here's your chance Jake. I won't tell your wife. Come on, come on…"

"Stop it, Des. Fucking stop it! This is not the Des I know and love" He grabbed her hands.

"Huh, She's fucking gone – this is the new Desiree Beaumont. Every fucking man in my life hurts me, even Matt… Well, *no fucking more*!"

"Come on, Babe, you're pissed"

Jake took her home. He rang Sandra to tell her what had happened and she asked if he wanted her to come over. He told her he needed her to be there, so Jake and Sandra stayed all night to watch her when she fell asleep, to make sure she was alright.

Chapter 28

Desiree's behaviour was getting worse. She started being late for interviews and photoshoots. She seemed to be in the news a lot, all bad. She wasn't eating and started to lose too much weight. She was scheduled to perform on an awards night but failed to show and then was so out of it at a singing awards that she fell out of the limousine onto her knees, cutting them.

She was distracted and shaky. Her attitude was defiant and she got sent home from yet another film set. Desiree went home alright – she got drunk and took some pills and went out to party and, as ever, she partied hard. Brett Gregson was at the club and saw her on the dance floor. He made his way over, stood behind her. He wrapped his arms around her, pulled her close to him and started kissing her neck. She was so drunk she didn't know what she was doing.

"Let's get out of here"

They left the club together. He helped into the taxi, his hands all over her as they went back to her place. Brett was a good looking man, mousy brown hair and brown eyes, but he was a womaniser. He liked no strings attached sex– nothing more than pure physical pleasure. Desiree was on his list of women to have, he had wanted her for a long time but he'd never even got close before.

As soon as she had fumbled the door open, he was straight to it, no messing around.

"Come here, baby" He summoned her. "I've wanted this night for so long"

"Brett, I don't…" slurring her words.

Before she could say anything else he kissed her, his tongue exploring her mouth.

"You brought me back to fuck you and that's what I'm going to do"

He moved closer to her and rubbed himself against her. She could feel his erection rubbing up her leg. He took hold of her hand and moved it into his open trousers, pressing down on his bulge.

"Feel that baby, it's all yours"

He slid his hand up her skirt, unclipped her panties and pulled her leg up to his waist as his pushed himself into her, there up against the wall. It was all over in seconds. He led her to the bedroom where she fell on the bed, then they had hot frenzied sex again.

Next morning, she was horrified. She'd woken up with her usual black feeling of despair, then saw Brett next to her to make it even worse. She kicked him out of bed with both feet.

"What the fuck?" as he fell on the floor with thud.

"GET OUT!" She screamed at him.

"Chill babe… you loved it, you couldn't get enough"

"Get out! Get out of my house"

"What's your problem? You whacky bitch"

"Get the fuck out of my fucking house!"

You weren't saying that last night baby you were begging for it"

She slapped him across the face, leaving her handprint on his cheek. He looked angrily at her and then slapped her back, cutting her above the eye. Seething, he got dressed and left. She couldn't remember much of the previous night, all she knew was she felt like she had betrayed Matt. She felt dirty and ashamed – she *hated* herself.

Desiree sat down and cried. She couldn't believe what she'd done. When Mae arrived she was crying uncontrollably. Mae looked at her and saw the cut on her right eye. It had begun to swell up and blacken. She sat down beside Des and held her close.

"Mae, what am I doing?" She sobbed.

"Oh, Miss Beaumont"

"I hate myself Mae. I'm going back to bed – I might die if I'm lucky"

Mae was really worried and stayed longer than she needed to make sure Des was alright. When Des woke, she was still there

"Mae, what you doing still doing here?"

"I wanted to make sure you were alright"

Desiree went over to Mae and kissed her on the cheek.

"Thank you… but you'd better go home now"

When Mae had left she started drinking again to blot out Brett. As a result, she had another evening where she was off her head. She was sinking deeper into a really bad place. She wasn't seeing anyone and the only friend she really spoken to was her pal Lori, and she'd even upset her. She wasn't coping with losing Matt, she missed him desperately.

Lori was so worried about Des she decided to call Delmar. She asked him for Staffan's number.

"Is this about Des?"

"I know this is not his problem and they are not married any more, but I don't know what else to do. She's on a self-destruct mission"

"Yeah, Staffan read about her in the papers. It's tearing him apart"

"Please give me his number"

"Lori, its taken him a long time to get where he is"

"Please Delmar I'm desperate I don't know what else to do"

"OK I know she not in a good way at the moment, but what do you think Staffan can do?"

"I don't know. She might listen to him… I *hope* she'll listen to him"

Lori rang Staffan. They spoke for a long time as Lori told him all about Des and how bad things were. Staffan agreed to ring Des and he did the next day. Mae handed the phone to Des mouthing that Mr Templeton was on the phone and Des got very excited.

"Staffan?"

"Hiya, Des"

"Staffan" she sounded really pleased to hear his voice.

“I’m so sorry about Matt”

“Thank you… What about you – are you OK?”

“Yeah, great”

“Staffan, thank you for ringing me, it’s really nice to hear your voice. I thought you would never talk to me again”

“Hey…. I can’t stay mad at you”

They had a very lengthy talk. He even managed to make her laugh a little, which took some doing these days. He hoped he had made her feel better.

“When you’re next here, maybe you could come and see me or have dinner? That's if you want to, of course…”

“Yeah that would be good. See you soon and Des… look after yourself”

“Yeah, thanks Staffan, thank you for ringing. Don’t forget dinner when you are next here”

“I won’t… I’ll call you. Bye”

Staffan put the down phone and softly sighed, *'I love you, Des'*. He wanted to go to her but he didn’t think he could take the pain of seeing her. It had taken a long time to get where he was and he wasn’t sure he was strong enough for that yet.

Chapter 29

An ending, 1985

Lori and Scott were finally divorced, a long and messy time. She and Ethan had folded when he found out that she had been seeing Paul Best. In her unhappiness she was missing Des but she was still mad with her for the things she had said. Des was still drinking but she had been seeing a doctor and he had managed to get her off the pills. The drink would have to be next to go but for the moment, it was still very much a problem. No directors wanted to take her on. She was still a nightmare to work with when she'd been drinking.

Lori finally decided to go and see Des. Des was so happy to see her she flung her arms round her and told her she was sorry for the hurtful things she said, she didn't want them to ever fall out again. Lori quickly forgave her and they were soon back to their old selves. They were soon going out every night partying and Lori wanted to have some fun.

Meanwhile, things had been going great for Staffan and Fallen. It seemed to be pretty serious between them and Fallen wanted to get married. She'd planned to ask him on a romantic weekend she had booked. After a romantic meal, they sat soaking up the atmosphere when told him she loved him.

"Staffan, will you marry me?"

Staffan was stunned. He didn't want this, and said so.

"No… No. I can't"

She told him that she wanted to get married and have children one day soon.

"Well it's not going to be with me"

He got up hurriedly from his chair and made his way to the elevator. Fallen followed him.

"But why?"

She wondered what she had done to deserve him getting up from the table so abruptly.

"I've been married – I'm not ever doing it again"

He went back to their room and started packing his bag.

"I think it's time to end this, now"

"Why are you doin' this? Just because it didn't work with Desiree, it doesn't mean it won't work with me"

"It won't work with you or anyone else, because I'm still in love with Desiree"

"But…I thought…"

"Well, you thought *wrong*"

And that was the end. He just couldn't settle down with anyone, he certainly didn't want to get married. She had wanted him to commit to her on a more permanent basis but he didn't love her enough.

Staffan was never short of women but Des did something to him that he just couldn't get over, no matter what he tried, he couldn't shake her off. This made his mind up for him to move back to New York. He'd been umming and ahhing about it for a while, now he was sure. He told the guys he was moving back. Delmar said it was fantastic news. Edvin told him he would be back just in time for his wedding to his long-time girlfriend, Adda Navn. He asked Staffan if he should invite Des.

"Yeah its fine"

"Are you sure?"

"We're going to bump in to each other sometime, Edvin. We'll deal with it"

Edvin's Wedding

The day of the wedding was going to be difficult for Staffan seeing Des, especially if she brought a date. They hadn't seen each other for quite some time and, when the time came, they just stared at each other, not knowing what to say. It was a lovely day and Edvin and Adda had been together a long time and were very much in love.

Riley had also been invited and had seen Desiree and gone over.

"Hi Des, as beautiful as ever, " he said and leaned in to kiss her.

"Riley, Hi"

Riley moved really close to her and put his hands round her waist.

"Des… Des….Des you are a hard woman to get over, baby" he whispered.

Riley took hold of her then kissed her. Staffan was watching when Johnny asked him what he was looking at.

"Riley's all over Des"

"Why don't you tell her how you feel?"

"No it's over. She doesn't want me"

Lori was sat at the table talking to Jake when Des was making her way back over to them when Staffan took hold of her arm. Smiling, she turned round.

"Des"

"Staffan… It's so good to see you. I saw you earlier and wanted to come over – but I didn't know whether I should…"

"It's good to see you too. And of course you should have come over. No date Des?"

"No. I'm here with Lori. I didn't want a date… What about you? I'm sorry it didn't work out for you and Fallen"

"Shit happens"

"I'm going back to the table for something to eat, are you coming?"

He gave her cheeky smile, Des smiled back.

"Come on" She took his hand and led him to the table.

"Hi Lori"

"Staffan, it's nice to see you," taking hold of him and kissing him on the cheek. "Oh, do you want something to eat?

"No – I'll take some of Des's when she's not looking"

Des smiled at him. They talked for ages. Lucas came over and asked Lori for a dance. They headed for the dance floor, leaving Staffan and Des at the table.

"So, Des…"

"So are you not dating at all, Staffan?" Des interrupted, eager to know.

"No. Fallen wanted to get married"

"Oh I see – were you not ready for that?"

"No…. I've been married, remember. I'm not doing it again"

"Oh Staffan, I'm sorry. Was I that bad I put you off?"

"No…no… I was only ever doing it once, with one girl"

"Staffan, I want to…"

"Do you want dance Des?" cutting her off before she could finish.

"Yeah I would," forgetting what she wanted to say.

He held out his hand and she put her hand in his and they made their way to the dance floor. He slipped hands round her waist and pulled her close. He could feel her skin next to his. He could also smell her perfume, a strikingly familiar aroma of sandalwood and amber. She smelt so good, she felt so good.

She was aware of him so close. She put her head on his chest. He too smelt so good, a masculine aroma, sharp and spicy. She played with his hair while they danced, his hands getting tighter round her waist. They were together all evening and at the end of it he offered to take her home. She accepted and soon they were in the house.

She offered him a drink. He really wanted to but said 'no'. She wouldn't listen, however, and eventually he accepted.

"One drink"

"OK, one drink it is"

Losing track of time, they talked for hours. Gently, he stroked her cheek until she started kissing his fingers. He leant in to kiss her and she responded to his kiss, pulling his shirt collar bringing him closer. His kisses were soft and sweet, she felt a throbbing running through her body. They looked at each other knowingly, both speechless with emotion. They both knew what was about to happen. She took his hand and led him to the bedroom where they slowly undressed each other. Her hands slid over his shoulders and round his neck encouraging a deep intimacy. She arched her back as he touched her, his eyes filled with passion.

He slid down between her thighs, his body slamming down on her. He moved his hands over the curves of her body as he moved back and forth making her groan with every movement. Her body tightened as she felt the relief of the orgasm. The sex was incredible. Her body jerked from the pleasure. She felt a warm feeling all over her body. Every time he touched her delivered a surge of heat. He came and collapsed lifelessly on top of her. They both fell asleep holding each other in the ruffled sheets.

When the sun rose the next morning, Des woke to Staffan trailing his finger up and down her back.

"About last night, Des"

"We are both adults – we knew what we were doing"

"Right?"

"We both had a good time, Yeah? Great sex…"

"Right… yeah, great sex"

He was confused and a little disappointed so he got dressed and told her he would see her soon. He had left by the time Mae had got there. It was her birthday and Des had bought her a little car because Mae walked everywhere and couldn't afford to buy a car. Des managed to stay off the drink long enough to make a birthday lunch for her.

"Oh Miss Beaumont, this is too much"

"I wish you would call me Des, Mae"

"Well I could do, Miss Desiree"

Des thought a lot about Mae. She looked after Desiree no matter what. When Desiree got so drunk that she didn't know what she doing, Mae was always there for her. Mae loved Des like a daughter and she worried about her. She'd never had any children. Her husband had died and she never married again Mae only ever loved one man.

Desiree loved that Mae had loved only one man. Mae told Des that *she* really only loved one man, too. Des looked at her a bit confused, not sure what she meant. Mae was referring to Staffan Templeton but she didn't think it was her place to point this out. She hoped that Desiree would realise this one day and tell him she was still in love him so she could be happy.

Mae knew Staffan was the one for Des – she'd had heard it in her voice when she spoke to Staffan on the phone.

For weeks and weeks Des had been partying hard and one particular night she was in the Horizon night club at the same time as Daniella Winton and Brook Owen from the girl band *Miss Naughty.* Daniella was talking to Brook about Des, telling her what a mess she was. Brook told her to keep her opinions to herself

"Come on, she's finished – she's a mess"

"Daniella"

Jenny had overheard what Daniella had said and went over to tell Des but she hadn't thought about would happen next. Des staggered over to Daniella and tapped her shoulder. Daniella turned round.

"Oh Hi, Des…"

Without warning Des threw out her fist, connecting with Daniella's face. Blood pooled round her mouth. Daniella reacted, throwing her own punch. The bouncers ran over to separate them. As they were parted, Des grabbed Daniella by the hair, ripping a handful out. Daniella screamed in pain

"Don't Fuckin' Mess with me, Bitch!" Des shouted viciously before she was removed from the club.

Daniella Winton slapped a law suit on Desiree for physically and verbally assaulting her. To be fair, Desiree had blackened Daniella's eye and split her lip – requiring three stitches in her lip and four over her right eye.

Jake had to go with Des to court. It had only been two days but she couldn't remember any of it. The judge found for Daniella and awarded $15,000 in damages. As Daniella walked passed Des on her way out, she gave her a very cold look indeed. Des was not one to push too far these days. The press, however, wanted to know everything and fired question at her from all angles.

"Des… Des…"

Des put her head down to try to hide but as soon as she stepped out the flashed bulbs blinded her

"No comment, just go away"

Jake opened the car door and helped her in.

"Just take me home, Jake"

Jake looked straight at Des and asked what was happening with her but she didn't know.

"Please, just take me home, Jake"

Chapter 30

Jake he was really concerned about Desiree so he rang Staffan. He'd heard about the two of them spending the night together after the wedding and he thought that if anyone could get through to her, it would be Staffan.

"Staffan mate, how are you?"

"Yeah, good. What can I do for you?"

"What makes you think I'm after something?"

"Jake, how many times do you ring me?"

"OK… well I'm worried about Des. She's still drinking far too much. I know that she's not your problem but…"

"What do you want me to do?"

"See her"

"Jake, do you know how hard it is for me to see her? Every time I see her… Oh man"

"I know Staffan, but I'm really worried. Lori has tried talking to her but she's not listening"

"OK Jake, where does she go at night?"

Jake told him a few places she might be so Staffan went looking for her.

Eventually he found her. She was really drunk and the man with her was all over her, he just wouldn't leave her alone and she was too drunk to get rid of him. Staffan spotted her and went over.

"Des, Babe, what the fuck are you doin?"

"Staffan… Oh baby, I'm so glad to see you"

He told the man to disappear. He wasn't too happy when Staffan told him she was going home with him.

"She's with me"

"No she's not, so why don't you just fuck off"

The man stood up and got in Staffan face.

"She's with me"

"Don't fuckin' think so, you see she's my wife and don't get in my fuckin' face again"

"Or what…? You fuckin' rock stars"

"You'll wish you hadn't, that's fuckin' what, needle dick. Come on let's get you home Des…"

He pulled her up and put his arms round her waist. The man suddenly lunged at him. Staffan dropped Des on the floor, turned round and thumped the guy in the face.

"Now Fuck off!"

Picking Des up off the floor he took her home. He didn't like seeing her like this. She was so out of it she hadn't even realised that Staffan had brought her home. With difficulty, he got her into the house, made some coffee and sobered her up a bit.

"You look a bit more with it now"

"I look a mess don't I?"

"Des, you're beautiful even when you're pissed"

"Come on…" he took her in to the bed room put her on the bed and started taking her clothes off

She looked at him said, "You still want me?"

She kissed him and moved on his knee, one leg either side of his, and started whispering very suggestive things in his ear.

"Des, Don't! "

He was trying desperately not to get aroused by what she was saying to him.

"Do you want to take me to bed and have really hot sex?"

"You're pissed, babe." as he pushed her back on the bed but it was too late. He was aroused by her and he was struggling to keep his hands off her.

"I know that you do Staffan"

She kissed him again she moved her hand slowly up the inside of his leg to his crotch she could feel his erection.

"You do still want me, don't you Staffan"

She opened the zip on his jeans, put her hand in and rubbed over his manhood, he was so turned him. She kissed him again and now he kissed her back, he couldn't help himself. She started to take his clothes off and her hands explored his body and he responded to every touch she made. He took the rest of her clothes off and began to touch her tenderly. He'd missed her so much, he began to kiss her again. They were always good together, there was never any doubt about that. He was so smooth and muscular and her body had missed him. He ran his fingers up to her hair, grasping, pulling gently, pulling her head to his he ran his tongue over her lips

"Ahhh Staffan"

She groaned and arched her back with the need to be touched. He moved closer, pressed his body against her, kissing her neck then moving his tongue down her body. They were both hot and sweaty. The sex was hot and frenzied, very passionate. They fell asleep in each other's arms.

When Staffan woke the next morning he just lay on his side watching her sleep. He loved her body, her legs, her face – just everything about her. She opened her bleary eyes and smiled. It had been a long time since she had woken up without that feeling of black despair.

"Thank you for bringing me home"

"It's fine"

"No, it's not your problem. You could have been with some hot girl, not babysitting your ex-wife"

"I *was* with a hot girl – the sex is always fantastic, babe"

"Yeah, we were always good in bed together"

"Stay there Des, I'll make some coffee or tea – which one would you like?" and he kissed her head gently.

"Coffee"

Staffan put his jeans on and went in the kitchen to make the coffee. He was standing there bare chested with his jeans open, his hair all over the place, looking very sexy when Mae came in.

"Oh sorry…" she said.

"Mae?" He asked as he zipped his jeans up

Mae smiled and nodded.

"Hi, I'm Staffan Templeton"

"Oh Mr Templeton, nice to meet you"

"Yeah, nice to meet you too, Mae"

"Miss Desiree hmm?"

Staffan told Mae she was still in bed and he was taking the coffee in to her. Mae nodded knowingly and told Staffan that she was going shopping and then left. Staffan took the coffee back into the bedroom. Des sat up and drank her coffee, then got out of bed and headed for the shower. Staffan's eyes followed her until she turned her head round, looking down seductively, inviting him to join her. She got in the shower as the steam billowed all around her, Staffan followed her in, the water was running all over her body as he stood behind her. Running his hands over her body he kissed the back of her neck, sending ripples down her body.

"You're so fuckin' hot!"

With the pleasure rising in his voice, he turned her around to kiss her. He grasped her leg, pulling it up around his waist and made love to her.

"Oh yessss, Staffan aaargh!"

"Oh yeah, baby… you feel so good"

When he was dressed and leaving he told her he thought she should get some help with her drinking. This only made her angry.

"It's not your problem… just because you shagged me does not give you any rights, they stopped when we got divorced"

Staffan looked stunned.

"Yeah you're fuckin' right, you're not my problem – you're a fuckin' *mess*. Go on, drink yourself to fucking death – I don't give a fucking shit! " and stormed off, he was so angry with her,.

She was so upset she went straight to the booze and then out came the pills.

When Mae came back she didn't disturb Des, she thought Staffan was still with her, so she put all the shopping away then left. She was taking the rest of the week off to visit her sister so nobody saw Des for three days.

Jake rang Staffan.

"Have you seen Des?"

"No… Last time I saw her we had a massive argument and I stormed out"

"Nobody has seen her for three days – Lori has tried but no answer"

"What nothing? OK… I'm on my way.

Staffan went straight round. He couldn't get any answer at the gates so he climbed over them, the alarms were going off like crazy but he needed to get in there. He ran up the drive. BANG! BANG! BANG! On the front door.

"DESIREE!… Des!… Des!" He shouted but no answer.

Des was at the back of the house. She'd taken a hand full of pills and drunk most of the bottle of vodka and was off her face hovering over the pool. She was very wobbly right on the edge and she suddenly passed out. As she fell she hit her head on the pool edge and landed face down in the water.

Staffan was frantic with worry, he couldn't get any answer so he went round the back and he saw a naked Desiree face down in the pool.

"Des… Fucking hell Des"

He jumped in the pool, grabbed her and dragged her to the side giving her mouth to mouth as he went.

"Don't you fucking die on me Des… Don't you fucking dare, don't fucking leave me, I love you so much. Please, Des come on. Come on!" He shouted, desperation in his voice.

The alarms to the house were still going off and the police and then the medics arrived. So did the press. Staffan took his wet shirt off and covered her, the medics took over and put her straight in to the ambulance. They rushed her to hospital and Staffan insisted he stay with her. He stayed with her all night. He called Jake to let him know what had happened. Jake rushed over.

Staffan told him she was going be fine but he couldn't do this anymore.

"She's tearing me apart. I can't watch her destroy herself like this, I love her so much… I just can't…"

Jake understood. He wasn't sure how to tell Desiree that Staffan wasn't going to see her any more but he knew he had to break it to her somehow.

Next morning Des was all over the front pages. She woke up feeling very groggy and asked for Staffan. Jake told her that he had gone, then told her what Staffan had said to him: that he couldn't do this anymore and he wasn't coming back. Desiree put her head down. Tears started to roll down her face, she was heartbroken. It slammed home that she had lost him for good.

He was right, she did need help. She decided to admit herself to rehab.

She was in rehab for months and had a bad time coming off the booze and the pills. She suffered shakes and sweats and underwent months of counselling, learning to cope with stressful situations. She had starved herself for some time, the booze and pills had taken their toll on her. When she was discharged from the clinic she started getting back in shape. That beautiful body was back.

Still, no directors want to take the chance on her. Her career her had taken a big nose dive until Mac Willows took a chance on her and put her in his film.

One Day In Life turned into a massive hit. She starred with Darrel Rawlins, Martin Laurence, Jenny Blake, Steven Russell and Judy Scott. She was grateful to Mac for giving her that chance – Desiree Beaumont was back, better than ever, back on top and back on track. She'd been through hell and back but she'd got through to the other side.

She started doing rock videos again. Riley was the first to get in touch and asked her to do another video with him and the band. She wasn't sure she should but he persuaded her to do it. It was good, she enjoyed it and so did Riley – they even went out to dinner and talked about old times. He told her he was putting her on their album cover. When the other rock bands saw it they thought this was great idea.

She started getting offers for more and more rock videos, even some pop stars started to ask her for videos as well. She was even approached by Scott. She wasn't sure about this, what with him being Lori's ex but Lori told her it was just a job.

She wasn't bothered, she was well and truly over Scott.

"I don't want you to think ..."

Lori interrupted her, "I don't"

"After everything that's happened… the way I was… I'm lucky you're still my friend"

"You were in a bad place; Matt suddenly being taken away from you like that it was just too much to take"

Staffan was romantically linked with Kady Marshal, a famous porn star, not too serious and that's how he wanted it. He kept getting updates on Des through Jake but he didn't want her to know. Whilst *Dominance* were on tour he rang Jake regularly to see how Des was doing. Jake told him she was doing great and he should come and see her but Staffan didn't think that was a good idea although he was really pleased she was doing well.

"She looked great when I saw her in the paper"

"Yeah the old Des is back, Staffan"

"I'm really pleased"

"You should see her, Staffan"

"I can't Jake… I really can't"

Lori flew over to England to see *Dominance.* They started their opening music and Staffan shot up from underneath the stage. They were fantastic and Staffan got Lori up to sing with them.

Back in New York, Des was in *The Party House* nightclub, the place to be if you wanted to pump and grind to thundering sounds and high energy beats. Des had been circulating when she bumped into Andy Marsh from *Eclipse*. As they talked he asked what she had been working on and she told him that she'd just finished a video with *Lightning* and was about to start one with Scott Danials.

"Wasn't it a bit awkward… working with Riley?"

"No … I thought it might have been but, no, it wasn't"

"It was great when you worked with us"

It was so loud in the club they couldn't hear each other without shouting so Andy suggested they went back to his hotel suite where it would be a little quieter. Des nodded in agreement so he took her hand and headed to the hotel.

He was about open the door when he turned his head and looked at her with a hot, intense expression. He had a sudden urge to kiss her. She responded without hesitation, passion running through their bodies like an inferno as they fell into the room, pulling frantically at each other's clothes.

They staggered and stumbled to the bedroom. She fell back on the bed and he looked lustfully down at her. Then he kissed his way down her naked body, right down to her toes then all the way back up again. He teased her with his tongue making her arch her back with need. The feeling rocked her body as he kissed her neck and finally pushed himself into her.

She moaned softly as he thrust deep inside her, then more loudly. She was driving him crazy, he needed to come but he didn't want this to end. He had to allow himself to release, he couldn't hold back any longer. Pulling out, he rolled on to his back and the both lay breathless, giggling at each other. They must have fallen asleep because the next thing they knew it was morning. Neither was looking for romance, they had just wanted one night of passion.

Lori flew back to New York the next morning. She was so angry with Lucas – she had gone backstage and found him making out with one of the fans. She had been there before and wasn't going back, she finished it there and then. When she got back she went out that night with Des and soon forgot about Lucas. They'd met up Hadley and Callan from *Connections* and spent the evening with them.

Des and Callan left Lori and Hadley talking while they hit the dance floor. Placing his hands on her hips, Callan could feel her soft skin, she felt so good. They swayed sexily together, in fact they danced most of the evening together.

He moved closer to her and whispered, "You're thrilling…"

She smiled, showing her pearly white teeth, and he just gazed into her eyes.

"You have the most beautiful, chocolate brown eyes I have ever seen"

She giggled and thanked him for the compliment. They made their way back over to Lori and Hadley who were obviously getting on really well. Callan told Des that Hadley had liked Lori for a long time.

Chapter 31

1986

Desiree had decided to write her autobiography. When it was released in the shops, she went on tour to promote it. She travelled all over Europe and America. When she got back to New York to do her last lot of signing, she had a face from the past. She had done so many book signings that see could hardly see straight any more, so when Johnny Barren hovered over her and asked her to sign his book she looked up at him not realising who he was. She asked him what he wanted her to sign so he told her he wanted her to sign 'TO JOHNNY THINKING OF YOU, DESIREE XXX'. She was half way through signing the book when she suddenly looked up.

"Oh my God, Johnny Barren"

He smiled and said, "Don't forget my kisses"

"No I won't," she said as she giggled.

"Do you get a break?"

"Yeah I do"

"Would you like grab a coffee or something?"

"Yeah… that would be good"

Johnny smiled at her and said, "Good"

Johnny was real smooth and he was also was very good looking, very sexy. He had shoulder length blonde hair with bluey-green eyes. He had recently gone through a divorce and he wasn't dating anyone at the moment. Though they had only really been acquainted through presenting an award together, he always thought Des was beautiful. His band was taking some time out and he'd been doing a bit of acting, well a couple of TV programmes. He liked acting and wanted to do more.

"It's funny. We were in the same circle of friends but we never really got know each other," he said smiling.

"No. All I knew about you was you were Staffan's friend"

"You never did a video with us…"

"You never asked me"

"Well I'm asking now"

"I'd love to"

"I always thought that Staffan was a lucky guy, you are so beautiful"

"Why, thank you" and she let out a little giggle.

He smiled at her. He had such a beautiful smile, showing off his beautiful pearly white teeth and she could see why he was such a big hit with the ladies. She was quite attracted to him so she was quite funny and flirtatious.

"Would you like to go for dinner tonight?"

"That would be nice"

They exchanged numbers and he called her later and arranged to meet her. After dinner they moved to the lounge bar and had a drink. Des only had a soft drink, she wasn't going down that road again. They chatted for ages, about their failed marriages, even about Matt. Matt was always there in her heart. They spoke about their careers and what they liked and disliked.

"I can see why Staffan fell for you. You're very addictive

"So are you, Mr Barren"

When she smiled at him, he seemed to be overwhelmed. When he saw Hadley the next morning he told him he'd had dinner with Des and that he couldn't get her out of his head and he really wanted to see her again.

"Call her"

"Staffan is our buddy..."

"Staffan is dating someone else..."

Johnny thought about it for a few minutes.

"OK I'm going to ring her"

Before he did though, he spoke to Staffan and asked him if he was OK with him asking Des out to dinner. Staffan said he was, telling Johnny she was a free agent, she could see anyone she pleased. Lucas, Delmar, Edvin were all listening in, they looked at him and Barny told him he should have been an actor. Staffan told them that he was fine with it. They wanted to know who he was trying to convince, them or himself.

Johnny decided call Des and asked her if she wanted to go out that night. She said yes, so he picked her up at eight and they went for dinner at The Satin Palace. The press was all over this hot new scoop, Desiree was dating another rock singer.

The press had jumped the gun. Des and Johnny were just friends, nothing had happened between them, they were just enjoying each other's company. Whatever Desiree did the press wasn't far behind, Johnny had the same problem so them seeing each other was a very big scoop for the papers.

Johnny even got stopped going in to the studio. He was totally bombarded with flashbulbs and questions flying from all directions.

"Johnny, are you and Des dating?" One shouted.

Johnny didn't comment and just tried to pass.

"Is it serious?" Another shouted.

It took him all his time to make his way through all of them, then when Des turned up they went wild. They crowded round her, they just wouldn't let her through.

"Are you romantically involved with Johnny Barren, Des?"

"Guys, there's nothing to tell" Des shouted.

They surrounded her so she couldn't move. Johnny appeared and took her hand and pulled her through. Masses of flash bulbs went off at this point. Eventually they made it inside.

"Wow, that was crazy!" Johnny said, placing his hands on his head pushing his hair back.

"You two are hot news" Hadley said.

Desiree had been invited to do an interview with talk show host George Vernon. When she asked who else would be on the show, George said there wasn't anyone else. It was to be just her – a special on Desiree Beaumont. She said she'd love to do it.

The George Vernon Show

"Welcome to the George Vernon show, everyone – Tonight we have the one and only, the beautiful... DESIREE BEAUMONT!"

The crowd applauded as she walked out in a black minidress that was strapped up at the back showing off her beautiful figure. She not only looked stunning, she was back to her beautiful, witty self.

"Welcome, Desiree"

"Hello, George.

"Desiree, I'll start with your autobiography. You've been touring everywhere with this book, it's selling very well – it's sold two million copies so far and still selling"

"Yeah, I was shocked it's done so well"

"It's about how you got started, your loves, your life and your ups and downs"

"Yeah, that's right"

"Did you ever think you would get so famous?"

"Hmm, no"

"Did you ever think you would get to be a sex symbol?"

"Not in a million years"

"Why not? You are very beautiful"

"I just didn't... I never thought of myself that way"

"Can we talk about your childhood? You didn't have a happy childhood, did you?"

"Hmm no, I had a dreadful childhood. My mother left me with a father who beat me – it was horrendous really"

"That must have awful"

"Yes it was... I was in one foster home after another – I couldn't have had a worse start in life"

"Now your marriage to Staffan Templeton… that was a whirlwind wasn't it? You met… you dated, then you were married"

"Yeah, when we met we were very attracted to each other and we fell in love rather quickly. It was never boring," she giggled.

"He's a very sexy man, women love him – did that bother you Desiree?"

"Yeah… sometimes… because he is a sexy man"

"Now the break-up… that must have been painful"

"Yes… painful for both of us, I would say"

"Then you had a romance with Riley Watson.

"Yep, another sexy rock guy"

"The world thought that Riley was husband number two. You both seemed to be in love"

"Yeah, that just didn't happen"

"Talking of husband number two, your marriage to the late great Matt Adams… that was surprising to the world. You were so young and he was much older, did it hurt when they said you'd married him for his money?"

"Yeah… I don't know why it was a shock – he was a beautiful man and I loved him very much"

"When Matt died you gave everything to his son and you ended up on a dark path"

"Yeah… I went down a very dark path. I just crashed and burned… I just couldn't accept that I had lost Matt"

"How did you get yourself back on track? It took a quite a while… you even went into rehab…"

"Yes. I was in a really bad place for some time and big thanks to Staffan, he saved my life – *literally*. I will always love Staffan, he is a very special man"

"So is there a man in your life at moment?"

"Hmm, not in a big rush really for romance"

"You've been seen with Johnny Barren – is there a budding romance there?"

"We are friends"

"Well Desiree, thank you for agreeing to do this interview and letting me asking you some very personal questions. Ladies and Gentlemen – *The beautiful Desiree Beaumont!*"

Staffan watched the interview. Now she was back to the Desiree he met and fell in love with – beautiful, funny and very easy to love. His relationship with Kady Marshall had hit the rocks and he quickly grew bored with the other girls he dated. He wanted to see Desiree again, he hoped she would be at the awards that were coming up.

Chapter 32

Sure enough, a few weeks later the awards saw Des and Lori arriving together. The limo pulled up at the theatre and they stepped out to lots of screaming fans. They signed a few autographs and had a few photographs taken with fans then headed inside. Staffan was already there, having a good time with the guys and slowly getting drunk. Johnny had spotted Des and Lori and made his way over, putting his hand round Des's waist and moving his fingers up her back before telling her she looked very sexy.

"You're looking pretty hot yourself"

"Oh, you think so? That's good to know"

"You, my friend, are *very* sexy"

"Ah well, maybe you'll take advantage of it one day," and winked at her, smiling that sexy smile.

Des thought Johnny was just fooling around he'd never made a move on her, they were just friends. Johnny knew that Staffan was still in love with her and that bothered him, Staffan was his buddy.

"Have you seen Staffan yet?"

"No"

"I'm sure you will. I'll see you later… I need a chat with Callan" and he kissed her.

Des smiled at him.

"Yeah, see you later," and kissed him back.

"Yeah you will" and blew a kiss at her.

Staffan had seen Des from across the room. She was looking very sexy in her tight leather jeans and sequinned halterneck top. Staffan told the guys he was going over. He staggered his way over to Des. She hadn't seen him and he came right up behind her and put his hands round her waist. He kissed her neck and whispered in her ear.

"Hi baby…"

Johnny had seen Staffan with Des and he suddenly felt jealous. Andy noticed him staring.

"You dig her don't you?"

"We're friends"

"Yeah, right!"

Des turned her head round to Staffan.

"Hi Staffan"

He pressed himself up against her and kissed her neck again, sending shivers through her as he held her tighter still. She could feel him pressing himself closer to her, he was making her feel how she used to.

"I want to come home with you tonight"

"You're drunk Staffan"

"Not so drunk I can't get it up babe"

"I have no doubt about that, Staffan"

"You know you want me… *bliv hos mig*"

"Staffan?"

"I said to stay with me, so can I come? I'll talk Danish to you all night… I know what it does to you, baby"

"Staffan"

"I won't disappoint you"

"You never did"

"No… and I never will"

She turned round and he swooped in and kissed her again. Lori looked around with her head in the air.

"Get a room, guys!"She said.

"Lori babe… you're looking good… Yeah a room Des, we need a room – you're so fucking hot I just want you to myself and what I'm going to do to you"

"Staffan, please…"

"Des, you don't need say please … I'm going to *give* it to you baby"

Lori just laughed uncontrollable laugher

"Fucking hell, you've got your hands full tonight babe"

Staffan looked at Lori and smiled a cheeky smile, raising his eyebrows. Lori told Des she would leave her to it and go and mingle, so she disappeared and found herself talking to Steve Russell. Johnny was feeling really jealous by this time but what could he do? It's not as if he and Des were an item or anything, so he couldn't really say anything. At the end of the night he had to watch Staffan leave with Des. Staffan was all over Des, kissing her, touching her.

In the limo and then when they got back to Des's, Staffan was beyond control. He started taking his clothes off as soon as they got in the house.

"Come on baby get them clothes off – I want that body"

"Staffan what's got in to you?"

"You baby. You're so fucking hot. Arrrrr I know what you want. You want me to strip you, don't you?"

He grabbed her and picked her up and wobbled his way to the bedroom. She was laughing at him uncontrollably as he staggered around with her in his arms before he dumped her on the bed.

"Stop laughing…" as he smiled at her, half laughing himself.

"I can't help it."and she laughed louder.

"You won't be laughing in a minute…"

"Oh and why's that?" She said in a sexy voice.

"You'll be moaning with pleasure, wanting *more*"

He pulled her leather jeans off and fell down on the floor. He was on his knees looking up at her. She could do nothing but laugh as he pulled her top off. His eyes moved down her body, his hands followed.

"Fucking hell, you are so fucking hot"

She pulled him towards her and kissed him, running her hands down his chest down to his thighs.

"Umm," he groaned. "I knew you wanted me, Des"

He began passionately and hungrily moving his mouth over her body, she was a habit he couldn't break.

"Huh hmm," she moaned with pleasure. "Oh Staffan, hmm…"

This man knew just how to get the most out of her. He grabbed her hands tight and moved between her thighs, pushing himself into her.

"Tell me you want me Des"

She looked straight in to his eyes. "Oh yeah, I want you Staffan… you are the sexiest man I've ever met" He was a habit she couldn't break either.

He run his hands and his mouth over her breasts, down her body – teasing her with his tongue then biting her gently. He looked up at her with an intense burning, sexy look. Her whole body surged. He was driving her crazy, he was so hot as he thrust deeper the louder she groaned. It was the hottest sex they'd had so far, the passion was extreme. He wouldn't stop until she climaxed over and over then they lay naked together Staffan moved onto his side to get his breath back.

"Ready?"

"Ready for…?" as she got her breath back too.

"Ready to go again, Des?"

He moved closer and started biting her neck.

"You're incredible, Staffan. Not bad for someone who's drunk"

He grinned at her. "Not that drunk, baby"

She reversed positions and sat on top of him. She started to bite his neck, then his nipples and then moved her nails down his body, digging them in as she went.

"Oh yeah, baby!"

"Like that, Staffan?"

"Ahhhhh yeah… Oh yeah"

She started to move her mouth down his body his body jerking as she moved her mouth slowly further down.

"Oh fucking hell Des hmm just… just make love to me"

She made love to him passionately. She hadn't felt like this since the last time they were together. Next morning, Des made a pot of coffee. Mae had just come in and seen all Staffan's clothes all over the floor and winked. Des smiled and headed back to the bedroom to wake Staffan who looked at her and smiled.

"No – *juice*! I'm really thirsty"

He jumped of bed and made off to the kitchen totally naked, not knowing that Mae was in there, Des shouted to him.

"Staffan… Mae is *oops…* in there"

Mae looked at Staffan, smiled and said, "Good morning"

Staffan ran back in the bedroom shouting "Hi, Mae"

Mae just giggled as she stared at his perfectly-shaped firm backside.

"Des"

"Yeah?"

"I've just flashed at Mae – now she's seen as much of me as you"

"I tried to tell you Mae was there," bursting out laughing. "I'm sure she was impressed, baby, I know I am"

"Des… please," he laughed as he got back in bed. "That's not funny"

"Oh but it is"

"Are you dating Johnny?" He just suddenly blurted out. "… because you said in your interview you were just friends"

"We *are* friends, that's all – he's not interested in me like that"

"Yeah, he is Des"

"No, he isn't"

"Des, do you ever wonder why we always end up in bed together?"

"The sex is fantastic"

His face dropped and he had an angry glint in his eyes.

"The sex, the fucking sex. You're fuckin' jokin, you're just fuckin' messing with my fucking head, you're driving me fucking crazy!"

With that he got out of bed and got dressed and stormed out. Des threw her hands up in the air. She was stunned, She didn't understand what she'd done or *said,* for that matter. She got out of bed and apologised to Mae for Staffan flashing at her.

"Oh Miss Desiree, he's gorgeous. I can see what the attraction is!"

"Oh Mae, you naughty girl"

"He *is* gorgeous – if I was only a bit younger"

Desiree laughed. "Oh, Mae" Mae just smiled.

Des had some appointments in town so she went to meet Lori for lunch.

"Good night last night Des?"

"Oh yeah, always is with Staffan… just the morning that was odd"

"Why?"

"Staffan shouted at me"

"Why?"

"I don't know. He shouted at me, got dressed and stormed out"

"Hmm… Anyway, guess who I ended up taking home last nigh – the actor Steven Russell, the very energetic actor…"

"Steve Russell? Why are you walking funny?"

"Don't fuckin' ask"

"Well you know I'm going to now"

"We had sex in the hall, kitchen, on the piano, the bed, up against the wall last night and in the shower this morning. I lost the use of my legs, fuck he can go. I couldn't take any more, you have to be a fuckin' contortionist to have sex with Steve Russell!"

Des burst into uncontrollable laughter. She was crying and her stomach ached from laughing so much.

"Oh, I'm glad it's so funny"

"I'm sorry but your face just then…"

"I've only just got my legs working again"

And again Des had a surge of laughter, spitting her water everywhere. It came out of her nose she was laughing so hard.

When Staffan got to rehearsals he was still really angry and the guys asked him what was wrong.

"That fucking woman – she's driving me insane!"

They all looked at each other as to say 'Desiree' and they were all thinking the same thing at the same time.

"I'll show her I can get any girl"

Staffan went in to overdrive with different girls. The press had a field day, he was with a different girl every other night. Eventually, Des decided to call him and asked him what she'd done and to ask what's with all the girls.

"You're fucking with me Des"

"No I'm not"

"Yeah, you're fucking with me… well, *no more!*"

"Fuck you Staffan!"

Staffan slammed the phone down. Des was stunned and thought to hell with him but she could just leave it there. She needed to give him a piece of her mind, she wasn't having him talk to her like that so she called him back.

"What?" He shouted.

"Don't ever talk to me like that and, furthermore, don't call me again!"

"Don't worry about that, I won't!"

Chapter 33

Johnny had a chance to star in a film and he jumped at it but he didn't realise that Desiree was auditioning for the same the film. If they both got their parts they would be playing lovers.

"Hi Johnny, what are you doing here? Desiree asked.

" I'm auditioning for the lead. Don't tell me you're auditioning too"

"Yes, I am"

"If we both get the lead parts we will be lovers, you know that?"

"Yes, we will"

"I think we would play lovers very well, don't you? He said with a gleam in his eyes

"Hmm yes I do," she said with an approving smile.

As it turned out they both got their parts. Johnny was excited about the thought of being Desiree's leading man – he would get to make out with Desiree Beaumont! Johnny suggested that they learnt their scripts together which Desiree thought that was a great idea and told him she was really looking forward to working with him. The more she was with him, the more she got to like him.

Johnny asked about Staffan.

"Well, you seemed to get on very well with each other at the awards"

"Yeah, we did"

"He seemed to be full-on with you"

"Were you jealous Johnny? " expecting him to say No.

"Yeah, I was…"

"Oh. I wasn't expecting you to say Yes"

"Why not? You are very beautiful, Des"

Johnny was relieved to hear there were nothing between Staffan and Des. He liked her and hoped that something could materialise between them. He was determined to go for it. He asked if she would come out for dinner that night.

"I would love to"

"Great, I'll pick you up at eight thirty"

Johnny turned up at eight thirty. Mae was still there and let him in and let Des knew he had arrived. She came out of her bedroom dressed in a black crop top, tight jeans and a little silk jacket

"WOW! Des you look great!"

"Thank you. You look great yourself"

Mae came out in to the hall and told Des she was going.

"Oh meet Mae, Johnny. She's like a mum to me" She put her arms round her

"Hi Mae" Johnny said and smiled at her.

Mae went weak at the knees when Johnny smiled at her, she thought he was *another* gorgeous man. Des and Johnny they had a good time over dinner then they sat and talked about lots of things, Desiree's past and the drink and pill problem she'd had.

"We've all had something, Des"

"Yeah, well I'm never going back there"

Before they knew it, the hours had rolled by, she felt so comfortable with him and they were the last out of the restaurant. Johnny dropped her off at home, said good night, kissed her and left.

Next morning Mae arrived with a paper in her hand to read on her coffee break. Des was up and dressed.

“Morning, Mae”

“Morning Miss Desiree. You made the headlines again this morning”

“Really?… With Johnny I presume. What did you think of Johnny?”

“He’s gorgeous isn’t he …and *that smile”*

“Yes he is isn’t he – and yes that smile!”

Des had an appointment with the film director about the film they had auditioned for. Johnny was there as well.

“Morning, Johnny”

“Hi Des… Am I going to see you tonight?”

“Yes you are”

“Good, that’s what I wanted to hear”

They started to see more of each other, for the moment still just as friends. The gossip about them, however, was spreading far and wide. They started work on their new film and were due to go on location. They started rehearsing their lines together and became quite inseparable. The press thought this was the next big romance for Desiree and they wanted all the gossip.

Lori caught up with Des just before they set out for location; they hadn’t seen each other for a while.

“What’s going on with you and Johnny ? Come on Des, tell me” nudging her repeatedly.

“We like each other… we're friends”

“Come on Des, give…. Johnny is hot… friend *my ass”*

“We *are* friends but… maybe, who knows? I’m sick of failed relationships – the only one that didn’t fail was Matt. I don’t want a romance. Sex yeah, but no romance”

“I thought you and Staffan would…”

“No. I don’t know what happened there. He got so mad with me when I called him and we argued…. No, me and Staffan are well and truly over”

“That's not what I see”

“Anyway, what’s going on with you Lori? You’ve been seeing Hadley, so what’s going on there then?”

“Well Des, there *is* a romance going on there!”

“Oh Wow, Lori!”

"And hey, talking of romance…. Riley got married"

"Oh wow… good luck to him I'm pleased for him… when?"

"Two days ago, didn't you read about it?"

"You know me and papers"

They had lunch and discussed another concert to raise money for endangered animals such as tigers and lions, this time with lots of different stars involved. She had been so overwhelmed with her endangered species tour in Africa, Asia, and the Mediterranean she wanted to do something big for this charity. Lori said that when she'd finished her tour and Des had finished filming then they should organise it.

A couple of days later, Johnny and Des set off to Maui on location for their new film, called *STRANGERS*. It was such beautiful place for the film, at the water's edge; surfer's paddling out to the waves, playful green turtles and Humpback Whales cruising the horizon and, at the beach, towering waterfalls plunging into shimmering pools. Spellbinding sunrises lit up the island's natural beauty.

After shooting their scenes, Des and Johnny would go out for dinner at the Maui Bistro, set perfectly on the boardwalk with beautiful ocean views – perfect to watch the sun set in a chilled out atmosphere. Occasionally, they were recognised and they happily signed a few autographs here and there.

One night, after weeks of shooting scenes, they went back to Desiree's trailer as usual. They'd had a heavy day and they were tired so they ordered dinner and went over some lines for the next day's filming. Johnny suddenly stopped and gazed at Desiree as she sat on the bed. His mouth dry, he took a deep breath, he was going to make his move. He bent over her and kissed her. His smile lit up his eyes when she kissed him back. He pushed her gently backwards and he fell softly on top of her, kissing her more passionately this time, moving his hand up her top.

"I'm not acting now," he whispered sexily.

"No… neither am I"

"I think you're so fucking beautiful, Des – you are unbelievably hot I've always thought so"

Johnny started to kiss her again, more intensely. He pulled his top off and she moved her hands over his chest. He started to kiss her neck, moving closer pressing his body into hers.

He removed her clothes slowly, gently moving his tongue over her soft skin.

"I've wanted you for a long time" He kissed her again.

She felt dizzy with the sensation. Her heart was beating so fast as he ran his fingers up her thighs. She moved to his touch, a warm feeling running all through her body.

"Aargh hmm…" she groaned.

Johnny was getting really turned on by her obvious pleasure.

"Oh Des, I want you!"

He pulled her close, pushing himself between her thighs, it was crazy hot and intense. His passion was overwhelming as his hands slid over the curves of her body, gripping her thighs tight as he pressed himself deeper into her. Each touch sent shivers down her body, and she pulled him into her so she could feel every inch of him. Their bodies moved together in a hot frenzied fashion – the harder he thrust into her the more she groaned. Her mouth was dry and her hands clammy, their sweat mingled as she ran her hand down his taut smooth olive skin. They made love for some time, climaxing together several times until they fell asleep eventually in the messed up sheets.

Next morning they woke to the sun peering through the slightly open blind and gave each other a knowing grin, Johnny snuck off back to his trailer before anyone could see him. As it was, everyone seemed to know anyway. They found it hilarious, filming sex scenes, as they had been doing it for real just a few hours ago. After shooting their scenes they would disappear. They couldn't keep their hands off each other. Johnny borrowed an open top car and parped the horn. Des opened the trailer door.

"Get in!" Johnny said, patting the seat.

Des jumped in and they headed off, Johnny driving fast through the country roads. The breeze swept through Des's hair and she stretched her arms up into warm air. Her laughter was warm and vibrant, happiness shone from her eyes. Johnny was captivated by her, he smiled with contentment. Could he be falling for her?

"Oh Johnny, this is great, where are we going?

"The *Shoreline Hut* restaurant"

It was on the beach and when they arrived they were both recognised instantly. People started going over to talk to them.. Johnny hadn't thought about people recognising them, he just wanted to be alone with Des.

"I'm sorry Des, I really didn't think this through"

"It's OK"

"Come on, let's get out of here"

They got back in the car and drove to the nearest burger bar they could find.

"This is good Johnny"

"No, it isn't"

"It is… I haven't done this for *ages*"

Then they headed towards a part of the beach Johnny knew, a spot that was very secluded, surrounded by rocks. The shallow water was so clear you could see the fish swimming in the turquoise sea. It was so hot, there wasn't a cloud in sight and a light breeze just caressed them gently as drops of sweat made their way down their faces. They made their way to the sea to cool down and waded in the cool water. Des felt invigorated and alive.

Johnny watched her playfully splashing in the water. He took hold of her, pulling her towards him. Without saying a word, he kissed her then gently pushed her over to an nearby rock. He kissed her again trailing his lips over her neck while he lifted her wet dress. She sighed with excitement, turned on by his soft kisses.

Dropping his hands, he unzipped his jeans and pulled out his manhood. His hand moved over her inner thigh, pulling her panties to the side. She could hardly breath as he pushed himself in to her, moving back and forth, keeping a steady rhythm, penetrating deeper – their mouths locked together as they both found orgasm.

Back in New York, Staffan and Delmar were partying hard with Tim and Riley after they had bumped into each other. It was funny, not so long back Staffan and Riley couldn't stand being in the same room together. Now here they were, knocking shots back together and picking women up. They were even giving each other signals for which women they wanted – left tug on the belt was for blondes, right tug was for redheads and middle tug was for brunettes.

"Hey, she looks like Des" Riley pointed out.

"Yeah… but it isn't – she's with Johnny, isn't she?" Staffan said drunkenly.

"Johnny… now there's handsome bastard – all the Sheila's want to bang him"

They all ended up in a hotel suite with a big crowd of people, mainly women, partying till the early hours.

Over the water in England, Lori had decided to have a night in with her favourite TV programmes on the VCR. She had loads to catch up on because she'd been touring so much and now she had some well-deserved time off. She spent the whole evening with her chocolate popcorn and crisps in her PJs in front of the TV. Finally, she was so tired that she couldn't watch any more. Her eyes were just so heavy so she headed off to bed, falling asleep as soon as her head hit the pillow.

She hadn't been asleep long when she heard a loud noise coming from the lounge. She jumped out of bed and she crept warily through the hall. As she made her way to the lounge she flicked the light switch on the wall and there, sat in the dark, was a young woman.

Lori looked at her, stunned, her chest tightening up she tried to control the tremor in her voice.

"Who are you? And how the fuck did you get in here?"

The young girl held up a screwdriver.

"I wanted to see you, I'm your biggest fan"

"What do you want?"

"To meet you … "

The girl started fumbling in her pocket and Lori was starting to feel uneasy

"Right stop pissing about – what do you want?"

"I wanted to meet you… and my name is Cathy"

A fake smile spread over her face and her voice had chilled She blew her breath out.

"Errrrr! You should be more grateful to your fans ,ya fuckin' bitch"

"It time you left, Cathy," Lori's blood started to run cold and the hair stood up on the back of her neck. She took a step back.

"Tut… tut…tut…" Cathy hissed. "Puh-leeze Lori, let me spend time with my favourite singer" as she grabbed Lori's hand.

Lori felt so helpless, she didn't know what to do, she didn't know what this girl was capable of doing to her. She let out a choked cry.

If it hadn't been for the night security guard doing his security checks no one would have heard her.

He called the police and told them that he'd heard a strange noise coming from Lori Miller's apartment and he wasn't convinced she was alright. The police came and banged on the door

"Miss Miller. Open the door please"

Cathy told her she should say she was her friend. Lori open the door and gave the officer a frightened look. That's all it took, the officer knew there was something wrong and demanded to be let in. When Lori spluttered that the girl had broken in, the police arrested her. She didn't go quietly either, she punched one of the police officers and kicked one of the others.

The news of the intruder hit the *Global Express* and the *News* back in New York. The guys finally rose out of their pits late next day and staggered into the lounge. Staffan and Riley looked blearily round the room at all the naked women. The room smelt of stale booze and cigarettes, their heads dense with dope, struggling to focus.

"Who are all these people?"

"I don't know"

"What the fuck did we do last night?"

"Fuck knows… I think we had a blow in"

"A what…?

"A party"

"No shit"

Riley looked round and saw Tim with his flower.

"Bloody oath… What a ripper!"

He nudged Staffan who noticed the flower between Tim's cheeks and laughed Delmar suddenly raised his head up from a girl's chest.

"What a fuckin' night!" He scanned the room and pointed at Tim. "Umm!"

"Fuckin' hell… we need to get rid of all these people" Staffan said swiftly.

"Fare dinkum…" Riley said standing motionless his stomach churning in a very unfriendly way. "I think I'm gonna hurl again – dunny here I come!".

Once Staffan and Delmar had got rid of everyone, they woke Tim. He got up from the couch and walked over to the other bathroom. He put his hand to his arse and looked puzzled.

"What the fuck is this?"and he pulled the flower from his bottom. "How the fuck did that get there? Not fuckin funny, guys!"

Riley reappeared. "I need brekki"

While they all sat having breakfast feeling sorry for themselves Riley spluttered and nearly choked when Staffan read out about Lori.

"Is Lori OK?" He spewed.

"I don't know… it doesn't really say, just that she's shaken up"

"Fuckin' hell there are some crazy people out the" Delmar said angrily

Tim agreed with him they decided to call her to make sure she was OK. Lori reassured them she was fine, just shaken that's all.

Chapter 34

After their film was done, Des and Johnny went to see Lori to make sure she was alright after her ordeal. When Des got back home she took some time out to relax and soak up the sun. She was stretched out on the sun lounger in her bikini, topping up her tan and drinking a refreshing lime and soda, when Mae brought Johnny out.

"Hi babe"

"Johnny come here …. kiss me"

Johnny sat down on the lounger next to her and kissed her, placing his hand on her leg and stroking her in a circular motion.

"You're very hot Des"

"Yeah, well it's a hot day" teasing him.

"You know what I mean"

"I know, I'm teasing you"

"You're not funny" he said kissing her, trying to keep his grin at bay.

"Oh, I thought I was"

He moved his hand further up her legs.

"You're really…"

"I'm really what Johnny?" interrupting him.

"… breath-taking"

Just then Mae came out and told Des she was going. Des told her she would see her tomorrow. Mae let her know she'd left dinner for her and said there was plenty for two. Johnny smiled at Mae.

"Bye Mae…. Where was I?" Johnny mumbled.

"Breathtaking"

"Oh yeah, breath…taking…"

He trailed his fingers back up her legs, kissing her softly. She pulled his T-shirt off and moved her hands over his chest, her brown eyes gleaming with mischief. He reached over to her, pulling her to him. She ran hand over his shoulders, over his tight stomach then down to his thighs, opening his jeans.

"Oh Des…" He got up held his hand out to her."Come on"

He took her into the house and led her to the bedroom. He took his off his jeans and laid her down on the bed before peeling her out of her bikini. She closed the distance between them by pulling him to her, smelling his aroma with a sweet undertone of sharp and spicy after shave. The chemistry between them was extreme.

Things started to really heat up like an inferno. Frenzied sparks flew, his hunger for her was overwhelming, his kisses deepened while his hands glided over her curves. He moved his mouth down her body. Her whole body surged, she sighed a long drawn-out groan as he teased her with his tongue until he made his way back up. Pulling her knees up as he parted them, he gently eased himself into her. His body flexed and moved over hers, both trapped in his rhythm.

"Ohm… yessss!" She purred.

"Oh yeah, baby yes… yes…"

Her stomach tightened, her legs stiffened as she felt the relief of her orgasm. He was ready to explode as his thrusts deepened and moved faster. His eyes rolled to the back of his as he shot his load. Breathlessly, they relaxed.

"I love being with you Des"

"We have fun, that's for sure"

"Des, I…"

She placed her fingers over his mouth and stopped him talking.

"Just sex... we agreed"

"But... I"

Des interrupted again "just sex"

He felt more for her than just sex and he wanted her to feel the same. He had fallen in love with her.

⁂

What happened with Lori had scared Hadley more than he could have believed. He realised that he was in love with Lori – he wanted her with him and he wanted to protect her. Taking the plunge, he asked Lori to move in with him.

"Oh Hadley, Yes"

"Good, I'm glad"

"Why?"

"I've fallen in love with you and I want you to be with me"

"I love you too"

Lori sold her apartment in England and moved over to New York with Hadley in his beautiful penthouse home on the Upper East Side on a sun flooded corner. Asher marbled floors in all the rooms, beautiful state of the art kitchen, a big well-lit terrace looked out onto the sky line. The view at night was spectacular. They were so loved up, Lori was hoping that Hadley was the one and she'd got it right this time.

⁂

Love was certainly in the air with Jake and his wife Sandra celebrating their silver wedding anniversary. Anyone who was anyone was going to be there. Des went with Johnny and as usual she looked stunning in her black sequinned backless dress. She wore her hair scrunched up, even her makeup was perfect – white eye shadow with thick black eye liner – long black lashes and full red lips. She smelt good too, a sensual musk. Johnny pointed Staffan out to Des and, when she looked over, he was with a stunning blonde. Staffan was introducing the blonde, Darcy, to Lori. She wasn't a model, or even famous for that matter, he had met her backstage at a gig and he had been seeing her off and on for the past few weeks. Lori mentioned that Des was there.

"Yeah I'll go over and see her, we parted with an argument last time we spoke to each other"

"She looks good, doesn't she?"

"Yeah she's…"

Then Darcy interrupted. "Is that Desiree Beaumont?"

Lori and Staffan both said in unison, "Yeah"

"Oh could I meet her. I want be just like her, she's so beautiful"

They walked over to Des. Johnny had his arms round her, whispering in her ear and she had her head bowed down joyfully, giggling at Johnny.

"Uh…Des?" said Lori.

Des looked up and there was Staffan looking all over sexy with this beautiful blonde on his arm. Des suddenly felt really jealous. She quickly mentioned the charity concert she and Lori were organising and asked if they would be part of it. Staffan and Johnny both said they would. She turned to Darcy and told her she would have to get used to all this talk of showbiz and other women, lots of women, if she was to be with Staffan.

"Are you gonna sing with me Des?" Staffan asked.

"Do ya want me to?" She said abruptly.

"Yeah… we had fun last time didn't we?"

"Then I will" her answer was so matter of fact.

Staffan looked at her. "Are you angry with me?"

"No. Why should I be? She threw back at him quickly.

Johnny noticed her making odd little digs at Staffan, how her mood had changed and didn't understand why until Staffan moved away and he mentioned how gorgeous Staffan's date was. Now, was she jealous at the fact he had said it or was it the fact that Staffan was with her?

"Hey Johnny"

"Riley… how ya doin?"

"Ripper… sweet as"

"She's still in love with Staffan, isn't she?

"Are we talkin' about Des by any chance?"

"Yeah… Time to let her go"

"You've fallen in love with her, haven't you?"

"Nah… We were just foolin around. Maybe if I call it a day she and Staffan can sort themselves out, tell each other how they really feel"

"Sorry mate…"

"What are you sorry about?"

Riley knew that look and what it meant.

Jake and Sandra had really enjoyed their anniversary. The evening had gone beautifully. Afterwards, Des and Johnny went back to back to her place. Johnny asked her why she had been watching Staffan all night.

"I wasn't…" and walked away.

"Hey…" He shouted. "You were jealous weren't you?"

"No!"

"Yes you were…"

"If you want to call it a day Johnny, don't use Staffan as an excuse"

"Yeah, it's time to end it, I think" he put his head down and walked away.

"Don't you fucking walk away from me…"

Johnny turned round to look at her, shock his head and left. When he got home he rang Staffan and told him that Des was still in love with him. Staffan told him he was wrong.

"No I'm not"

"What about you and her – if that's true.

"I've ended it, Staffan. You two need to be honest with each other"

The papers reported that Des and Johnny had split up *'…and it was an amicable split and they remain good friends,'* a close friend said.

Chapter 35

Lori and Des got to work on the charity concert, giving all the acts the dates to make sure they could come along. It took some time for Des and Lori to sort out the stadium big enough and to get it fixed up. They wanted it to be videoed so they had to have loads of camera crew and loads of hi-tech equipment. Jake was the man to sort all that out.

There were so many stars wanting to be involved. Des wasn’t sure if Johnny would still do it, she hadn't seen him since he walked out but the band insisted. Staffan and the guys were also able to do it, even Scott signed up and there were so many others.

Lori was to go on with Johnny and his band, Johnny and Staffan were going to do a set together with both bands. Des was going on with Staffan and they also had some comedians and some film stars making appearances. They had managed to get a big name line up; it had turned in to a massive event. Riley was also on with his band and Andy with his band and Paul best and his band. Des and Lori were so excited everybody put so much work in to this concert. The charity was for endangered species all round the world so they needed it to work and raise loads of money.

This charity was close to Desiree’s heart.

The day the concert and everyone was ready, sound checks all done,everyone had been rehearsing, costumes all hung up ready. They were all having a great time together. Lori and Des had ordered lots of food and drink for everyone. Famous comedian Tommy Carlen introduced Des and Lori on stage. The stadium was packed to the rim with screaming fans. They in turn introduced Scott first, then lots of other stars like pop singers Anita Scully, Julia Ellison, then new romantic bands such as *Vertical Change*. A bit later on, Lori went on to sing with *Connection. S*he had a great time with the guys then Johnny and Lori sang a sexy song together. The audience loved it. *Eclipse* and *Sharp Edge* went on together too.

The crowd roared when Riley went on and when he unexpectedly called Des on they went wild. Riley and Des sang the song he wrote for her, she totally loved it, and when they came off she kissed him and congratulated him on his marriage, she was really pleased for him. He told her that she was a nice girl.

"Well, I wasn't getting you back was I? I think that there's only one man for you, Des"

Des went back on, this time with *Dominance* and she and Staffan did a love song, then a sexy song with some very sexy moves. It took Des right back to when they married and how much she loved him then.

Johnny was waiting to go on with Staffan and their bands, he was watching Staffan and Des do their song at the side of the stage. When they came off he grabbed Des's arm.

"Hi Des"

"Hi Johnny"

"Are we still friends?"

Des smiled at him. "Yeah, of course we are," and kissed him on the cheek.

Johnny and Staffan ran on stage with the guys and all the girls in the stadium went crazy. Des was smiling, watching them. Lori asked who she was watching.

"Staffan, I love watching him"

"Staffan…?"

"Yeah…" Realising what she'd said. "The guys – I love watching the guys"

"You said Staffan, Des"

"Yeah, I know"

"Des…. you're going to lose him totally if you don't tell him"

"I know, I'm going to do something about it"

The guys come off stage. Hadley grabbed Lori's hand and took her to his dressing room and locked the door.

"What you doing Hadley?"

"You babe, "grinning from ear to ear at her.

"We can't"

"Yeah we can"

With that, Hadley dropped his jeans and pointed downwards.

"What do ya want me to do with that Hadley?"

"Oh baby, you know…" and grinned again.

Lori and Hadley were in the dressing room for some time. Staffan went over to Des and asked the question they were both thinking.

"What do ya think their doin'?"

"Well, at a guess…"

Staffan laughed, "…the same as we did when you came on tour with me?"

"Um… Yeah…. They were fun days"

Lori and Hadley came out and looked at Des and Staffan.

"Have you been outside here since we went in?"

Staffan laughed, "Pretty much, yep" winding them up.

"Fuck off!" Hadley said, grinning at them.

Des and Staffan went into fits of laughter, tears were rolling down their faces.

Lori said, "Oh God, fuck off… Anyway, it's no worse than you and Staffan in the pool in Vegas"

Staffan looked at Des and pulled her close. "What we got up to that night was amazing"

Des smiled, "Yeah, I remember"

Johnny came over and asked what they were all laughing at.

"These two horny bastards – we've just caught Lori and Hadley at it"

"Fuck off" Hadley said laughing.

Johnny shook his head, tut-tutted and smiled then smiled again at Des and pulled her to one side

"Des... Tell him.... I know he still loves you"

The concert came to the end it was huge success and it had raised a huge amount of money and they all had fun doing it.

A few days later, Des was in the studio with Jake talking to him about doing a calendar for a charity. She was going to talk to Lori about it, she knew Lori would be keen to do it. Jake thought it was a fantastic idea.

"Des... phone. It's the hospital" Lyn shouted.

"The hospital?"

She rushed to the phone with all sorts were going through her head, what on earth could it be? The nurse told Des that Mae had been attacked.

"I'll be right there – Jake!" She shouted in a panic.

Jake asked what was wrong and Des explained about Mae, she needed to go to the hospital. Jake took her but the paparazzi was all over Des. They followed her all the way and it was all over the news and the radio that Desiree Beaumont had been rushed to the hospital. Staffan heard it on the radio and headed straight over to find her. He had to know if she was alright

"Oh Staffan, it's Mae – she's been attacked"

"Mae.... What.... How?"

As Des was telling Staffan what had happened, the doctor came in to speak to Des. Mae was OK, a bit battered and bruised and very shaky. He looked a bit sheepish and told her that Mae didn't have medical insurance. Des told him that she would cover it, that was not a problem. "

"Just get her better..." Des didn't know what she would do without Mae. "She's OK ,isn't she? Can I see her?"

The doctor took Des in to see Mae. Mae looked up at Des.

"I'm sorry Miss Desiree"

"Mae, why are you sorry?"

Mae had been beaten quite badly. She had put up a fight, though. She'd suffered a couple of broken ribs and her eye was black and blue. It was so swollen that it had closed completely.

"They took the grocery money"

"Don't worry about that, Mae"

"I'll pay it back out of my wages"

“You’ll do no such thing Mae Green”

Mae told Des she couldn’t say in the hospital but Des told her it was all taken care of.

“Mae, let me do something for you. You're always there for me – it’s my turn to be there for you”

“No…no… Miss Desiree”

“Yes… Mae… you mean the world to me”

Des kissed her on the cheek and Mae stroked Des’s hair.

“You are a lovely girl, Miss Desiree. I wish you could be happy with the man you really love”

Des smiled and told Mae she would be back to see her next day. Just then, Staffan popped his head round the door.

“Hi Mae”

“Mr Templeton,” she winked at Des and whispered, “He’s the one”

Des smiled then they left Mae to rest.

“What did Mae mean, 'he’s the one'?”

“Hmm…” She wanted to change the subject., “Staffan thanks so much for coming”

“I was worried about you, Des”

She leant in and kissed him on cheek. “That’s nice”

On the other side of New York, Hadley planned to ask Lori to marry him over lunch at the *Rock Joint* restaurant.

“Lori?

“Yeah?”

Hadley took a box out of his pocket and put it on the table.

I found this"

Lori looked at the box, “What’s in it?”

“Look inside”

Lori smiled at him, took a deep breath and opened the box.

“Oh Hadley it’s beautiful”

“Will you marry me?”

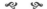

"Yes…yes…yes…

Hadley put the beautiful twenty carat diamond ring on Lori's finger. She held her hand out to admire it. Hadley broke in.

"I want six kids"

"Yeah right… in your dreams baby!" and she kissed him.

Hadley just laughed and kissed her back.

Lori and Hadley told Des and Johnny first, then they announced it to the world at a press conference. It hit the front pages all over the world.

Chapter 36

Des called Staffan and invited him to dinner. She had finally decided to tell him how she felt.

"Yeah that's great – see you tonight"

She had cooked everything herself. She prepared a Danish beef pot roast in a creamy mushroom sauce and *aebleskiver,* a Danish dessert very much like a doughnut but much sweeter, served with syrup. There was a beautiful aroma of flowers and scented candles coming from the dining room. The atmosphere was romantic, now all she had to do was just get ready. She took a bath then walked through a mist of perfume, the sensual smell of ylang ylang. She sat at the mirror, piling her beautiful long black hair on the top of her head to apply her makeup – a smoky brown eyeshadow outlined with black eyeliner. She fluttered her long black lashes and pouted full glossy red sexy lips. She picked the sexiest dress she could find, an ivory glittery dress with a very low back, revealing her body beautifully.

Staffan buzzed her so she could let him through the gates. As he came up the drive, she saw the headlights and started feeling very nervous. He parked and checked himself out before he rang the bell. He'd put black trousers on with a white shirt and he'd made sure he smelt good, of musk and spice.

"Hi Des" He kissed her.

"Staffan, I'm really glad you came"

"What's the occasion?"

"No occasion"

Staffan really enjoyed his meal. Des could cook and she made him Danish food specially. She knew how much he liked her cooking.

"Wow, that was very nice, Des"

"Good. I'm glad you liked it"

To push her a little, he asked about her and Johnny. She told him it was never serious they weren't a couple – they just enjoyed each other's company.

"Staffan… I want to…"

"What?" He interrupted her.

"I…I…" she totally bottled it. "Do you want some coffee?"

"Yeah… I'm just going to the bathroom"

"OK"

Staffan went to the bathroom and paced up and down. *'Come on Des, come on'*, he thought to himself. He wanted her to say she wanted him, that she loved him. She had to do it, she needed to do it. Des was in the kitchen making the coffee saying exactly the same thing to herself. *'Come on Desiree, tell him!'*

She made the coffee and poured two cups. As she poured, she stared at him from underneath her eyelashes. He smiled at her.

"You look very beautiful"

"Thank you…"

"Actually, I've got to go Des, early start tomorrow"

"OK…. Staffan – I just want to…" then she hesitated again. "…say thank you" changing her sentence quickly.

"Yeah, It was great. Thank *you"*

She walked him to the door. He stopped and looked at her and then kissed her, touching her face tenderly. He walked to his car and got in.

Shutting the door after him, she slid down to the floor. *'Why didn't you say it?'* She was so angry with herself. Then, out loud.

"I love you Staffan, there I said it!"

Why couldn't she tell him she loved him, that she'd always loved him?

Staffan was very disappointed too, sat in his car pondering how the hell he was going to get her to say she loved him. Finally, he got out and walked back towards the door. Des was still sat behind it, she could feel a sheen of water building up behind her eyes. Staffan hovered his finger over the bell then pressed it. She jumped up and opened the door to him. Staffan looked deep into her eyes, stepped forward and took hold of her, kissing her very passionately. Pushing her back, he slammed the door behind him, snatching Des up in his arms and carrying her to the bedroom. Gently, he lay her on the bed and hovered over her. He bent his head down to kiss her and she reached up to his face and kissed him back. They undressed each other slowly, item by item. Caressing her face with his fingers, she pulled him on to her. She could feel his arousal and knew he wanted her as much as she wanted him.

"I want you so much Des"

As he moved his hand down her neck towards her breasts, down her stomach, she arched her body with pleasure.

"Oh… Oh… yeah, Oh Staffan, ahh hmm"

"Oh yeah baby, that's it – show me how much you want me"

"Baby, I do want you"

"You are the sexiest women I ever met. There's nobody like you"

He ran the tip of his tongue over her lips, trailed his hot steamy breath down her body sending ripples through her

"Arrr… Oh… Oh … Staffan…"

He hovered over her body, releasing the passion that had been building all evening.

"I want you Desiree," his voice low and commanding.

Their bodies were hot and sweating. He moved his hand down the curves of her body before sliding it between her thighs. Her eyes glittered feverishly as he used his lips, tongue and teeth to tease her. She couldn't take any more – she wanted him and she wanted him now. She folded her legs around him, pulling him to her.

"Oh Des, it's been a long time"

"Too long Staffan"

Kissing her again, he made love to her with passion. The sex was hot, frenzied and carnal and went on and on, orgasm after orgasm ripped through them. They wanted to please each other and they did…

Next morning, Des made coffee and toast while Staffan showered and dressed. He went in to the kitchen, pulled Des to him and kissed her before taking a swig of coffee and a bite out of his toast.

"Got to go… but we need to talk Des"

"Yeah, we do. I'm away tonight but I'll be back tomorrow evening"

"OK, tomorrow we talk.

"Yeah"

Staffan kissed her and said, "… a *serious* talk"

She walked him to the door. "Staffan… I love you"

"I love you"

Then he kissed her again, smiling at her, he went over to his car and was about to open the door when he turned and headed back to Des, smothering her with butterfly kisses.

"See you tomorrow"

"Yeah… can't wait!" She said smiling at him.

Staffan left a very happy man. Des grabbed her bag and headed off to see Jake but before she left she called Delmar.

"Hello?"

"It's Des. Will you meet me for lunch at Rockets?

"Yeah, sure"

"Don't tell Staffan you're meeting me"

"OK. This sounds interesting"

At lunch time Staffan went round to Des's. He knew she wasn't there but he'd still brought strawberries and champagne.

"Hi Mae.

Mae looked very puzzled.

"It's OK – champagne's for me, strawberries for Des"

She still looked very confused.

"Are you celebrating, Mr Staffan?"

"I think we could be Mae – keep your fingers crossed"

"Oh, I hope so!" She was crossing her fingers with excitement.

"Come in a bit later tomorrow, Mae" He winked.

"But what about…?"

"Don't worry, it'll be fine… Got to go"

At Rockets, Des and Delmar were having lunch. They were pictured holding hands and kissing. It looked a very romantic setting.

The next day, Staffan flicked though the paper and caught sight of the picture. He stopped in his tracks, his blood starting to boil. He didn't understand what the other night was all about. *Why did she sleep with him? Why was Delmar with Des? Why were they kissing?*

When Delmar appeared in the studio, Staffan threw the paper at him.

"What the fuck is this?"

"What…?" Delmar asked, wondering what Staffan was on about.

"This… What the fuck are you doing with Des?"

"Having lunch"

"Fuck you… that's a bit more than fuckin lunch, you're fuckin kissing her! You know how I feel about her, why would you do that to me Del?"

"Staffan it's not what it looks like

Staffan didn't talk to Delmar all day. Edvin and the guys asked Delmar what was going on. He told them that Staffan had got it all wrong but couldn't say why just say yet. After rehearsals, Staffan was making his way out of the studio when Delmar grabbed him by the arm.

"Staffan…"

"Fuck you!"

"You've got this all wrong"

"Have I?"

He pulled away and left.

Chapter 37

That evening Des got back, took a shower and put Staffan's old shirt on. She made sure she looked sexy and smelt good, light and feminine. She waited for Staffan, she was so excited she was like a teenager

When Staffan arrived at the gates he buzzed her and he sounded really angry Des wondered why but let him in and he steamed straight into her, shouting at her.

"What the fuck are you playing at?"

"What? Staffan don't shout at me like that"

He grabbed her by the arm firmly, "What the fuck are you playing at?"

Staffan pushed her against the wall, poking her with his finger

"Tell me, what was last night about?"

Des grabbed his hand. "Stop it Staffan, and tell me what I've done"

"Delmar…" pulling the paper out of his back pocket.

"Delmar, yeah?"

"Fuck you Des… you've got your tongue down his fucking throat .Ya know what – I'm fuckin' *done*"

He started to walk away.

"Staffan…"

"WHAT?" He shouted, turning back to her. His eyes had started to fill up. "You're not doing this to me anymore, I thought last night was… fuck, it doesn't matter." His voice was shaky he was so angry and hurt.

"Oh, for fuck's sake… *gifte dig med mig?"* She blurted out.

Staffan stood with his mouth open.

"Did… did you ask me to marry you just then?"

"Yes Staffan … *jeg elsker dig*"

"You love me?"

"Yes… but this wasn't how it was all meant to happen. And for the record, I didn't have my tongue down Delmar's throat"

He moved his head closer to hers and ran his fingers through her hair. He kissed her very tenderly.

"Des, I love you too, very much"

He looked at her

"Is that my shirt?"trying to take everything in after his shock.

He kissed her again, pulling her even closer to him As he kissed her passionately, he ripped the shirt open.

"See what you do to me, Des"

His hand moved down her body, peeling off the shirt until she was naked. He stood up and towered over her and took his clothes off too. His lips moved down her body. She responded to his every touch, his fingers trailing down her body. He gripped her tightly and looked at her triumphantly, moving between her thighs. She licked her lips seductively and he traced his fingers over them as she licked them.

"Ahhhh, baby…" he said, his eyes wide with promise. "Des I want you so much"

"I'm all yours…" her voice sounded sexy,

He kissed her slowly. He wanted her so much. She could feel his breath on her neck then he made love to her, their bodies moved together in a frenzy. Their sweat mixed together, their bodies spasming after they climaxed together. They lay in each other's arms, entwined on the floor.

Staffan got up, picked Des up and took her in to the bedroom. She pushed him down on the bed and sat on top of him. He beckoned her closer and smiled.

He kissed her and bit her lip sexily.

Her whole body surged, she sighed a long drawn out groan. Holding his hands above his head, she kissed him passionately, digging her long red nails into his chest.

"Ahhh babe…" he sighed as his body jerked with pleasure.

He swiftly reversed the position, lifting her leg gently – caressing it and kissing it, trailing his tongue down at the same time. It was sending shivers all over her body. Again he moved between her thighs and made love to her. They sent each other into another frenzy. The sex was electric but then again, they had always been good together in bed.

Next morning Staffan rang Delmar and told him he was so sorry. Delmar asked if everything was alright and Staffan told him that Des had asked him to marry her.

"But you knew that she was going to do that didn't you"

"Can I tell the guys?

Staffan said, "Yeah"

Des called Lori and told her that she and Staffan were getting married again. She was so excited and pleased for Des. She screamed down the phone.

"Oh Des… Des…"

When Mae arrived, Des and Staffan announced they were getting married again. Mae was so pleased. Staffan told Mae to take the rest of the day off as they would be out all day. They were going shopping for a ring and they were arranging to move Staffan's stuff in.

EPILOGUE

The Hotel Capri was the venue for Lori and Hadley's big day. Her dress was a figure-hugging, long-sleeved, lace ivory dress. Her hair was swept back away from her face leaving cascading curls at the back with a beautiful crystal headband. Hadley looked very handsome in his black suit. Des help Lori with her wedding dress. She looked so beautiful. Des smiled at her best friend then told her that she and Staffan were getting remarried.

"I'm really happy for you, Des"

She grabbed Des and kissed her, clapping her hands and jumping up and down. After Lori and Hadley's wedding, Des and Staffan announced their happiness to the world.

Des and Staffan remarried on the beach in Fiji in front of a majestic deep blue ocean. A light breeze offered slight relief from the blazing sun, the sand shimmered in the sun light, sparkling like diamonds. Everyone commented on her dress, a sheath/column V-neck appliqué Chapel satin dress, netted and pearl buttoned to her waist. Her hair was curled and twisted into a side ponytail, cascading down in front of her, with a pearl crown chain headpiece to finish it off. She was simply stunning. Everybody was buzzing with excitement as she held out her bouquet and stared deep into Staffan eyes. They had a beautiful wedding reception at the *Hotel Zentina* just off the beach with all their friends there this time.

Well, they are still married to this day and proud parents of twins, Camitta and Derri. Camitta followed in her father's footsteps as a successful recording artist while Derri is a successful photographer. He has photographed some very famous models, including taking headshots of his mother. Staffan still tours (though not as much) and Desiree still does commercials and TV shows.

Staffan's love for Desiree never faded even though they'd been parted for several years. He knew he would get her back one day.

So Desiree finally put her demons to rest and got a happy ending.

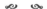